Absolution

And Other Stories

BY

Neal James

Short Stories Volume Six

First Published in 2022 by:
Lulu Press Inc.

Absolution
Copyright © 2022 Neal James
ISBN13: 9781387716098

Cover artwork and design by Inhouse Graphic Design Solutions

Neal James has asserted his right under the Copyright, Designs and Patents Act, 1988, to be identified as Author of this Work.

www.nealjames.webs.com

Lulu Publishing
627 Davis Drive
Suite 300
Morrisville
NC 27560
United States

Dedication

In Memory of Christine Pryor (Redfern)

6th August 1957 to 22nd October 2020

'Sister, Friend, Aunty, Wife. Loved by us all for her generosity and kindness, but most of all for her wicked sense of humour.'

- Diane Webb

Acknowledgements

For the excellent artwork and cover design, I am indebted to Inhouse Graphic Design Solutions for stepping in at short notice to produce a book cover matching all my requirements.

My appreciation goes to Mark J. Edmondson for the help and guidance he provided in an area where I lacked the necessary skills. The time we spent on format and layout will be of great benefit to me in the future.

To my beta readers, Lesley Riley and Heather Clements, my thanks for the time that they took to scrutinise the manuscript and correct inconsistencies in the text, and for assuring me that the anthology held together.

In completing this, my latest collection, a number of readers have aided the process by suggesting story titles. They are:

Deafening Silence (Linda Bennett), The Last Train (Alistair Blackett), Mind My Toes (Julie Brown), Why Me? (Mitchell Chanelis), Do It Again (Karl Clements), Stunned (Sheila A Donovan), Absolution (Matt Earl), Blood and Sweat (Julie Finlay), Never Too Late (Prissy Govender), When I'm Gone (Marinda Hatcher-Grindstaff), Thunder and Rain (Terry Hetherington), Parrots and People (Julie Hunt), Life's An Illusion (Jenny Jeffrey), The Lion and Harriet (Geoff Kirkman), L'Appel du Vide (Jessie Masoner), Time To Travel (Heather McBain), The Long Mile (Guy McKenna), The Ghost in the Garage (Yvonne Moore), Revenge Time (Sandra Nelson), Winter's Creeping Chill (Angela Shepherd), Bridge of Dreams (Ankush Soni), The Optical Road (Deidre Stephenson), The Lemon Tree of Life (Amie Taylor), Red Shoes (Sharon Teece), The Dancing Clouds (June Wayland).

Finally, my wife, Lynn, who has lived and breathed all of the stories, and offered constructive advice at all stages of the writing. Where would I be without you?

Other Books by Neal James

A Ticket to Tewkesbury

Short Stories Volume One

Two Little Dicky Birds

Threads of Deceit

Full Marks

Day of the Phoenix

The Rings of Darelius

Twelve Days

Three Little Maids

Short Stories Volume Two

Short Stories Volume Three

Edge of Madness

Overmorrow

Contents

Absolution

David Samson his name is, this psychowhatsit guy that's come to decide if I'm crazy or not. Well, I'm not; I'm about the sanest man that I know, and I know a lot of people. It's the dreams that're doin' it – that's one of the reasons I ended up here in this Goddamned awful place. Psychiatric hospitals they call 'em; used to be lunatic asylums when I was just growin' up, but that's a long time ago, now.

I never sought Absolution. Absolution found me an' I wish to God that it'd never bothered. Dreams; did I say dreams? Well, maybe I was wrong – they're more like nightmares an' I wake up screamin' when they come a-callin'. The authorities put me in this padded cell until they think I've calmed down an' not goin' to hurt anyone – particularly me. I take a deep breath as the guy gets out his notepad an' pen. We're sittin' in a room just along the corridor from the cell, but I'm on the other side of a Plexiglas screen in case… you know. He sets himself up and smiles. I have to smile back – that's the rule.

"Well, Mr French," he begins. "How are you today?"

Dumb assed question if you ask me, but I have to be positive. "About as good as I can be, considerin' what happened," I say.

"Yes," he says, lookin' down at his notes. "Quite a show from what I heard. Another occurrence?"

'Occurrences' he calls 'em. He'd call 'em somethin' else if he came along with me an' saw for hisself. We've met for three times now, but this will be the first instance that I've felt clear enough to let him into what I've been goin' through. The last 'occurrence' was two nights ago, an' they only removed the straightjacket this morning.

"Yessir," I say. "Another one of them there."

"Can we get to the cause?"

"You mean can I tell you the story?" I reply. "Hell, yes; what're we waitin' for?"

I'm Tobias French. It was back in '64 that me an' Jimmy Rae Hollis went on a boy's weekend up in the mountains. We'd planned a few days huntin', fishin' an' generally doin' the kind of things that men do when they think that they're still teenagers. Our wives were none too impressed, but it seemed like the last fling before settlin' down an' bein' sensible, so they let us off the leash. We'd driven out from Portland after work on the Friday, an' headed east on Route 26 for the Mount Hood National Forest. Jimmy Rae's mom an' dad had a cabin up in the woods near Alder Creek, an' we turned off onto South East Alder Creek Road – the place was a couple of miles further on.

"Why don't we start with the day Jimmy Rae... disappeared," Samson said.

"You mean when they say I murdered him?" I asked. "I served twenty-five in Salem for somethin' that I didn't do, an' now they label me as a crazy an' lock me up for the rest of my life."

"If you want to get out of here, you need to be more co-operative," he said.

"Have it your way. We'd been on the road for a while an' turned off 26 onto the track leadin' to the cabin. Jimmy Rae was drivin', an' suddenly this thick mist comes down an' we could hardly see where we were goin'. He's slows down so's we could follow the route an' the mist lifts a little. That's when we saw the sign."

"Sign? What did it say?"

"Absolution," I told him. "It was a town sign; you know, the kind that you see on any highway as you drive along. This one was just a beat up old sign an' we stopped the car an' got out to take a look at it."

"Go on."

"Well, there it was, by the side of the road. All it said was 'Absolution' and 'Pop. 512'. We peered into the distance but all we could see was the mist. I'd never heard of the place, an' Jimmy Rae said we should take a look, so we did."

"And when you got there?"

"Place was like somethin' out of the Wild West, 'cept there was nobody around. Whole town looked abandoned; dust everywhere an' tumbleweeds rollin' down the street. Jimmy Rae parked up outside what musta been the saloon an' we got out of the car. The breeze stopped an' you coulda heard a pin drop – it was real spooky."

"What did you do?" Samson asked, scribblin' away at his notepad.

"Went up the steps to the saloon an' walked inside. Them doors squawked like they'd never moved in a hundred years. Man, it was dirty in there. Place looked as though folks had upped an' left in a real hurry – chairs knocked over an' glasses still on some of the tables, an' all. I said we should leave an' try to find a way back to Route 26, but Jimmy Rae smiled that smile of his an' it was suddenly like we was both kids again."

"What did he want?"

"He says to me 'C'mon Tobias. How often d'you get to look around a real old ghost town?' Well, we'd nothin' better to do, an' it was kinda creepy, so I said okay. We had a look around the bar room an' then headed up the stairs. That's when we heard the noise."

"Noise?" Samson said, looking up at me. "What noise?"

"Freaked us out back then, an' we stopped half way up them stairs. Jimmy Rae laughed an' we carried on. It was a kinda growl, but like no growl that I'd ever heard. It was comin' from a corridor to the right of the head of that stairway, an' I suppose we thought that it might have been some wild animal trapped in one of the rooms."

"And was it?" Samson asked. He'd stopped takin' notes by this time.

"Never really got to think about that. Things happened kinda fast. Jimmy Rae looked back at me – he was in the front – an' then there was this… thing comin' hell for leather down the corridor. Jimmy Rae never stood a chance, an' then it had him by the shoulder. I stood frozen to the spot – musta been no more'n ten feet away. Then there was blood gushin' all over the place, an' Jimmy Rae screamin'."

"What? What did he say?"

"I'll never forget them words. 'Run Tobias! Get the hell out…' an' that's all he had time for. I was covered in blood by then an' just turned an' hightailed it out of there."

9

"The police…"

"Cops found me later back on 26. Oregon State Troopers passin' by saw me just starin' right ahead. I had no idea how I'd got there. Car was smeared in Jimmy Rae's blood an' they took me in. They never found Jimmy Rae and the DA made a case for me killin' him an' disposin' of the body. That's about it; I served the time, but I didn't kill Jimmy Rae; whatever there was in that saloon did that, but nobody believed me."

"Tobias," Sansom said. "I checked up on Absolution in the Oregon state records in Portland. The place doesn't exist. I even went down to the county records level, but there's no mention of any place by that name and the files go way back into the nineteenth century."

I thought about that for a while; Sansom looked as though he was tryin' to believe me but he just shrugged an' started to put away his stuff. As he rose to leave there was only one thing left for me to do.

"I guess there's only one way that I'm goin' to convince you. Why don't I show you where it is? Think the hospital will let me out if you an' some others come along?"

I could see him weighin' it up, an' it really was my last card – my final chance to prove to them all that I wasn't nuts. He put his bag on the table an' looked me right in the eye.

"I'll see what I can do. I have to check in with Doctor Porter before I leave, and if you agree to take a couple of cops along with us he might just go for it."

He did.

We started the drive from my old home in Portland an' followed the exact same route at the exact same time of day as me an' Jimmy Rae had way back in '64. We didn't talk much durin' the drive, an' when the turn off for Alder Creek came up, I started to get this weird feelin' deep inside like we'd stepped right back in time. When the Oregon Police Camaro suddenly hit a bank of mist, I could feel the tension inside the vehicle go through the roof. We slowed down, just like Jimmy Rae had done back then an' pretty soon the town sign

10

came into view. There it was, tellin' us the same information from over fifty years earlier – at least I thought it was at first, but the count was up by one:

Absolution

Pop. 513

Samson had the troopers pull over an' got out to take a look. He stood there shakin' his head like he couldn't believe what he was seein'. He got back in the car an' looked at me.

"Am I going as nuts as you?" he asked.

"Glad you joined me," I replied. "Better late than never. Shall we?" I nodded my head at the windscreen, an' he told the troopers to move on.

The town was just as I remembered it, even down to the tumbleweed rollin' down the main street. We pulled up outside the saloon an' the four of us got out. I took a deep breath, almost expectin' Jimmy Rae to come runnin' outta that building screamin' for his life, but there wasn't a sound – not even a bird in that Godforsaken place.

"What now?" Samson asked.

"It was in there," I said, pointin' at the saloon. "Up the stairs an' down the corridor on the right. That's where we go if you want to see if I've been lyin'. Don't forget that you said this place didn' even exist."

The three of us, me, Samson an' one of the troopers, made our way up the steps an' into the bar room. Officer Devon – that was his name – brought along his pump-action shotgun. Guess he thought it was his insurance policy. We left the other trooper in the car. We shivered as we pushed through the swing doors – even me, an' I was ready for it.

"Up there?" Samson asked, noddin' at the stairs an' the darkened landing at the top.

"Yessir," I said. "Want me to go first?"

"I'll go," Officer Devon said, cocking the shotgun. "Never know who might be waiting for us."

"Knock yourself out," I replied, followin' his lead an' happy to have him as a shield. Samson might not know what was comin' but I

11

had a good idea. It was time to face my demons an' get revenge for Jimmy Rae.

We'd reached the top of the stairs, an' Devon had taken a few steps down the corridor when we heard the sound. It was the same growling rumble that I'd faced all those years ago, an' I hesitated so suddenly that Samson ran into me. Devon continued his walk, stoopin' a little in that way that cops have when they're on a raid. The movement wasn't so fast this time, but the effect was pretty much the same. The steps came slowly, one foot – if that's what it was – draggin' behind the other.

"Come out where I can see you!" Officer Devon called, bringin' the shotgun up to waist level.

The sloughin' steps paused, an' the growl deepened as if whatever was down that corridor was weighin' up the odds. Then the action quickened an' Devon gasped in surprise. His surprise turned to blind panic as the thing emerged into the half-light. I'd seen images of demons in any amount of movies an' TV horror shows, but this thing was like nothing from any of them – it was the eyes; glowin' yellow in the shadow an' then brightenin' as the thing stepped forward. Samson peered over my shoulder an' screamed. Officer Devon was lifted off his feet an' his head rolled across the floor as the thing bit it clean off. The shotgun clattered away towards my feet an' I picked it up.

"Now's the time to go, Samson," I yelled, bringin' the weapon up an' into line with the thing's body. "This is my fight, an' I'm takin' this sucker down for Jimmy Rae!"

I'm a psychiatrist – I deal in the provable, the believable. The job title is there on my certificate just below my name 'David J. Sansom'. Nevertheless, I ran from that saloon as if I had wings on my heels. The state trooper by the car started asking questions but I just jumped into the vehicle and told him to drive. He paused, and that's when we heard another scream and the sound of the gun shot. I'd seen the brown stains of the blood that I now know had belonged to Jimmy Rae Hollis and I wanted out of there. The trooper got out of the car and drew his gun.

"You fool!" I yelled. "Get back here and drive!"

It was no use; he was through the saloon doors and I heard him clumping up the stairs. That was when I heard the third scream that day. I shifted across the car, turned the ignition key and floored the accelerator pedal. I was down that road faster than I'd ever believed I'd drive. Now I knew that Tobias French was telling the truth and yet, according to all of the literature and records, the town of Absolution simply does not exist. By the time I'd got back to Portland and parked up the police car, some semblance of my rational mind had returned to me and I stopped off at the city library as I had done when first checking out French's story.

"Well, like I said before, Mr Samson," the librarian said, "I don't believe that such a place has ever existed, but we'll take a look in the local history section again. Come this way."

He led me through a labyrinth of bookshelves until we came to the section he wanted. He paused and I could see a look of surprise come over his face.

"Well, I certainly don't remember seeing *this* one before," he said, pulling out an old brown book from the end of one of the shelves. "Maybe it will help you in your search."

With that, he left to return to the front desk, and I sat down at one of the tables and opened the book. It smelled kind of musty and there were no stamps to record when it had last been taken out on loan. The pictures were old – some of them going back to the turn of the century, but I was about two thirds of the way through the pages when my heart seemed to jump to my throat. There it was, just as Tobias French had described it to me – Absolution, Oregon. A township of some 516 souls which had been left to decay when the railroad bypassed the area on its way to Portland.

The picture that particularly caught my attention was an old sepia print of a group of men standing outside the town saloon. They were a mixture of ages but there, at the right hand side, was the unmistakable face of Tobias French. I'd seen his mug shot from his police and jail records and there was no doubt that it was him. No doubt, also, that the young man to his left, and towards whose head Tobias was pointing, was Jimmy Rae Hollis. I looked back again at the head count on the description – 516! It had been 513 when we first saw the town sign.

13

The dreams began a week ago. They were odd at first more than scary, but now they're becoming terrifying. This can't be happening to me; I'm a sane man – a logical man. And yet I'm scared to death to close my eyes each night; I see the sign: 'Absolution. Pop.516'. Unlike Tobias French I *did* seek Absolution… and now it's coming for me.

Bridge of Dreams

Joe Martin sat outside his cottage and stared at the setting sun as it fell slowly behind the trees of Carr Wood. His view of the bridge from this point was uninterrupted – the bridge where he and Alison used to dangle lines into the canal and fish for sticklebacks when they were children. Leaving the cottage at seven each morning, he drove the three miles to the surgery in Highridge where he was the senior partner in one of the town's two GP surgeries. Returning home eight hours later after hearing the moans and groans of his daily list of patients, he shut off all thoughts of work and imagined Alison walking up the lane from Aldersford to Stonebridge.

Stonebridge, the Derbyshire hamlet, was now his home; Aldersford, the nearest village, was the place where they had both grown up and from where they had made their way to school all those years ago. They were inseparable back then; from the age of five to the time that they both went away to university there hadn't been a day when they had not seen each other.

"Mrs Martin. Mrs Martin!" Alison had exclaimed one day when they were having tea at Joe's house. "Me and Joe are going to get married when we're grown up, and we'll have lots of children, and we'll have a big posh house!"

They were six at the time, and Joe smiled now as he relived those scenes from their past. Alison had been so adamant about the plans back then, and it seemed to both of them that it would be the natural order of things.

"Is that right, love?" Joe's mum had said, wiping her hands on her pinafore after washing up.

"Yes!" Alison went on. "You and Mr Martin and my Mummy and Daddy will come and live with us so that we can take care of you like you take care of us now."

Life was so much simpler back then, and although Joe and Alison had other friends, it was to each other that they gravitated outside of school. At weekends, it was not unusual for them to walk the three miles to the old canal site at Stonebridge where, with sandwiches and lemonade, they would spend an afternoon fishing

15

off the bridge – their 'Bridge of Dreams' they called it, and they wouldn't make their way homewards until the sun had begun to set. Holding hands all the way, they laughed and giggled at the daftest of things – things that only the innocent would understand.

As they grew older, the attractions of the canal were replaced by other forms of entertainment. Evenings out at the pictures in Highridge had become a favourite pastime, and Alison would sit with her head on Joe's shoulder as she wept through the latest Hollywood tear-jerker to hit the local screen. He'd put an arm around her and smile – there was never a thought in his head of where that act may have taken him; to Joe they were just friends and this was the way that friends behaved – wasn't it?

In later years, before they went their separate ways to university, Joe had wondered whether he had missed something. If he had made that first 'grown-up' move, would she have left him? Was his lack of action taken as disinterest? He'd had a few girlfriends at college, but none of them had meant anything to him compared to the way that he felt about Alison. She always seemed to be there at the back of his mind, and somehow he couldn't feel the same about anyone else.

They met up, of course, during the college holidays, and Alison always came looking for him as soon as they had both arrived home. They would exchange talk about their courses, the cities where they were living, gossip about college and a myriad of other things. They talked a lot about each other and how their friendship would never end. Even then, Joe wondered whether she was, in some way, sending him messages – he just never seemed to pick up on them.

Then, one Christmas, she brought Peter home with her. He was a postgraduate student working for his master's degree. They had met up in the period between Alison's last holiday and the current one. Joe felt a pang of regret, and his missed opportunities now came home to him. They appeared to be happy and comfortable in each other's presence and Alison introduced Joe, rather coolly he later thought, as *'one of my best friends from home'*. To Joe, the smile seemed a little less sincere and warm, and Alison and Peter did not stick around too long.

It was at the Easter break, when Peter made another appearance, that Joe spotted the bruises. He had been one of a group of former Grammar School pupils out for the evening at a reunion at The Bell,

16

a small pub in Woodhouse, a village just outside Highridge. Joe had stepped into the ladies' toilet by mistake (the gents' was the next door along) and Alison was facing the mirror with her top pulled up, inspecting her side. The discolourations were purple and still quite fresh. She turned at the sound of the door opening and pulled the top down.

"Wrong door, I think," she said with her trademark smile. "Out! Martin," she ordered in mock outrage.

Joe stood his ground and frowned. He pointed at her side. "What are those?" he asked.

"Oh, I just..." she said, her voice fading away and she coloured up.

"Is he hitting you?" Joe stepped forward and she was in his arms, crying.

"He doesn't mean it," she said, wiping the tears away. "He drinks too much and then gets angry at the silliest thing. He always apologises afterwards..."

"How many times, Alison?" Joe asked. "How many times has he hit you?"

"Not often, and he does love me..."

The rest of the conversation was lost upon Joe and they resumed their places in the bar room of the pub. He sat for a while, fuming and wondering what to do. The question was resolved when Peter rose from his seat and headed for the toilets. Looking to one side, he could see that Alison was otherwise occupied in talking to someone else; he rose from his chair and followed. There was a broom in the corner of the mens' toilets, and Joe shoved it through the door handle to prevent anyone else from coming in.

Peter turned at the sound and smiled. "Oh, hi," he said. "You're Alison's friend Joe, aren't you?"

Joe was across the room in a split second and had Peter pinned up against the wall, his hand firmly gripping him by the throat. Peter's surprise was total and he had staggered backwards under the onslaught.

"Listen to me," Joe said, menacingly. "Listen, and do it carefully. I've seen Alison's bruises. You're a real piece of shit, Peter; is that what it takes for you to get a thrill? I want you out of this place right now, and tomorrow you're going to leave the area. If

17

I ever hear that you've even breathed the same air as Alison again, I'll beat the crap out of you and feed it back to you. Understand?"

Peter nodded – in truth there was very little else that he could do. He left by the pub's side door, headed back to Alison's house where he picked up his gear and departed without leaving a message. Alison would be upset, Joe thought, but she would get over it. Maybe then she would see where her true friends were; maybe then Joe would have the courage to tell her... maybe.

He didn't. Procrastination allowed Alison to slip through his fingers once more and it was to be a further five years before he met up with her again. The holiday breaks that had seen them meeting up no longer happened, as she took to spending her time out of college abroad. Joe received postcards from as far afield as Thailand and San Francisco as he plotted her travels around the globe. It was during this period of his old friend's absence that Joe met Caroline.

A fellow GP, she had arrived at the practice in Highridge as a locum for one of the partners who had taken time out to care for his elderly parents. Joe and Caroline quickly struck up a friendship based on common interests and were at ease in each other's company. It was eighteen months later that he asked her to marry him; she accepted and, at a small ceremony at the local register office, they tied the knot a few weeks later. Alison crash-landed back in Highridge a fortnight before Christmas.

Discovering that he had left his parents' house in Aldersford, she arrived at the surgery asking to see him. Faced with a receptionist resistant to her demands, Alison created such a fuss that she was quickly ushered into a side room where Joe arrived moments later.

"Alison!" he said, surprised. "What...?"

"You have to help me!" she said, rising from her chair.

Joe was staggered by her appearance. Gone was the healthy complexion, the rounded cheeks, the bright sparkling eyes. Her hair was dull and appeared matted; her face was pale – almost waxy, and her cheeks had the hollowed appearance of someone clearly addicted to illegal substances.

"What have you done to yourself?" he asked, quietly, gently pushing her back into the chair.

"I need... have you got something? I mean, you're a doctor, aren't you? You always have stuff lying about. Can't you...?"

"What are you taking, Alison?"

"Nothing much; just a little... okay, so it's Crack. Happy now!?" she snapped.

"You need to get into rehab," Joe said. "Wait there."

He was back a few moments later with some leaflets in his hand. He placed them on the table in front of her and watched as she flipped through them.

"What are these?" she asked, sharply.

"Clinics, Alison," he replied. "Places where they can help you to come down and get yourself clean, and then..."

"I need something right now, you fool!" she shouted. "Don't you understand that!?"

"You need to calm down," he said.

The suddenness of Alison's appearance and the belligerent nature of her approach were so far removed from the Alison that he had known, that Joe Martin was struggling to see the friend that this person used to be. Picking up the phone, he called reception and told them that he would be out for the remainder of the day. Gathering his coat from his room, he took Alison by the arm and led her to his car.

The clinic in Derby admitted her without question. Joe Martin was recognised throughout the county as one of the best GPs working in the local NHS Trust. Despite Alison's protestations, the staff persuaded her to stay for treatment and Joe promised to call in and check on her progress within the next few days.

"Do you think that she'll stay the course?" Caroline asked him at home that evening. She had covered all of Joe's appointments for the afternoon.

"Hard to say," he replied. "This is so unlike her. I don't even know where she's come from this time, and I'll have to go to Mum's to pick up her bags – she just dumped them there without warning."

Joe's fears were confirmed two days later. He and Caroline had been sitting outside the cottage in Stonebridge where they had set up home. The weather was cold but fine and the view towards the bridge was more or less the same as it had been for many years. The telephone call from the Derby clinic had his heart sinking. Alison had left the place having broken into the pharmacy and taken all of the stock of morphine. The local police had been alerted but no-one knew where she had gone.

Alison's sudden appearance and departure had set Joe Martin thinking about the way that things might have turned out had he paid more attention in years gone by. His marriage to Caroline, though comfortable at first, began a slow decline after three years and their divorce, though amicable in the end, seemed to Joe to have been inevitable from the day that Alison entered his surgery.

Reports of Alison's death from an overdose of heroin came to him six months later through a friend at the Nottingham Post. She had been found in a squat in Gateshead.

In the warmth of an early summer evening, Joe sat on the bench in front of his cottage and looked across at the Bridge of Dreams – the place where, as children, he and Alison had planned out their lives together. There was no longer any regret, only sadness. Alison had left him on a number of occasions due, it had to be said, to his own lack of action. That, though, was a thing of the past – she would never leave him again; now they would be together as they had said all those years ago.

Picking up the urn containing her ashes, he walked slowly over to the bridge. The final sadness was the fact that Alison had no family; her parents had died a few years earlier and she had no brothers or sisters. Joe supposed that he was the closest to a relative that she had. This was the place where he would remember her; he was sure that she would have wanted her remains scattering here.

While Shepherds Watched

Huddled against the cold, Gary Hopgood had settled down to keep watch over the flock of sheep which was gathering against the north wall of the field. He and his brother, Geoff, had bought the farm some years back with the redundancy pay from the Coal Board after the closure of the local pit. It had taken them a few years to make the place home, but after a period of adjustment to their new lives, the flock had steadily increased in size and was now providing them with a steady income from both lamb and wool sales. However, with finances still tight, they had to watch every penny. Their fortunes appeared to have turned a corner, but that had been before the rustlers had homed in on the area.

Reports on the East Midlands News bulletins had alerted the brothers to the activities of what seemed to be an organised gang moving around the Derbyshire Peak District, and farms in the area of Hartington had been raided over the previous month. They had decided to take preventative measures after their neighbour, Barry Weatherstone, had lost a dozen sheep a week earlier, and the 'watch' had been set up between the two of them. So far, there had been no return of the rustlers, but Gary had convinced his brother that it would only be a matter of time before their turn came around.

"We'll take turns on watch," he said to Geoff. "I'll take the shotgun for company."

"Don't go doing anything stupid," his brother replied. "It won't be like with Tony Martin, you know."

Tony Martin was a Norfolk farmer who had been harassed by a couple of burglars over a period of time. He shot and killed one of them in his home after the young man, Fred Barras, broke in. Initially charged with the murder of the intruder, the offence was reduced to manslaughter. Martin served three years in jail.

"Don't panic," Gary replied. "It'll just be to scare them away, and you can come running if you hear it go off."

Geoff was not convinced, but let the matter drop as his brother has been so insistent, and after a week of no activity he had almost forgotten their disagreement on the subject. On the following Wednesday Gary had started out from the farmhouse, flask and sandwiches in a back pack and the shotgun broken over his arm, heading for the field where they had moved the flock to newer pasture. He was settling down for the night as the dusk turned to a darker shade.

Their farm was well off the beaten track, being served only by a rough roadway which ran off Hide Lane; the nearest settlement was Hartington itself – there was nothing else for miles around, making it a perfect target for the sheep stealing gang. Gary was no slouch with the twelve bore, but he reckoned that the noise on its own would be enough to frighten away any thieves. It was almost two in the morning when the sound of an approaching vehicle had him focus all of his attention to the south. It was pitch black, but the night vision field glasses that he had bought revealed the approach of a car along Hide Lane. Gary frowned; a car wasn't going to be of much use to anyone hoping to make off with half a dozen sheep, but when a noise from the north caught his attention as well, the glasses enabled him to home in on another vehicle – a Land Rover this time – coming from the opposite direction. He shook his head in puzzlement; with no trailer behind it, this would also be useless for the task which he supposed they had in mind. The two vehicles stopped at a distance of around twenty yards from each other, and two men got out of each of them.

"What the…?" Gary whispered to himself. He pulled his mobile from his coat pocket. "Geoff!" he whispered. "I'm in the south paddock; get down here quick, and keep quiet – we've got visitors."

Geoff Hopgood was at his brother's side in minutes, and looked through the field glasses in the direction Gary had indicated. "What are they doing?" he asked, quietly.

"Dunno," Gary replied. "They've been standing like that since I called you, but I can't hear what's going off – they're too far away."

"Not the rustlers, then."

"No chance," Gary said. "No trailer for the sheep, but that one down there…" he pointed to one of the individuals near the car, "has got a case of some kind in his hand."

22

At that precise moment, there was a flash from the muzzle of a gun, and one of the men from the Land Rover fell to the ground. Return fire from his accomplice's automatic had one of the opponents lurching backwards, fatally wounded. The stand-off came to an end when the surviving pair turned their weapons on each other. After another burst of fire, there was complete silence and no-one left standing. Gary and Geoff remained frozen to the spot, stunned at the violence that they had just witnessed.

"What in hell was that all about?" Geoff asked.

"No idea," Gary replied. "Think it's safe to go and take a look?"

They waited for a further quarter of an hour before venturing from their cover close to the wall, and made a silent but cautious approach across the field towards the scene of the action. The sight that greeted them could have come straight from the pages of 'The Godfather'. Of the two men from the Land Rover, the first had taken a hit direct to the centre of his chest; the second had blood pouring from a wound in his neck – they were both dead. The brothers turned their attention to the two from the car but, with a similar set of wounds, they too lay lifeless on the road.

"What now?" Gary asked.

"Well, there's nothing to be done for any of them, so I suggest we take a look at what they brought with them," Geoff replied. "What's that over there?"

Gary walked across the road to the place his brother had indicated, and came back with a briefcase. They walked along the road to the Land Rover and put it on the bonnet. Geoff flipped the catches to open it, and they stood in silent wonder at the sight that the torchlight revealed to them.

"Cash," Geoff said, picking up one of the bundles. "Fifties, and in bundles of fifty," he said, having counted the notes. A quick tally of the number of batches, and he shook his head. "There must be over a quarter of a million in used notes here, Gary."

"And there's this as well," his brother replied, pulling another case from the passenger side of the Land Rover. He opened it at the side of the other case. "Has to be heroin," he said. "This was a drug deal gone bad."

"Now what?" Geoff asked. "Four dead criminals, a stash of class 'A' drugs, and a load of readies."

Gary took a deep breath. "Geoff," he said. "This could be the answer to all of our prayers."

"What do you mean?"

"Think about it, bro," he said, slowly. "The cash must be untraceable, right? The drugs we can chuck down that old mine working at the back of the north field and no-one will ever find them."

"But the bodies…" Geoff began.

"Can either be left here and we phone the cops, or they could follow the drugs down that mine shaft. We can take the vehicles and park them at the Hartington visitor centre; there'll be nobody there at this time of night and we can walk back here. What do you say?"

"What if we do that and someone comes looking for them? We're the nearest farm and they'd be bound to come here."

"I can take the tractor up and down the road to clear out the tyre tracks – there'd be nothing to show that they had ever been around here," Gary said. "Come on, Geoff – decision time."

"What if we take half the money, ditch half the drugs, and tell the police about what we think we saw. That way we could keep part of the cash to spend on the farm," Geoff replied.

The argument went on for a further half hour before Gary forced the issue by pointing at his watch. "We're running out of time, Geoff. We need to do something right away, before morning."

It was a fortnight before the tranquility of the Hopgoods' part of Derbyshire was interrupted. Gary opened the farmhouse door to a man dressed in a suit, and carrying a briefcase. He smiled and held out his hand.

"Morning," he said. "I wonder if you could help me. I'm looking for a couple of friends who may have passed this way a week or so ago."

"Well, we don't get many strangers around this part of the Peak," Gary said, shaking his head. "A couple of weeks, you say?"

"That's right. We were supposed to meet up in Buxton, but I fear that they may have lost their way. I haven't heard from them since."

"Sorry, mate. Apart from our local suppliers, neither me nor my brother have seen any strangers for ages."

"I see," the man said, frowning. "That's very unfortunate for me. They were my business partners and it's extremely important that I contact them without delay. However, if you haven't seen them I must be on the wrong track."

"Looks like it," Gary said, closing the door, but watching the man from the window as he made his way to his car. He stood at the side of his car and took out a mobile phone. After a brief call, he got into the vehicle, drove down to Hide Lane and headed off northwards in the direction that the Land Rover had come from.

"Gone, is he?" Geoff said, coming from the kitchen.

"For the moment," Gary replied. "Don't think he believed me, though, and the phone call that he made might be to bring in reinforcements."

"What's the plan?"

"Load up the shotguns and wait," Gary said. "We know the lie of the land – they won't. Having regrets?"

"We agreed on the decision," Geoff replied. "Now's not the time to get cold feet. It's not like we haven't got supplies. No need to go anywhere, and we'll see them coming a mile off if they do return."

Geoff Hopgood's words could not have been more prophetic. Four nights later, a vehicle came to a halt on Hide Lane. It parked up at the side of the road just over the crest of a rise, the other side of which would take them down the hill to the Hopgood farm. Four men got out of the car, checked their weapons and silently approached the farmhouse.

"Sure this is the place?" one of them said.

"Positive; I saw from the look on his face that he was hiding something," the one addressed replied. He was the suited figure who had questioned Gary Hopgood about his missing 'friends'. "No idea what could have gone wrong with the deal, but I'm as sure as hell that he knows. Come on, we need to get the cash and the consignment back."

The leader, now at the farmhouse door, raised a gloved hand and counted down three fingers. As that last one fell, the door was smashed in. Their invasion of the building was met immediately with a number of stun grenades from the kitchen.

"Armed police! Drop your weapons and get down on the floor!"

The room was a cauldron of noise and smoke as the tactical firearms squad swamped the area. All of the intruders were disorientated and helpless against the overwhelming force ranged against them. The confrontation was over in minutes, with all four now in handcuffs.

"You made the right decision, Mr Hopgood," DI Fallon said as Gary and Geoff left the Buxton police headquarters the following day. "I don't suppose for a moment that you considered keeping the money, did you?"

"Of course not, Inspector," Gary replied. "That would have been dishonest, wouldn't it?"

"It certainly would, sir," Fallon said, as the brothers got into their car. "The street value of that stuff would have been half a million. Good job we got our hands on the two hundred thousand as well as the heroin, isn't it?"

"Yes, it is," Gary said. He smiled and waved as they left the car park and headed off home.

"Half a million?" Geoff remarked. "Imagine that."

"I am imagining," Gary said. "That copper had no idea how much was actually in the briefcase. Clever ploy though, him putting it out on the news that the quantity of the drugs and cash recovered was nowhere near the quantities we found. Those guys were bound to come looking for the rest of it, and the cops only know what we told them."

"How much did it leave us with?" Geoff asked.

"Just short of sixty grand, bro," Gary said, smiling. "Should set us up nicely for the future if we're careful."

Never Too Late

"Referee!" I yelled in frustration. "Are you blind?! He must have carried the bloody ball five yards!"

I'm Ian Hancock and I've been watching Highridge United with my mate, Colin Butcher, for over fifty years. We've suffered some ups and downs with the team in that time, and this season was having its fair share of the downs. My anger had been simmering all through the first half as the inept official seemed incapable of spotting even the most blatant of rule breaches. He took no notice of my latest outburst, which was clearly audible in a crowd of less than two hundred on a cold, wet Wednesday evening at the Town Ground.

"Save your breath, mate," Colin said. "You'll only end up with a sore throat. I don't know how these guys get their badges, but it'll even out through the game."

His words, wise as they were, did nothing to quell my annoyance and I shoved my hands deep into the pockets of my overcoat and prayed for half time and a hot cup of tea. Thankfully, the whistle soon signalled the end of a tedious first half that had been completely devoid of any meaningful action. We trudged off to the tea bar, got our brews and returned to the terrace at the half way line.

"Remember the old days?" I said. "Back in the sixties when we really had a proper team; not one like these comedians now."

"I do," Colin said with a sigh. "Then came the Northern Premier League and we, in our wisdom, said a polite 'No, Thank You' to the invitation to join and it was all downhill from there. It's too late to do anything about it now, though."

"It's never too late, Colin," I said with a wink. "Mark my words; it's never too late."

Highridge was a club with a proud tradition. Sadly, and to most supporters' dismay, that ended back in 1968 when the club turned down the opportunity to join the fledgling Northern Premier League. Many of the Midland League teams that had formed the backbone of a very tough competition had joined, leaving Highridge behind in a poorer division. The club lost many of its players as a result of the committee's decision, and fortunes went downhill. Colin and I stuck with it through thick and thin, but it was a torrid time. The current fixture against Chelsworth Town was fairly typical of where the club presently stood.

The League system runs to over twenty levels with the Premier League at its summit; Highridge was currently playing at level nine in the Midland League Premier Division – not bad, but not good either. Our league position of tenth summed up the abilities of the present team; on a good day we were a match for anyone else in the division; on a bad one we were abysmal. Chelsworth were propping up the table with almost half the season gone, and Highridge was making heavy weather of putting them to any kind of sword.

"What this bloody club needs is an injection of money," I said to Colin. "We're never going to get anywhere with things as they are."

"Yeah," he replied. "But who's going to be daft enough to plough cash into a setup like this?"

I nodded towards the far end of the main covered terrace and he followed as I wandered away from anyone who might be within earshot. I looked around to make sure that we were alone.

"Somebody with a shed load of cash and nothing to spend it on," I said, quietly.

"And just where do you think that we'd find that kind of idiot?" he asked.

"Remember last month's Euro Millions Lottery?"

"Yeah," he said, frowning in concentration. "It was a rollover, and a mystery winner scooped the whole lot. Can't remember the exact amount, but it must have been about…"

"One hundred and thirty-three million, four hundred and twenty-five thousand, four hundred and two Euros," I finished the sentence.

Colin stood, momentarily, stuck for something to say. Then he asked "How do you remember that?"

"Because…"

"Bloody hell!" he hissed. "Not you!?"

"Me," I replied. "And it's been sitting in my bank account just waiting for this kind of opportunity."

"What are you going to do, exactly?" he asked.

"Tell you later over a pint in the supporters' club bar," I said. "They're coming out for the second half; stand by for more torture."

It wasn't quite as bad as the first period, but with five minutes to go, missed chances and a clear penalty appeal denied had us both heading slowly through the sparse crowd towards the exit. Suddenly, a murmur of anticipation ran through the terrace like some scared rabbit. We turned to see our winger clear of the covering defender and haring off for the edge of the Chelsworth penalty area. Pausing just long enough to look up to see who had been running up field in support, he fizzed a wicked cross towards the penalty spot where it was met with a diving header from one of our strikers. The net bulged before the goalkeeper had even had the chance to move. One flash of brilliance and the three points were ours; you had to feel a little sympathy for Chelsworth – just a little, and not for too long.

Feeling more relieved than happy, we took a couple of pints to a table in the bar at the end of the social club room.

"Okay, Rockefeller," Colin said. "Spill the beans. What is it that you've got planned?"

"I'm going to buy the club," I said, smiling and taking a large swig of my beer. "The Chairman's over there talking to Tommy behind the bar. I think we'll invite him over here for a quiet chat, don't you?"

"Me?" Colin said. "What's it got to do with me?"

"Because, my old friend, you are going to be my financial advisor. You're still an accountant, aren't you?"

"Yes," he replied. "But I'm retired."

"Still got the certificate? Still paying your subs?"

"Yes."

"Then it doesn't matter. You are who I say you are, and I'm the man with the money. Come on – no time like the present."

"Mr Hanley," I said, holding out my hand. "Ian Hancock – season ticket holder."

Patrick Hanley looked at me suspiciously but took the hand offered. He glanced over my shoulder at Colin and frowned. "Who's he?" he asked.

"This," I said, standing to one side, "is my friend, Colin Butcher; also a season ticket holder."

"Look," Hanley said. "If you've come to give me some grief about the state of the first team and the way that they're playing, you can forget it; I've heard it all before."

"Not at all, Mr Hanley," I said, holding up my hands in mock surrender. "In fact, if you'd like to join the two of us for a drink there's something that I have to say that may well be of interest to you."

"You want to do what?" Hanley looked at me in astonishment. "Have you any idea what it is that you'd be taking on?"

"Yes, Mr Hanley," I said. "I'm quite aware of the enormity of the task that I'd be facing."

"Where on Earth would you get the money?"

"That's not something that you need to worry about. Are you and the rest of the board of directors prepared to sell your shares? That's the only question facing you. If not, I go away and the club would probably fold within three years. If you agree, I'd take over the club and the limited company, and set them on the road upwards through the Football League Pyramid."

"I can't make that decision here and now," he said.

"Of course you can't," I replied. "Take the time to put the proposal to the board and let me know. Shall we say in one week's time?"

"All right. I'll convene a special board meeting early next week and let you know."

"Good," I said. "If the board agrees, my friend, Colin, will conduct a Due Diligence exercise in order to value the assets that the company has. Then I can table an offer which the board can consider."

Shocked as he was at my unexpected proposal, but buoyed by the win which had pushed Highridge United two places higher in the league, Patrick Hanley spent the rest of the evening contacting the rest of the members of the board of the limited company which owned the football club.

"Think they'll bite?" Colin asked me when we'd left the ground.

"Almost certainly," I said. "Just from the size of tonight's crowd I can't see how the club's doing much more than paying the players' wages. Where are we now? Ten home games into the season and an

30

average attendance of around two hundred. Taking into consideration that half of those coming through the turnstiles will be either kids or pensioners, I reckon that the takings can't be more than a thousand quid."

"And they still have rent, repairs, loan interest… they're in deep, aren't they?"

"They certainly are. They'll be crazy if they don't snatch my hand off."

"So we wait," Colin said.

"Yeah, but don't be surprised if you get a phone call from me before the weekend's out. You'd better brush up on those accounting skills of yours."

As it turned out, I got a call from Patrick Hanley on the Friday after the midweek game: the board meeting was set for the following day – a Saturday! Things were certainly moving fast.

I stayed close to the phone that afternoon. With the team playing away, I sat watching rugby on the TV and trying not to think about Highridge United's plight. It was around tea time that Patrick Hanley called: Colin and I were invited to attend a meeting of the full board on Monday morning at nine.

"Mr Hancock," Hanley said as we entered the boardroom. "It's very good of you and Mr Butcher to come along at such short notice, but bearing in mind our brief discussion last week the board felt that it would be in the interest of all to get this matter sorted out as soon as possible."

"I agree," I replied. "When would my associate be able to carry out the Due Diligence?"

"Immediately," Hanley replied. "I've spent some time with members of the board compiling the records that we feel you'll need, and they're all here." He waved a hand to the end of the table where a stack of papers had already been prepared for us. "Would you be able to begin right away?"

"If I may interrupt," Colin said. "I've already taken the liberty of checking your company records at Companies House and have the files relating to the last six years of trading for the limited company."

"How can you…?"

"I subscribe to the Companies House site, and for a fee can request the accounts for any company registered with them. I'll still need to see the detailed schedules prepared by your accountants, but essentially I already know what the state of affairs of the company is. I won't need more than a couple of hours to confirm the reports that I already have."

"If you could let us have use of the boardroom in private for the next few hours," I said, "I think that we could have a firm offer to put to you by the end of today."

The board members looked stunned at the news, but Hanley merely smiled and nodded. Opening the boardroom door, he ushered the others out of the room and closed it behind them all.

"Okay," I said. "Let's get down to it, Colin. Shall I make some coffee?" I pointed at the percolator on a corner table and he nodded.

It took a little under two hours for my friend to confirm what he already suspected. The limited company was teetering on the brink of insolvency, and if it failed it would take the football club down with it.

"So, what's it worth?" I asked, as Colin put the last of the reports back into order.

"Well, according to the last six years' accounts, the balance sheet's been weakening each time. They've got assets all right – there are the new changing rooms for a start. However, the directors have been pumping in money over five of those years just to keep things ticking over."

"And last year?" I asked.

"No fresh injections of cash and the balance at the bank has gone into overdraft. There's no problem right now – it's within agreed limits, but I suspect that it won't be long before they're invited to have a chat with the manager about the company's plans for the future."

"So, the ball's in my court?"

"Absolutely."

"What's the net worth right now?" I asked.

"Twenty-five thousand," Colin said, grim-faced.

"That all?"

"Yes. What do you plan to offer?"

"What's the combined value of all of the directors' loans to the company?" I asked, steeling myself.

"A shade over fifty grand," he replied. "Not pretty, is it?"

"Actually, it's not as bad as I'd thought."

"What do you plan to do?" he asked.

I thought for a moment. I wanted this club. I wanted to take it out of the league where it was floundering. I wanted it back to the days when I cheered them on when I was at school; most of all, I wanted it in the EFL – football league status: an unfulfilled dream, and it was never too late to dream.

"I'm going to make them an offer that they can't refuse. I'll give them back all the money that they've ploughed into the club plus a bonus. If they don't take it I'll just wait until the company goes under and buy it from the liquidator. Trouble is, by that time there won't be much left to work with."

"Shall I see if Patrick Hanley's available?"

"No time like the present, Colin," I said.

The reconvened board took only moments to agree to the terms of the offer and, by the looks of relief on their faces, I worked out that they'd already kissed goodbye to any chance of getting back the money that they'd lent to the club. I was an instant hero.

"What will you do with the club?" Patrick asked as we toasted the deal with the last bottle of wine on the premises.

"I'll take all the shares that the board hold and become Chairman. I'll need some of the members to stay on, at least in the short term, and that will include you. Once the club is back on a stable footing I can look at the way that the company's structured to ensure that it never gets into this state again."

"What about the staff?"

"Nobody's going anywhere, at least unless they want to leave; I'll need everyone around me on the admin side who knows how things run. Then I'll start to modernise – the club can't stay on this site. It's old-fashioned and three-sided grounds aren't allowed in the EFL."

"EFL?" Hanley said in surprise. "Are you serious?"

"Deadly serious, Patrick. The decision that you guys made today is just the beginning. I'm going to talk to the coaching staff as soon as we've tied up the legal formalities. Things are going to change radically after the end of this season. We're going up the pyramid – call it the Holy Grail if you like, but in five years I want us in League Two."

Colin and I had already primed a Derby solicitor to handle the transfer of ownership, and two weeks later I was the sole owner of Highridge Ltd and Highridge United Football Club. I spent the first part of the following week briefing all of the employees from the cleaner to the accounts staff; after that, I had a long talk with Charlie Statham, the team manager. Charlie had been a semi-professional with a number of local teams before a broken leg ended a promising career – he had been the manager for the past three seasons and, in my opinion, had done well to keep the club where it was. He had little in the way of resources to attract a better class of player and had tried desperately hard to instil a sense of pride and enthusiasm into a team made up of raw youngsters and ageing journeymen.

"I'm leaving at the end of the season, Mr Hancock," he said. "I've been offered the Assistant Manager's position with a team in the National League."

He told me the name of the club, and I had to admit that he would have been foolish to have turned it down. They were an outfit going places and currently sat just outside the play-off places with games in hand on all of the teams above them. I was sad at the news, but told him that Highridge would be unable to match the terms that he was being offered. I now had a new team manager to find before the season ended in May. On the bright side, I knew precisely where to find one. I made the phone call that evening.

"So, what did he say?" Colin asked when I told him a couple of days later.

"He's coming to see us on Friday."

"You managed to get Bob Hart interested in managing the team?"

"He's curious to say the least," I replied.

Bob Hart had managed teams in the lower reaches of the EFL for a number of years and had taken one or two of them way beyond their abilities on paper. He was a tough, uncompromising coach who demanded total commitment from his players and complete trust and loyalty from his chairman. There had been occasions in his recent past where these two components had not worked smoothly together, and his latest position with a League Two team up north was a case in point. In answer to my question on that very subject, he was quite open with his answer: the chairman, whilst initially enthusiastic about the Hart philosophy, had relented when complaints from some of the team's senior professionals had the board of directors doubting the wisdom of his appointment. When confronted with the issue, Hart had refused to budge and he and the club parted company. He seemed to be just the type of manager that we needed.

"He's coming to the game?" Colin asked.

"What better way of assessing the problems that we may be facing?" I said. "We'll leave him on the terraces to make his judgement, and talk it over after the match."

"As I see it," Hart said, putting his pint on the table at the Hare and Hounds after the game, "you've got a couple of decent young lads at centre back, a pair of strikers who should be putting the fear of God into any defence in this league, and a midfielder who, if he can get his arse into gear, could split any side wide open. That's it; five players out of eleven worth keeping on. The rest seem to be just cruising; if the ball doesn't come to them they can't be bothered."

"Our manager's a good lad," I said. "He's been here for a few seasons but he's been given precious little to work with. He's leaving at the end of the season, so you'll have carte blanche as far as I'm concerned with regard to the playing staff. What do you need?"

"A decent goalie – one who's not scared to come off his line, a pair of wing backs who can actually run for ninety minutes, a stopper in midfield and another defensive guy to play alongside him. Then you need another pair of creative players to supplement the only guy who can make the team tick. The final piece of the jigsaw will be an experienced target man who can hold the ball without being pushed around."

"Where do we find them?" I asked.

Hart smiled. "Oh, I know a few blokes who'll come and play for me. They're the kind who aren't scared of a bit of hard graft and as long as you're straight with them, moneywise, they'll walk through fire for you."

"What about you?" I said.

"If you're serious about league status in five years, I want a contract that long and the freedom to pick my own backroom team. There won't be many – just a couple of guys that I know: one to scout for talent and the other to check up on the next opponents."

Colin and I hammered out a deal with Bob Hart and he went away to make some phone calls. When we saw him again on the Friday evening he was in the company of two other men. They stood on the terraces at the end of the main stand and just watched, making a series of notes as the game progressed. The result, not that it mattered, was a two all draw in which we threw away two points in the final five minutes due to some dire defending and a horrifying goalkeeping error. Hart and the other two signed contracts the following week and we waited the season out.

May came and Highridge's final game of the 2021/2022 season was a home fixture against Woodborough Athletic, our near neighbours and fiercest rivals. They stood second in the table and were heading for a play-off slot for promotion to the Northern Premier League's Division I (Midlands). Contrarily, the whole team chose that very match to reveal what they should have been capable of all season. We outplayed our more skillful rivals in every area of the pitch and ran out easy winners 4-0. The attendance was also a very satisfying 1,385. We had a leaving ceremony for Charlie Statham after the game and introduced Bob Hart to the players as their new gaffer for the 2022/23 season. With the evening drawing to a close and the players beginning to head for the door, Hart called them all back.

"Okay," he said. "Now that we've been introduced, I think that it's a good idea to let you all know how the land lies. This club is going places; it starts here and now. I want you all back here tomorrow for a training session."

"Season's over," one of the older guys said. "What's the point?"

"The point is whether or not you want to be a part of the team next season. You were all lucky tonight; Woodborough are already in the play-offs so they didn't need to try too hard. If you think you played well, think again; those eleven against you were more interested in avoiding injuries than getting a result – they didn't need a win."

"There's no alternative," I said, stepping in. "Bob's in charge now, and anyone not liking the idea has the club's full permission to look for somewhere else to play. Highridge United is changing – there are no soft options now that the season's over. Next year we're going to win this league instead of finishing up as also-rans; clear?"

The majority of the team filed out in silence, but I found it curious that the five who Bob Hart had singled out for next year all remained behind and were now involved in conversation with their new boss. I smiled at Colin and we headed to the bar for another drink.

May ended with Bob Hart conducting a series of training sessions aimed at integrating his new signings into the team. Those sessions were tough – I watched them all; aimed at increasing levels of fitness, they involved long runs through the local country park and intensive tactical routines focussed at keeping the ball and wearing out the opposition by making them chase, chase, and then chase again. The sharpness of the eleven that Hart singled out as a potential starting line-up was amazing when compared to the previous season. By the beginning of June, when Bob gave them all a month off, I had started to believe that we were on the cusp of something really special.

"How are you planning to keep up the momentum?" I asked him during the week before pre-season training was set to begin.

"Incentives," he said, bluntly. "Keep the players hungry; not physically but mentally. Make them want to win, but also make them desire to win well."

"What kind of incentives?"

"When I was a teenager I thought that I was good at this game," he said. "I was at Forest when Clough and Taylor were there. Never made the first team, but we had some decent kids in the reserves. Clough took me to one side one afternoon in training and said *'You're a decent player, son, but you're lazy. Look over there at John McGovern; watch what he does when we lose the ball; see? He's back in front of the central defenders. You don't do that;*

unless you're prepared to work, you won't be here long.' He was right; I didn't listen and they released me at the end of the season."

"I'm not following you," I said.

"The point was, that McGovern and the rest of the team would walk through fire for Cloughie. The club paid the players a decent basic wage, but the bonuses and incentives were phenomenal."

"Okay, say I agree," I said. "What did you have in mind?"

"Don't starve the team – pay them like Clough and Taylor did, but dangle the carrots before their eyes. Don't just pay win bonuses; supplement them with extra money for goals scored beyond a certain number each game – say three. Now pay them for each clean sheet; pay the goalkeeper extra if he saves a penalty. Incentivise them for bigger crowds."

"What about the downside? There needs to be something for breaches of discipline," I said.

"Fines for yellow and red cards; fines for arguing with the referee or abusing his assistants. Fines for missing training or misbehaving in public. Don't turn them into monks, but don't stand for any nonsense either. The players will respect us for it and we'll reap the benefits."

I loved what this man was saying and we drafted out a scheme for carrying out just what he had suggested.

"Get all the players on contract as well; no more of this holding onto their registrations on a yearly basis – all that means is that some bigger club can pinch them at the end of the season."

That was something that I discovered early on and had decided to reform, so Bob coming up with it merely served to reinforce my own thinking. When July arrived and the players reported back for training, all the incentives were lined up to present to them. It was hard to judge reaction but there were certainly no mutterings of discontent.

There were changes to the club outside of the playing staff. Marjorie, our senior admin lady, decided for personal reasons that she would no longer be able to run that side of the business. I brought Colin onto the board as FD and his wife, Angela, stepped into the breach to fill the hole that Marjorie left. Wendy, our younger admin clerk, took to the new regime like a duck to water. I offered her the role of Angela's deputy with a view to her taking over the role in a couple of years – that was the limit of time that

Colin's wife had said she would be prepared to work. We started Wendy on an AAT course and she lapped it up.

Gradually, the former board members resigned as they felt that they no longer had any influence over the progress of the company. Patrick Hanley was the last to leave.

"I'll stay until the end of this season if you don't mind," he said to me before the first game. "I want to see where you're going to take Highridge, but I don't fancy looking over your shoulder all of the time." He was as good as his word.

"What are you going to spend your time doing?" Colin asked me when I broke the news to him.

"Me?" I said. "I've got other stuff that needs taking care of. We can't stay on this site. The state of the ground will prevent us from going up the pyramid much further – we have to move to a new stadium."

"Where?" he asked. "Surely we can't move too far away from the town."

"There's a site just on the edge of Highridge and the council is wanting to sell it to plug a hole in their budget. It's no good for housing because it's a former industrial location and the clean-up costs for property development will be too high."

"I'm guessing that a football stadium wouldn't be out of the question, then," he said. "Think you'll get it?"

"I've already made an offer and they're thinking about it. Should be getting an answer this week. If they give us the green light, I reckon we can be at a new ground in time for the start of the 2023/24 season."

Oddly enough, we began our home league campaign of the 2022/2023 season against our old rivals, Woodborough Athletic. Their efforts at promotion through the play-offs came to nothing after an aggregate 4-2 defeat in the semi-finals. Most of their better players left and they were forced into a recruitment campaign from lower leagues. Bob Hart's team was electric; playing in triangles, they pushed and ran until Woodborough were chasing shadows. The game ended up with Highridge celebrating a 5-0 win. The season had begun with three away fixtures due to the nature of the ground – it was three-sided, the other long edge being shared with the council-owned cricket pitch; those games had resulted in two wins and a draw, and the four games played saw Highridge at the top of the table.

"Looks like all your hard work's paying dividends," I said to Bob Hart after the Woodborough game.

"So far, so good," he said. "Let's see what happens when the bad weather sets in. Ask me what I think at the end of February and I'll have a better idea."

He did have a much better idea. At the beginning of March, with only ten games left to play, Highridge topped the league by nine points. There had been defeats, of course, but the team bounced back with resounding victories each time. Discipline was outstanding – not a single red or yellow card had been handed out to Highridge players, and referees all reported on the exemplary behaviour of the team. Patrick Hanley died at the end of that month. His wish to end the season still on the board, and see how we fared, foundered as a massive heart attack took him whilst he and his wife were on holiday in Spain. Highridge won the league title and preparations began for life in the Northern Premier League Division I (Midlands). It had taken fifty-five years to right the wrong of the decision on that day back in 1968.

The summer months were once again devoted to training and tactics after a four week break, and the addition of a few new players saw the first team squad expand to twenty-two. It was at this point that Bob Hart suggested that we look more to growing our own talent from within rather than spending money in an ever costly transfer market. With the end of the 2023/24 season approaching and the team once more top of its division, plans were prepared for the formation of both reserve and youth teams for the forthcoming campaigns. Patrick Hanley would have been well pleased by progress – Highridge won the divisional title and would move up into the premier division of the Northern Premier League in August 2024. As for the proposed new stadium, it was a proposal no more. The ten acre site had been acquired from the local council for slightly more than the company was initially prepared to pay for it, but work had started after the end of the 2022/23 season. Estimates were that all safety certificates would be in place in time for our new campaign. The ground would hold ten thousand to begin with, but groundworks had been laid to a high enough standard that we would be able to build on the original structures and increase capacity to thirty thousand in due course.

"Where's the money coming from?" Colin asked me as we sat poring over the plans. "I know you had that enormous win on the Euro lottery, but surely that can't have been enough to fund *all* the plans that you've got."

"Careful planning," I said. "The majority of the winnings were placed in the hands of an asset management company that I use for my own pension funds. The portfolio I chose has grown the investments considerably over the last eighteen months. There's no need for me to fret about money – this club will earn a good return by the time we're in the EFL."

Considerable interest in the new stadium had been shown by local media, and with a lengthy feature on East Midlands News just before the start of the new campaign, season ticket sales received a healthy boost as a fresh wave of interest from local football fans hit the club. Highridge began the new season with a disappointing 0-0 draw and, initially at least, results were not what Bob Hart had in mind when conducting his pre-season schedule. He shifted his team selections around and things began to improve. A record crowd of 6,856 on Boxing Day saw Highridge put Whitby Town to the sword to the tune of a 5-1 win; at that stage, the team stood fourth in the league – six points behind the leaders, Lancaster City, but with two games in hand. Excitement had begun to build, but a run of four games without a win had the side losing ground slightly. Hart's team talk after the last of those games saw a dramatic improvement and the season ended with Highridge unbeaten in eleven games – ten wins and a draw. It was not enough to win the title and automatic promotion, but in a play-off final against Grantham Town, Highridge squeaked through 2-1 on aggregate. We were now only two steps away from the EFL.

"When you look at it," Bob Hart said to me on the eve of the first game of the 2025/26 campaign, "Crawley Town set the trend back in 2012 and Salford City did the same in 2019. It just goes to show that it's never too late for a club like Highridge to shake the dust off their boots and climb the ladder."

"It's a fine line between splashing indiscriminate cash and going bust, and breaking the Fair Play Regulations," I replied. "We're limited as to how much we can pay players in relation to the company's turnover. We're doing fine at the moment, but I'm guessing that you'll be wanting to plan soon for life in the Football league and its impact on player contracts."

"I will, and it'll go some way towards keeping our best players, both in the first team and the reserves."

That conversation was to come back onto the boardroom table at the end of the season as Highridge won the National league (North) by quite a margin. The 2026/27 campaign was to be a momentous year for the club as it made its final assault on membership of the EFL.

As for the company as a whole, Colin had joined the board and I'd allotted some share options to him as a 'thank you' for the work he'd done since our days in the Midland Counties League, and he'd been joined by Bob Hart – my attempt to tie him to the club beyond the initial five year plan. Wendy Stenson, the junior admin girl, had sailed through her AAT qualification and, with the 'retirement' of Colin's wife, Angela, she had taken responsibility for the entire admin/accounts department and now had a staff of three working for her; I had promoted her to Company Accountant reporting to Colin. She would be set to take over his role when the time came. Expansion of the non-playing staff had been carefully controlled – I'd seen too many clubs struggle after running before they could walk. Of the players that Bob had brought in to steady the ship in the early days, three had left and the remainder had joined the coaching team. The five that had survived Bob's initial cull had, despite his efforts, all moved on, at considerable financial benefit to Highridge, to clubs at higher levels; this is where Bob's youth policy had paid dividends. Their places had been filled by young, hungry individuals from our reserves – we were truly an organically grown club!

So, where are we now? Well, the side won the National League outright in the 2026/27 season and the ground was extended during that summer to bring it up to a 15,000 capacity. Season ticket sales suggested that we might fill it with each game in our first season in the EFL, and so it turned out as the club embarked upon its first assault on league football since its foundation in 1883. Our opening game against Newport County was a sell-out and the gates were closed well before kick-off. Needless to say we won that game; it wasn't easy and the 3-2 score line told the story of a cut and thrust encounter which was to be the hallmark of the first half of the season.

Highridge made it through the early stages of the FA Cup and I sat in shivering expectation on Saturday 6th January 2028 waiting for the teams to come out onto the pitch for a third round tie. Our only previous incursion into the 'proper' rounds of the cup competition had been on 16th November 1963 in a 3-1 first round away defeat to the now defunct Bradford Park Avenue; I was at that game with my father and cried all the way home. Now Highridge had a real chance at giant-killing; West Ham United play the kind of football that suits us – an open, attacking style which tends to leave gaps that we can exploit. It's never too late to dream, and I've done quite a bit of that over the years – this is where the dreaming stops and reality begins.

Parrots and People

"He's a pretty one," Polly said to her friend Katie Macaw. "Where did you get him?"

"Oh, I picked him up at the local shop last weekend," Katie replied. "The owner said that he's quite the best specimen of his type that he's ever seen."

"Does he talk? Have you been training him?"

"Well, I've only had him for a few days, and I have tried but he doesn't seem to have got the hang of it yet. You have to be patient with them, the shop owner said."

They peered into the cage that was standing on Polly's table and cocked their heads on one side in wonder at the small figure in the corner. It was eyeing them suspiciously and edged further away as they drew closer. Finally, it turned its back on them both.

"Oh," Polly said. "Doesn't seem very friendly. What's that noise he's making?"

"He does that when he's not pleased about something. I put a bath attachment on the cage door the other day and he made such a racket that I had to take it away. You should have heard him – wouldn't surprise me if he was swearing in his own way."

"Well, I suppose it's the new surroundings. He'll soon get used to it," Katie said. "Won't he be lonely on his own?"

"Ah," Polly said. "That's where I'm way ahead of you. I asked the shop owner that very question, and he said that he'd have some females coming in from his supplier next week – I think that might cheer him up a bit."

"I hope so for your sake," Katie replied. "You're going to end up with one very grumpy pet if he's wrong."

Polly did indeed buy a female companion for her male pet on the morning of her friend Katie's next visit. She perched herself in anticipation as Polly brought a small box with ventilation holes from the kitchen where she had left the rest of her shopping.

"Come on, then," Katie said, jiggling excitedly from side to side. "Get on with it."

"Patience," Polly replied. "They might not like each other; and do try to keep quiet, please. You might put them off."

Polly opened the door of the cage where the male sat sulking in the corner; she lifted the flap of the box, offering it up to the now open cage. Nothing happened at first, but then a figure emerged from its depths and a head peeked round the corner. She eyed the two of them for a while and then looked into the cage where she soon spotted the male in his corner. Stepping carefully over the edge of the box, she stood on the platform created by the cage door and then stepped inside. Polly closed the door behind her.

"Hi," she said, noticing that the male had turned his head slightly at the sound of the cage closing. *"I'm Teri; what's your name?"*

The male stood up from his crouching position and turned to fully face her. He frowned before answering. *"William. Where did they catch you?"*

Teri moved a little closer. *"I was just sitting out in the fresh air, and suddenly this net scooped me up. The next thing I saw was a kind of shop when they opened the box I was in. They plonked me into a small sort of rabbit hutch – it had a mesh front and I couldn't get out."*

"Yeah, that's what happened to me too," William said, his shoulders sagging in resignation as he realised that any kind of escape was unlikely. *"Looks like we could be here for some time together."*

"What do you think they're up to?" she asked, nodding her head towards Polly and Katie who seemed to be watching them in fascination.

"You're not going to like this, but I think that they're probably wanting us to mate."

"What?!" she exclaimed. *"Here? In daylight? In front of them??"*

"I dunno," he said. *"It's all got me very confused. Why else would it* (he nodded at Polly) *have bought the two of us?"*

"But I hardly know you," Teri said, recovering some of her composure. Her initial assessment of William had convinced her that he meant her no harm, but her mind was still reeling at the situation that she found herself in.

"Yes," he said. *"I'm not overwhelmed at the prospect myself, you know. You're pretty and all, but I have a family of my own back home..."* His voice trailed away as his eyes began to fill up.

"What do you think they're talking about?" Katie said.

"Oh, I think I could be on to a winner here," Polly replied. "She's moved in closer to him and he's come away from his corner. They do seem to be getting on quite well, don't they?"

"What about that loud noise she made just then?"

"I bet that was part of their mating ritual, Katie. I must admit I'm no expert, but he does seem to have perked up a bit and he's showing quite a lot of interest. Perhaps if I cover the cage up they'll get on with... you know."

"Hmm," her friend replied. "Maybe you're right. Anyway, I have lots to do. I'll call in on you in a day or so to check up on them. Must fly, now."

With that, Katie Macaw spread her wings and eased away from the branch where she had been sitting. Cruising effortlessly on the thermal that was rising from the forest floor, she headed for home, wondering why on earth parrots took such a keen interest in humans as pets.

Red Shoes

"We have a match," Peter Spencer said, entering Dennis Marks' office at New Scotland Yard. "The DNA samples that George Groves took at the scene came up with a name from our files."

"Not bad for speed, Peter," the DCI said. "Who is it?"

"Rosie McFee," DI Spencer replied. "Prostitute working the streets in Paddington, and according to our enquiries she went missing a week ago."

"Just waiting for Groves' autopsy report, now," Marks replied. "Let's take a trip to the lab and see if we can hurry things along."

"Your timing, as usual, is impeccable, Dennis," Groves said. He was senior pathologist at the Home Office and had worked closely with Marks and Spencer on a number of cases down the years. "The woman over here," he beckoned them to a table on the far side of the room, "is, as you are probably now aware, Rosie McFee, late of Paddington."

"Yes," he replied. "I got that from Peter. Anything else?"

"Cause of death," he said, pointing at the woman's neck, "was strangulation. She'd also been raped; abrasions around the pelvic area are quite severe."

"Any DNA matches for the assailant?" Spencer asked.

"Not possible, I'm afraid. Whoever did this had been very careful. Her clothing wasn't much help either," he said.

"Don't tell me," Marks sighed. "No transfer."

"That's right," Groves replied. "The assailant had been very aware of that possibility. In my opinion, she had been thoroughly cleaned, redressed, and dumped in Southwark Park, Bermondsey, where she was found. The kill site was elsewhere. I did find one curious thing, though," he said, stepping to another table where the woman's clothing and belongings had been laid out.

"Shoes?" Marks said. "A pair of red shoes? What's so special about them?"

"They're Gucci," Groves replied. "By the look of them, I'd say that they were top of the range when they were bought."

"Okay, George," Marks said, acutely aware of Groves' penchant for a puzzle. "What do you mean by 'when they were bought'?"

"Well, I managed to do a little digging around; this particular style was discontinued in 1990, so that means that they must have been purchased in the mid-to-late eighties."

"Doesn't narrow it down much, though," Spencer said.

"In itself, no, it doesn't, Peter," Groves replied. "However, there was a very faint label inside one of them, and I managed to lift a name from it."

"You traced the shop?" Marks asked.

"Ferris and Brown," Groves smiled, holding up an old label. "New Bond Street, and they're still in business. Shops like that tend to keep their records for quite a while - you never know; you might strike lucky."

"Yes, Chief Inspector, we do keep our records for all purchases of that range of Gucci shoes," Steven Prince said.

Prince was a man of discerning taste, and was very smartly dressed in a three-piece suit complete with button hole. He had been manager of Ferris and Brown for over thirty years and his tone was very much that of one of the suppliers to the aristocracy. He viewed Marks and Spencer with more than a little disdain.

"Could you tell us to whom you may have supplied these shoes?" Marks held up a plastic bag containing the pair removed by George Groves from the feet of Rosie McFee. "We also found this label inside one of them."

Prince removed a pair of spectacles from his top pocket, peered at the label, and took a long look at the shoes. "Hmm," he said. "I believe that I know the style, but we haven't sold them for quite some time. One moment."

Marks and Spencer looked at each other and shook their heads as the manager disappeared into a back room. They did not have too long to wait, however, and he returned with a smile on his face.

"Our records, Chief Inspector, are quite impeccable. Those shoes were sold, on 16th April 1987, to a Mrs Stephanie Cavendish-Brown

– one of our best customers if memory serves me correctly. Will there be anything else?"

"No, thank you, Mr Prince," Marks replied. "You've been very helpful."

"Something I've missed?" Spencer asked when they were back at the office.

"Not really," Marks replied. "Apart from the fact that I did wonder how a pair of shoes belonging to Stephanie Cavendish-Brown could have ended up on the feet of a London prostitute."

"What is it that you're not telling me, then?"

"Stephanie Cavendish-Brown disappeared in 2012," Marks replied. "We suspected her husband, Raymond, at the time but we had nothing to go on apart from the fact that theirs was a very volatile relationship. She was last seen in public at a dinner dance with her husband on 12th June of that year. They had a furious row in front of a roomful of witnesses. When we interviewed him, he told us that his wife had left him and gone abroad. Her clothes and passport were missing, but we were unable to trace her leaving through any of the ports or airports, and the case went cold. Now her shoes turn up on a murdered prostitute and we're no nearer to finding out what happened to Stephanie Cavendish-Brown or who killed Rosie McFee."

"Might be able to help you there, Dennis," Groves said, walking into the room as the conversation was ending.

"Go on," Marks said. "Please enlighten me."

"Well, when I took a closer look at Ms McFee's fingernails, I found small traces of skin under the middle two of her right hand. There was enough to put through a DNA test, and it appears to belong to this man." He handed Marks a file.

"Sammy Barks?!" Marks exclaimed. "I thought he was in Parkhurst."

"Hmm," Groves said. "Came out a few weeks back – good behaviour and all. Didn't look good for Rosie McFee, though."

"Peter," Marks said. "Get an address for our Mr Barks – I think we'll pay him a call."

It didn't take the detectives long to break Sammy Barks down. A former worker at the docks, Barks had been fired for being drunk. Marks had known him for a number of years, and the man usually found himself on the wrong side of the law as a means of feeding his addiction to the booze. A win at Walthamstow dogs had seen him celebrating in a number of pubs in Paddington.

"She came onto me in the Swan, Mr Marks," he said. "All fur coat and no knickers, that one. I was a bit the worse for wear; me and the lads had been drinking for a while and I thought 'What the hell, Sammy, she's up for it and the rate's not bad.'"

"So why did you kill her?"

"Kill her?" he said in amazement. "I didn't kill her."

"Your DNA was under her finger nails."

"We argued; she tried to con me on the price and when I wouldn't budge she went for me. Look – still got the marks." Barks pulled down the neck of his sweater and revealed an angry-looking set of scratches. "She was still breathing when I left her outside the boarding house – she'd set her eyes on this other geezer; smart-looking bloke he was. I suppose she thought she could make up the amount she was asking from me by overcharging him."

"Can you give us a description?" Marks asked with a certain amount of scepticism – he had been down this route with Sammy before.

Sammy Barks, despite being an alcoholic, was renowned for his memory – something which the booze had not appeared to affect during all of the years that he had been indulging. By the time that Sammy had finished at the side of a sketch artist, the detectives had a clear image of the man that Sammy said he saw with Rosie prior to her death.

"If that's not a good likeness to Raymond Cavendish-Brown I'll hand in my warrant card," Marks said. "We need to talk to our facial recognition experts and see what they can come up with from an old photograph of our man."

The likeness was astonishing in its accuracy, and Marks and Spencer were at the home of the aforementioned gentleman a couple of hours later. Faced with their evidence, Cavendish-Brown was, at first, outraged at their insinuations, but when threatened with arrest, he chose, instead, to go with them voluntarily to answer questions about his relationship with Rosie McFee.

"She was a tart, Chief Inspector. Nothing more, nothing less. Our meeting was quite accidental, but when she saw me, as she was coming away from another of her clients, I suppose she saw a further chance to increase her earnings."

"A little down market for you, wasn't she?" Marks said.

"You take what you can get where you can get it. I'm no longer the dashing young blade that I was, and she wasn't bad looking when the lights were out."

"She was found wearing your wife's shoes."

"Stephanie's?" Cavendish-Brown said, suddenly shaken.

"Indeed," Marks replied. "Now, how could that have happened?"

"I have no idea," he said. The self-confident air of less than half an hour earlier was now gone, and the two detectives saw instead the fear of a cornered animal.

"Let's just theorise for a moment, shall we?" Marks asked. "Peter," he said, turning to his DI. "If you wanted to dispose of a body somewhere away from Paddington, where would you choose so that your crime would be covered up pretty quickly?"

"Landfill, sir," Spencer replied. "I can pull up a list of sites quite easily. Shall we start with Springfield just off the M40?"

"Yes," Marks said. "I wonder if the rest of Mrs Cavendish-Brown's belongings are there as well."

"Here we go," Spencer said, a little later. "The council keeps detailed records of the pits that they use and the dates that they were sealed. Good Lord! There's one here that was closed in June 2012 – that's quite a coincidence. Wasn't that about the time that your wife went missing, sir?" Spencer said to Cavendish-Brown.

"Maybe if we obtained a warrant to search the site we might come up with some very revealing evidence, Peter," Marks said.

"I'm saying nothing more until my solicitor gets here," Cavendish-Brown said. "I think that I'm entitled to a phone call, aren't I?"

"So, we think that he dumped the body and all of his wife's belongings at Springfield?"

"We'll find out once we get the diggers in there, Peter," Marks said. "Mr Cavendish-Brown certainly became very twitchy when we started going down that road."

"If we do find anything, George Groves may have to work hard at it to give us something concrete to present to the CPS," the DI replied.

It did not take the excavators too long to scrape away the topsoil of a section of the Springfield site that was the last to be sealed. Once re-opened, belongings of Stephanie Cavendish-Brown emerged close to the surface; sadly there was no trace of the body of the lady in question.

"I'm still puzzled as to how the shoes came to be in Rosie McFee's possession," Marks said to George Groves the following week.

"Might be able to help there, sir," Spencer interrupted, coming into the office and holding up a DVD. "I found this in the evidence box in the case of Stephanie Cavendish-Brown's disappearance."

"What is it?" Marks asked.

"CCTV footage from Paddington Station on the day she went missing. Here," he said, inserting it into the player in the office, "look what I found."

The footage, even though not completely clear, showed the comings and goings of passengers making for the Dover train from the London station, and after a while Marks was on his feet.

"Go back, Peter," he said. "There! Freeze the frame; could that be Stephanie Cavendish-Brown? It certainly looks like her. Can we zoom in?"

Spencer closed in on the female in question, and Marks pointed at the screen. "Those shoes," he said. "Sharpen the image, Peter. See? I reckon those are the shoes that Rosie was wearing. But how did she get her hands on them?"

"That's where it gets interesting," Spencer said. "Watch what happens next."

The woman paused, looked at her watch as if checking something, and then headed for the ladies' toilets. She came out again a few moments later with the red shoes in her hand and a different pair on her feet. Checking her watch again, she dumped the shoes in a litter bin and headed off out of shot towards one of the platforms. The camera remained angled on the area of the bin, and another figure entered its field of view. Rosie McFee walked over to the bin and removed the shoes; she took one look at them and shoved them into her bag.

"Well," Marks said. "That proves how she got hold of them, but it doesn't help us find Stephanie Cavendish-Brown."

"No," said Spencer. "It doesn't."

"If Raymond was telling the truth, and that was his wife, she's long gone by now," Marks replied.

"If," Spencer said. "If it was her; however, it wasn't."

"How do you know?"

"Because a case containing more of Stephanie Cavendish-Brown's possessions was found at Calais by the French police. They've had them in storage since 2012 and didn't know what to do with them. When I asked for it to be opened they were only too willing. Stephanie Cavendish-Brown never went from Paddington to Dover that day. The woman you saw was a friend of Raymond's – Julie Stenson."

"Okay. How did you track her down?" Marks asked.

"Quite easily once I'd been through the address book that we found as part of our search after we'd brought Cavendish-Brown in for questioning. The warrant gave us all that we needed. Her name was in the back section. I went to her house and she told me everything."

"Everything?" Marks asked. "Why?"

"Apparently she and Raymond were going abroad together once the dust had settled, but he backed out – dumped her quite unceremoniously. She was livid and she's been looking for a way to get back at him ever since. She'll testify in court as long as we don't charge her with anything."

Marks and Spencer went ahead with charging Raymond Cavendish-Brown with his wife's murder, and the CPS agreed to prosecute the case on the strength of the circumstantial evidence that the detectives had unearthed. He was found guilty by majority verdict at The Old Bailey and was sentenced to life imprisonment. At sixty-five years of age it was likely that he would die in prison. Despite the efforts of DCI Marks, Cavendish-Brown refused all cooperation in the matter of the murder of Rosie McFee.

"Typical, Peter!" he cursed. "Tie up one cold case loose end and we're left with another. I hate the bloody things!"

Stunned

"Your trouble is that you never take any care with what you're doing."

The statement was delivered flatly, and in a careless way. In itself, it was not destructive criticism, but in Warren Sheldon's current state of mind it was the flame which lit the blue touch paper, and he sat there silently fuming at Cross's comments. He'd been seeing his lawyer and long-term friend regularly for a month since the guilty verdict at his trial and Cross had, seemingly, been working hard during that time on an appeal. Sheldon was convinced that he had been the victim of a miscarriage of justice. It was time to set things right.

"No," he replied. "My trouble is that I was innocent. Somebody set me up and I'm looking at life for something that I didn't do!"

"Jury thought otherwise," Cross said, making notes on his pad. "Evidence was stacked up against you. All circumstantial, of course, but the fact that you couldn't prove where you were at the time of your wife's murder didn't help matters."

How could Sheldon prove that he was out jogging at the time of Rebecca's brutal killing? He ran alone, usually late at night after working all hours at the mall where he was the manager of the local supermarket. To say that he was stunned at his predicament was the understatement of the century.

"Might have some good news, though," Cross said, looking up and putting away his pen.

"Hit me," Sheldon replied, not altogether persuaded that there was a way out of this mess for him.

"Turns out there was an eye witness to place you away from the scene of your wife's death."

Sheldon's heart skipped a beat at the news. He took a moment, and then replied.

"Yeah? How so?"

"Guy out walking his dog caught sight of someone answering your description turning left out of Crosby on Steadman's east side at the time that the ME's autopsy report gives for the time of death."

Steadman was typical of the kind of Southwest town that you're likely to pass through without giving it a second thought. Founded early in the late nineteenth century by cattle baron Thomas Jefferson Steadman, and set fifty miles to the north east of Arizona's state capital of Phoenix, it was a town that had been in steady decline for more than twenty years. Despite that fact, it had continued to survive as a stopover for those hardy souls seeking a vacation in the McDowell Mountain Regional Park, and a fledgling tourist industry had miraculously emerged to support what was becoming an increasing flow of visitors.

"Will he testify at the appeal?"

"Says so, and without him you could be looking at the death penalty."

"You're such a comic; know that? Ever since high school you've been pulling my chain."

"Quit worrying; it's all going to be fine. You'll be acquitted at the appeal and the cops will have to start all over again."

Warren, although initially trusting his lawyer's skill in the courtroom, had been disappointed at Cross's seeming inability to dig up evidence which should have proved his innocence. Now, out of the blue, this new witness seemed set to turn the tables in his favour, and he returned to his remand cell at the State Prison in Buckeye with a lot more optimism than before. It was the following month, when Cross came to relate the results of the appeal hearing, that the bottom truly fell out of his world.

"What do you mean the guy never showed?!" he yelled in frustration.

"Just that," Cross said, shaking his head. "Judge dismissed the appeal, and I went to the guy's home to find out what had happened."

"So, what *did* happen? Somebody get to him or something?"

"Heart attack the day before the hearing. He was dead by the time the medics got to him," the lawyer replied.

"I'm a dead man," Sheldon said, stunned, his voice now almost a whisper. "There nothing else we can do?"

"Afraid not, Warren. The guy was our only hope."

Sheldon's marriage to his wife, Rebecca, had been a tumultuous affair. Periods of calm were regularly punctuated by ferocious rows which had them almost at each other's throats, and neighbours had called the police out on a number of occasions when it seemed that their verbal battles were set to escalate into something far more serious. Rebecca's death at the hands of an alleged stranger while Warren was out jogging had shocked the neighbourhood. Police were quick to arrest Sheldon, and the fact that Rebecca had been shot using his gun which was covered in his fingerprints was the deciding factor in the case. His guilty verdict at trial had been unanimous, and the DA had lobbied for the death penalty. Now that the appeal had failed, Warren was set to face the lethal injection in a matter of a week or so.

On the morning of Tuesday 22nd June 1999, he boarded the State Prison transport vehicle for the ninety-eight mile journey from Buckeye to a cell on death row in Florence. On a straight stretch on the Ed Pastor Freeway close to the Gila River Indian Reservation, they were hit by an oncoming fuel tanker that had strayed suddenly onto their side of the road. The head-on impact drove both vehicles off the freeway, and the resulting explosion unleashed a fireball that consumed both of them and all of their occupants. By the time that emergency services reached the scene there was nothing left to identify any of the bodies save for the records held by those employing them.

Two men walked into Clancey's Sports Bar in Colorado Springs just south of Denver. It is now late fall in 2009, and the TV screen was broadcasting the Thursday night game from the NFL. They took seats in a booth to one side of the premises and ordered beers from the waitress who turned up to serve them. Alan Cross took a pull from his glass, wiped his mouth with the back of his hand and sighed in deep satisfaction. The drive from Phoenix had been a long one and the dust of the journey had left him dry.

"So, what d'you have next?" Ray Boulter said.

Boulter was the second man, and a lawyer like Cross. They had met up the previous evening and, headed for Denver, decided to take a break and stop over at a cheap motel just down the street.

"Fraud," Cross replied, leaning back into the booth. "Guy rips off his employer and thinks he can get away with it. IRS had different ideas when they caught him out on the tax returns."

"Pretty run-of-the-mill, then?"

"Yeah," Cross said, almost despondently. It had been quite a while since he'd had something that he could really get his teeth into.

As the evening progressed and interest in the football game waned, the two of them partook more than freely of the beer that Clancey's had to offer, and talk that would, under more sober conditions have remained cautious, slipped into the kind of carelessness that either would have considered rash had they been more clear-headed.

"Ever kill someone?" Cross asked, his voice dropping to an almost conspiratorial level.

"What? You mean self-defense?"

"Well, not exactly self-defense, but intentionally anyways."

"You?"

"Yeah; some years back when I was working out of Phoenix. Guy goes out leaving his wife alone. I thought we, that is me and her, had an understanding and I called after he'd gone out…"

"Hey, Pete," Clancey called, looking at his watch. "Kinda early today, ain't ya?"

The bar owner smiled as his general cleaner came through the door. Pete had been working casually at the bar for the past six months and it suited Clancey to pay him cash for the hours that he spent sweeping up and cleaning tables. The IRS would never know about the payments funded by under-declaring takings, and Pete was reliable – a trait that could not be said for some of the waitresses.

"Yeah, well," Pete replied. "Doreen's gone to her mom's and it beats staring at the wall all day."

He was typical of the kind of drifter who still made a living moving from town to town throughout the Southwest, picking up laboring or cleaning jobs for cash and then moving on when boredom set in. He had been staying with his current partner,

57

Doreen, at a boarding house on the east side of town, and neither of them was young enough to think that the relationship was anything more than temporary. He had arrived at the bar half an hour before the two, now fairly inebriated, lawyers in the booth against the wall, and was currently standing in an adjacent section of the room listening intently to the somewhat slurred conversation.

He bristled sharply at Cross's words, and had recognised the guy as soon as he entered the premises. Fuming, with fists clenched and knuckles turning white with the rage that was building within him, he awaited his opportunity. Having passed unrecognized as he made his way around the room, gathering empty glasses and wiping away beer stains, he paused abruptly as the second man rose from his seat, bade farewell to his companion, and headed for the door. Pete watched closely as Cross himself rose and made his unsteady way to the restrooms. Glancing towards the bar where Clancey was engaged in conversation with another customer, he followed.

Cross never saw the left hook that rendered him unconscious as he turned back from the urinal. Pete caught him as he fell, cushioning the fall to reduce the sound of Cross hitting the floor. Taking a quick look into the corridor outside the john, he pulled Cross up, slung one of his arms across a shoulder, and dragged him to the fire exit a few yards away. Once out in the open, he laid the lawyer against the wall and walked across the car park. He smiled; Clancey had left the keys to his pickup in the ignition.

He pulled off the road half an hour later and headed up Bear Creek as far as the pickup would go, and then pulled in out of sight of the rough track. He stepped out of the cab and walked round to the rear of the vehicle. Cross was lying in the flat bed where he had been since they had left the bar. The tarp had concealed him from any prying eyes, and Pete had used a length of rope from the truck to tie the man up. He was still out. Pete took a pack of Marlboro from his pocket and lit up, waiting for his captive to regain consciousness.

It took Cross a further half hour to recover from the punch, and he shook his head in confusion as he tried to clear his thoughts. It was then that he became aware of the gag across his mouth.

"Back with us, huh?" Pete asked. "Well, make the most of it, Cross."

He dropped the tailgate and pulled the recumbent figure out of the back of the truck. Pushing Cross before him with a piece of pipe that he'd found in the back of the flat bed, they made their way deeper into the trees and completely out of sight of Clancey's vehicle. They had been walking for around ten minutes when Pete called a halt. Backing Cross up to a pine in the middle of a clearing, he tied the man's arms around the tree and secured his legs in a likewise fashion. It was only now that the gag was removed. Cross, still slightly stunned, spat on the ground to clear his mouth.

"Who the hell…?" he began, and then gaped in surprise as Pete stepped into a shaft of evening sunlight streaming down from between the branches of the trees. "Sheldon!" he spluttered. "But I thought you was…"

"Dead?" Warren said, smiling grimly. "Yeah, you and the rest of the justice system. Explosion from the tanker threw me clear of the crash. The other body must have been a passenger in the rig. By the time that help arrived I was long gone. Been bummin' around for the past ten years – not something that I can recommend when you realise what I lost."

"Why am I tied up?"

"You killed her, didn't you? I heard you telling that guy in Clancey's. You murdered Rebecca and let me take the fall."

"No!" Cross exclaimed. "It was an accident. I thought that she… I mean, I was hoping that the two of us…"

"You and Rebecca?" Sheldon asked. "She despised you."

"Yeah, I saw that when she came out of the bedroom with your gun. She got too close and I made a grab for it. Damned thing went off; I didn't mean to…"

"You could have owned up; why send me to death row? Was there even a real witness that night?"

"No," Cross sighed. "Made that up when I realised I was in too deep. It was you or me."

"Well, now it's you," Sheldon said, pulling the bindings tighter and cutting away Cross's clothing.

"What are you doing?" Cross asked.

"Well, see, come nightfall there's any number of scavengers in these woods, and if I nick you in a couple of places they'll be quick to pick up on the smell of blood. Rats'll be first I'd imagine; then maybe a javalina. Shouldn't be surprised if you got a coyote come visiting, either."

"What!?" Cross said, eyes wide in fear. "You can't be serious."

"Serious as hell," Warren said, slipping the gag back into place.

"You'll never get away with it!" he raged before the cloth cut him off.

"Sure I will. I'll just leave the truck here and hitch a lift at the freeway. There'll be no folks to come helping you out here in the dark, and I'll be long gone by the time they find what's left of you. So long, sucker."

The Lion and Harriet

"What are you doing?" Jean Fretwell had returned from shopping to find her husband, George, packing away things in one of their upstairs rooms.

George stood up from his kneeling position on the floor of the bedroom and took a deep breath. Stretching his aching back, he smiled sadly at his wife and stepped away from the box that he had been filling with a collection of soft toys. There were other boxes lying around the floor, containing other groups of belongings – clothes, books, and pictures that had formerly hung on the walls.

"You were right," he said. "It's time to put it all behind us. I've been a fool all these years for believing that she'll come back to us one day. You've been right all along. What is it? Twenty years now?"

"Twenty-one," Jean replied, sitting down on the bed that had been their little girl's. "She'd be twenty-four now."

Harriet Fretwell had disappeared one sunny, summer afternoon in 1989 – she was three years old at the time. It was a Wednesday, and the two of them had been in Markeaton Park in Derby. George had been at work, and it was usual for Jean and her friend, Beverley, to take their two small children out one day in the week; Wednesday was the designated day, and this particular one was clear and sunny. They had brought a picnic to the recreation area where the children could play and splash around in the paddling pool. Such a perfect day – such tragedy to unfold.

No one had witnessed the little girl's disappearance – she had run to retrieve a ball from some bushes and Jean had only taken her eyes off her daughter for an instant, believing that Harriet would emerge, smiling, with the ball in her little hands, ready to resume the game that she had been playing with Beverley's son, Robert.

The initial feeling of apprehension had quickly been replaced by a sinister foreboding that all was not well. The remainder of the day had passed in a blur as Beverley summoned the police whilst trying to calm her distraught friend. Response had been rapid and dramatic as uniformed officers flooded the area in search of the missing toddler. It had all come to nothing as the weeks went by and, amid nationwide coverage, the lives of the Fretwells came under intense scrutiny. Police enquiries, after the initial appeals for information had produced nothing of consequence, homed in on the parents. This too yielded no leads as to the location of the little girl and as the years passed, fewer and fewer officers remained on the case until now, in May 2010, only two CID staff were listed as detectives handling enquiries into the disappearance. The case had gone cold.

"We need to let go," George said. "You said so yourself ten years ago but I wasn't listening. Someone will find a use for all of this stuff. We can take it to the Brinsley car boot sale – there's one this coming weekend."

"What's that in the top of the last box?"

"Lion," George said, picking up the soft toy and holding it up to his nose and inhaling deeply. "He was her favourite. She took him everywhere with her; I still can't believe that he would have been left lying on the grass at the park that day. Whoever took her would have had a hell of a job on their hands, and yet nobody saw or heard anything."

"Come on," Jean said. "I'll help you finish up and we can store them in the garage ready for Saturday, then."

"Right. Are we all set? Everyone know what they're supposed to be doing?"

DI Steve Redwood concluded the squad briefing at Hucknall police station. It was Saturday morning and his team, acting on a tip-off, was set to hit the car boot sale at Brinsley. He pointed to the white board, emphasising to all present exactly who the targets were.

"Dave Wragg and Mickey Taylor," he said. "On our radar for a while, but this is the first time that we've had good intel that they're offloading stolen gear. Let's make sure that we get the right people and catch them before they get wind of us and scarper. Okay; let's move."

As the room began to empty, he turned to his DS, Sharon Collins. Collins, originally from Leeds, had been promoted to

Detective Sergeant and posted to the Nottinghamshire Constabulary six months earlier. She and Redwood had hit it off immediately, and it was becoming accepted that when the DI moved to his new role of DCI with the Derbyshire force at Ripley, her promotion to DI would see her take over the reins at Hucknall.

"Good to go?" he asked, seeing the frown on her face. "Headaches no better?"

"Sir?" she said absently. "Oh, no; I'm all right, thanks. They're not serious, and my doctor couldn't find anything wrong. I went for a scan but nothing showed up."

"And the woman? You know, the one you told me about?"

"The dreams?" she said. "Oh, I've no idea. She just turns up from time to time. I haven't a clue who she is. All I can see is her face."

"Not losing your marbles, then," he said, smiling.

"No, it must be all the strain you're putting me under." She grinned, put on her coat and headed for the door. "You coming along?"

"Cheek!" he said, and followed her out of the room.

Sitting beside her DI in the unmarked car, Sharon's thoughts during the short journey returned to the annoying ache which had been plaguing her for the past few weeks. She had been experiencing a dull thumping sound at the back of her ears, and whilst not enough to distract her from daily duties, it was becoming a nuisance. Fluctuating during the day, there were times when she could almost believe that it was not there at all. On other occasions, it was as if a voice was trying to tell her something. Odd words popped up, but the one that she heard most frequently was 'line'. It made no sense to her, and she had tried hard to ignore it. The raid on which they were all currently occupied would require all of her concentration.

Three unmarked police vehicles rolled into the car boot sale half an hour after leaving their base and the occupants, twelve plain clothes officers, split up into less conspicuous groups of twos and threes.

George and Jean Fretwell had arrived at the Brinsley site on Cordy Lane just after half past six when the site opened for stallholders to set out their wares. The weather was fine, heralding a warm June afternoon to come. Having finished setting up their tables, Jean was placing the final items when she paused over a soft toy that had brought back memories.

"D'you think that we should keep just this one, George," she said, holding up the lion that had been the final item which he had placed in one of the boxes. "It was her favourite."

"No, love," he replied. "It really is time to let go. If we start making exceptions, we'll end up packing everything up again and heading off home. She's gone; it's been too long. We can't let the memories rule the rest of our lives. We've got the photos – that should be enough."

Jean Fretwell had been thirty-five when she found out that she was pregnant. She and George had been trying for a family, unsuccessfully, for what seemed like an eternity. They had just about given up hope when their miracle happened. It had been a difficult time, and complications during Harriet's birth had meant that they were not destined to have any further children – it made the loss all the more heart-rending. A bright and happy child, Harriet Fretwell animated each and every day with her presence, and her three years were filled with magical moments for both parents. Jean sighed, placed the lion in the middle of the left hand table and turned to get the flasks of tea from the bag that they had brought along with them.

"Do you remember, George, when we bought the lion? You wanted to call it Aslan after the lion in *'The Tales of Narnia',* but Harriet didn't like it, she wanted to call it just 'Lion' but couldn't say the word properly – it made her quite cross. She ended up calling it…"

"No, don't go there, Jean," he said. "We've been over this several times since we decided to sell all of this stuff. It won't do any good raking over the coals again."

"No," she said. "I suppose you're right. Somebody'll love him, won't they?"

"Yes, they will, and I'm sure that he'll find a good home," he replied. "Hey, now that we've got our teas, how do you fancy something to eat? There's a burger bar just across there."

"You're on," she said, brightening. "Make them large ones."

Sharon Collins turned as she heard the sudden commotion at one end of the car boot site. She was one of a group of three that included her DI, and it became clear that their two targets, Wragg and Taylor, had realised that they were in trouble and had decided to make a break for it. The six officers nearest to their stall had quickly closed in and cornered the pair at the bottom end of the playing field where the sale was taking place.

"Okay, let's go!" shouted Redwood to his group, and the three of them began to head in the direction of the disturbance.

Collins stopped suddenly; the dull thudding in her ears had now turned into a low roar. She shook her head. Yes, it was definitely a roar – the roar of a big cat: a lion maybe. The noise stopped as abruptly as it had started and turned into a soft, low baritone voice. She screwed her eyes tightly shut and concentrated.

'Line' it said, and then repeated the word with increasing volume.

She turned away from the pursuit that her DI had instructed and the volume diminished. She turned back again and it increased. Clearly there was some kind of message in the sound. The further she went in the opposite direction to the chase, the quieter the voice became. Following the voice, she came to the stall manned by Jean and George Fretwell.

"Something take your fancy?" Jean asked as the young woman stood staring intently at the items laid out before her.

"No; that is, yes," Sharon said, not understanding what it was that had brought her to this spot. "I'm not sure; there was a voice…" She picked up the lion and looked at it closely. She frowned and put it back on the table. "Line," she said.

"It's a toy that belonged to our daughter," Jean began. She stopped. "I'm sorry, what was it that you just said?"

"Line," Sharon repeated. "Line. That's what I'm hearing. No, it's gone now - I don't know what it means."

Jean Fretwell had staggered backwards, caught by the strong arms of her husband, George, and lowered gently into one of the garden chairs that they had brought with them.

"Jean, what's wrong?" he asked. He turned to Sharon Collins. "What did you say to her!? Why is she upset?"

"I... I'm sorry, it's just... the word – I heard it. What is it?"

Jean had recovered some of her composure and rose from her seat, staring intently into the young woman's face.

"Our little girl disappeared twenty-one years ago. The toy was her favourite and she called him 'Line' because she couldn't pronounce 'lion' when we bought it. The name stuck."

Sharon picked up the lion again and frowned.

"What's the matter?" Jean said, coming round from the back of the table and standing right in front of the young woman.

"I don't know," she said, staring at the toy in her hand. "It's... wait... there's another word now."

"What?" George asked, now standing at his wife's side.

"I can't quite... no, it's there," Sharon said. "It's clearer now - 'height'. Does that mean anything?"

"No," Jean said. "Not 'height', 'hi-yet'. Harriet couldn't get her tongue around the double 'r' and she pronounced her name Hi-yet. You misheard whatever the sound was."

Sharon held the lion close to her face and inhaled. The smell set the hairs at the back of her neck on end and goose pimples erupted along her arms and wrists.

"There's a park – lots of green; and a paddling pool. Who's Robert?"

"Oh my God!" exclaimed Jean. "Robert was the little boy that Harriet was playing with at Markeaton Park. He's the son of my friend, Beverley."

"What does 'moomy' mean?" Sharon asked, looking deeply into the eyes of the toy.

"That's what Harriet used to call me," Jean said.

"How much is this, please?" The voice interrupted the tableau, and Jean turned to face a man holding up an item from the table.

"I... I'm sorry; what did you say?" she asked.

"This box of building blocks," he said, testily. "How much is it? There's no price on it."

"I'm sorry," Jean said, turning to look back at Sharon. "None of this stuff is for sale. We're taking everything back home where it all belongs, aren't we, Harriet?"

The Code

The code didn't break when they found Mary Andrews hanging from a cord in the rented house on Tower Close in the Derbyshire village of Aldersford in 1989. It didn't break when her mother, Margaret, my maternal grandmother, passed away in 1995. It was only just before my own father died in 2017 that I discovered the truth that had lain buried within our family for over forty years. I was thunderstruck at what he told me, his head hung in shame, and I now needed a sounding board of my own before I would know what it was that I ought to do.

I chose Paul Beresford. We had been friends since we were nine years old and I trusted him as I trusted no-one else. I'm Peter Hayward and now the last member of the Hayward family who has knowledge of the secret.

"Okay," Paul said as we took our seats in the lounge bar of the Mitre in Highridge. "What's eating at you?"

The Mitre, now one of a shrinking number of pubs tied to a local brewery, still served its beer from hand pumps and it had been our local since our late teens. I took a generous mouthful of the pint of bitter, savoured its twang, and heaved a huge sigh.

"This has to be off the record, Paul," I said. "Can't have you making an official matter of it."

Paul Beresford was a DS with the Derbyshire Constabulary based at Butterley Park in neighbouring Ripley and should, if he was to follow protocol, follow up on the 'line of enquiry' that I was about to impart to him.

"Of course," he replied. "We're mates – it goes without saying. What have you done?"

"It's not me," I said, shaking my head. "However, I do have some information that may or may not lead to a police enquiry going back to the seventies."

"The nineteen seventies?" he asked, his pint poised before his mouth. He replaced it onto the table. "What are you getting at?"

I gave him a brief family history, and he sat for the most part in silence while I rambled on. Mary Andrews had taken her own life in July 1989. She was some years older than me and, as I grew up, had always been presented as my mother's younger sister. Mum had married a Longlea collier by the name of George Hayward, so we didn't really have much to do with the Burtons, my Mum's side of the family tree. What I did see of her, however, didn't make me want to spend too much time in her company. She was odd; according to my Dad, she was subject to bouts of extreme peevishness; she was a 'pincher' and more than a few of the neighbourhood kids bore the marks left by her thumb and forefinger. I was born in 1970 and she was eighteen when she met and married Douglas Andrews.

"Doug was a nice enough bloke from what I can remember," I said. "Mary was, I suppose, attractive when you ignored her temper and he couldn't see much beyond that, especially as he was very near-sighted."

"I don't see where this is going," Paul said.

"I'm getting to it," I replied, a little tetchily. "You need to understand the family background before I can let the cat out of the bag."

"Okay, I'm listening," he said, picking up his glass and taking a mouthful of beer.

"Mary got pregnant in 1970. She'd been seeing Doug for a few months and I think they had to get married. It didn't bother Doug, but Dad said that she was none too pleased at the news. Anyway, the baby, a boy they named James, was born in September of that year; I was born a month later."

"Not seeing the connection," Paul said, rising from his seat and picking up our glasses before heading for the bar. He returned moments later, by which time I had gathered my thoughts.

"James died in 1972," I said when he had settled himself once more. "He was under two years old at the time."

"And?"

"Mary pointed the finger at Doug, saying that he had mistreated the little boy over a period of a year or more, and that James's death had been the result of him being thrown down the stairs."

"What?" Paul said, now keenly interested as his copper's nose came into play.

"Nothing came of it in the end, but the matter dragged on for quite some time before the police closed their file. The autopsy confirmed cause of death as being due to a broken neck that had resulted from a fall. The coroner returned a verdict of accidental death and the matter was closed."

"But you think that there's more to it than that?" Paul asked.

"I was nineteen when Mary was found hanged in the house just around the corner from where we lived in Aldersford. Apparently she'd been living there for a couple of years without us even knowing."

"Alone?"

"Yes," I replied. "After James's death and the resulting inquest, Doug Andrews left the area. Some of the men in the Burton family had paid him a call at his rented flat in Marehay. A neighbour found him and called an ambulance. He'd been badly beaten and the doctor at the Derbyshire Royal Infirmary said that he was lucky to be still alive. Nobody's set eyes on him since - he must be in his seventies now."

"So, let me get this straight: James dies, either by accident or some deliberate act; the verdict clears anyone of blame, but the Burton family thinks that it was Doug who killed the little boy," Paul said. "Am I missing anything?"

"No," I replied. "That's what they were told by Mary, and blood being thicker than water they believed her." I paused and Paul raised his eyebrows. "It turns out that she wasn't my mother's sister at all."

"So?"

"Mary was the daughter of Margaret Burton's sister, Betty Southern. Betty died from cancer in 1956 when Mary was four. Ray Sutton, Mary's father, couldn't cope with bringing her up on his own – he was an alcoholic and couldn't hold down a job. From what Dad told me before he died, Mary was taken away from him after my Grandma Burton found out that he'd been abusing her. She brought her up along with her other five children and the whole thing was brushed under the carpet."

"Are you saying that Mary could have killed James as a result of some psychological damage done to her when she was still a child?" Paul asked.

"I don't know, mate," I said. "Experts nowadays say that it can happen that way, and all I can tell you is that, given the choice, I'd rather have been in Doug's company than Mary's. She had this look about her, and it used to send shivers down my spine on the odd occasion that I saw her. I was the same age as James and she'd stare at me and sneer as if there was something that she knew that I didn't."

"You don't miss her then?" he said, chuckling.

"What do you think?" I replied. "Look, I'm getting off track. I think the Burtons knew what had happened and covered it up. I think that Doug Andrews took the fall, in more ways than one, for what happened back in 1972. The newspapers certainly had a field day at his expense and all of his friends deserted him – he was an easy target for the Burton men when they decided to have their 'little chat' with him."

"So, who covered it up?"

"That's the thing, you see," I said. "Margaret Burton, my mother's mum, died in 1995 at the age of eighty-four. On her death bed she sent for the local vicar to hear a confession. The vicar was out of town, so one of the church deacons came along in his place. The deacon, a lay member, should have cleared the room but didn't – he wasn't aware of the rules."

"So, someone overheard."

"Yes; that someone was Joan Hayward, my Mother."

"And she told your Dad."

"Yes."

"Okay, what was the big secret?"

I took a deep breath. "Mama Burton knew all along that it had been Mary mistreating James and not Doug Andrews. Doug had come home from work at the end of the day and found James lying at the foot of the stairs. Mary was sitting at the top, staring down at the little boy and laughing."

"I see," Paul said, suddenly becoming very serious. "Are you sure of this?"

"I only know what my Dad told me just before he died in 2017. Mum had died the previous year leaving him on his own; I suppose he wanted to get the whole thing off his chest before… you know."

"Yes, I can see why he might want to put it to rest. However, from what you've told me, this all happened forty-seven years ago.

Mary's dead, and so are your Grandma, your Mum and your Dad. Are there any other members of the Burton family who knew about it that are still with us?"

"No."

"Well, that's it, then," Paul said. "There'd be no point in raking over the coals of a family tragedy that's lost in the mists of time, and as you have no idea where Doug Andrews is, even supposing that he's still alive, I'd advise you to let it go."

"I see."

"Unless," he said, "there's something else that's on your mind; something that you haven't yet told me."

I sat in silence for a few moments, gathering my thoughts and pondering whether to tell my oldest friend the rest of the tale. I finished the remainder of my pint and went to the bar to slake a thirst that was drying my mouth. I sat down again with a heavy sigh.

"Come on," he said. "Spit it out."

"Okay. On the day that James was alleged to have died, my Dad was suddenly taken ill and Mum had to go to hospital with him. Mama Burton was out at work – she had three jobs in an attempt to care for her family. Her husband, Sam, had been killed in the D-Day Landings, leaving her alone with five children. Mary had been asked to look after me until my Mum came back home."

"And?"

"There's no easy way to do this, Paul. I'm not my father's son."

"What? How can you be sure?"

"I did one of those Ancestry DNA test things, thinking that it'd be a bit of a laugh. It came back with a different family tree to the one I'd expected, so I asked a mate who's a surgeon to run a private test for me on the quiet. I pinched one of my Dad's cigarette ends and sent it away with a sample of my own saliva. The comparison came back negative – I'm not related by blood to George Hayward."

"So, who *is* your Dad?"

"I don't know, but if I'm not Peter Hayward who the hell am I?"

"You don't mean…?"

I nodded. "What if it wasn't James Andrews that died that day back in 1972? What if it was Peter Hayward who was thrown down the stairs by Mary Andrews? What if they all knew and I was given to the Haywards to keep them quiet? I know it sounds outrageous, but it was almost fifty years ago."

72

"Jeez!"

"Exactly!" I said. "I don't think that James Andrews did die back then. He's here sitting right before you, and there's a little boy in Marpond Cemetery whose grave has a headstone with my name on it!"

"So, what do you want me to do?" Paul asked. "We've already said that everybody involved is now dead; what's to be served in digging it all up again?"

"Not everybody, Paul," I said, quietly. "Doug Andrews may still be around; I'd like you to try and find him. I need to know for sure who I am, and he's the only one who can help now. This code of silence has gone on for far too long and I'm damned if I'll take to my own grave. I have to know the truth."

The Last Train

It was late. Gregory was sure that the train was late. It was dark, so that meant that the time was also late. He sat down on the bench against the wall of what he thought must be the ticket office, but there was no sign on its door to tell him as much.

Where was he?

How had he come here?

Why were there no other passengers waiting for the train?

He shook his head to clear his thoughts. Surely he could not be the only person at the station waiting for a train at this time of the day. He looked at his watch; the second hand was not moving and the time was fixed at 9.38pm. He looked around for the station's clock.

There wasn't one.

Anywhere.

Not even on the platform across the rails from him.

Gregory frowned – this was highly unusual. There weren't even any signs to tell him the name of the station where he was sitting waiting for a train that showed no signs of turning up. There were no destination boards either; in fact, there was nothing to give him the slightest clue as to what was happening to him.

He looked at the rails. One had to be the down line and the other had to be the up line, but without knowing which way was north, he had no means of ascertaining which of the two was the one that he should be using. Maureen would know – Maureen, his wife, was very good at things like that.

But she was not here.

Gregory frowned.

Where was she?

He didn't feel hungry, so clearly he had eaten in the recent past. Would it have been at breakfast that they last saw each other?

But where had he been in all of that time? At work? Doing what? He sighed in frustration – this was not making any sense at all.

"Hello!" he called out. "Anyone around?"

74

His voice echoed back to him from around the empty station, but apart from that there was no reply. Rising from the bench, he made his way along the platform until he found a door which led into what seemed to be the ticket office. There was a hatch in the far wall where it appeared that one could buy tickets, but the shutter was down.

"Hello!" Gregory called once again, but once more there was no answer to his hail.

The embers of a fire were glowing in the fireplace on the opposite wall and, suddenly feeling a chill, Gregory walked over to it and held out his hands to the burning logs, sensing the warmth soothing the ache in his fingers. The dying flames crackled but that was the only sound in the room and Gregory began to get the strangest feeling that he had been at this place before – maybe a long time ago; he was not sure.

He turned suddenly at the sound of the wind blowing the ticket office door open. Leaves swirled around the threshold on a previously calm day, and the sound of footsteps echoed along the platform outside, becoming louder as they approached the now wide open door. Gregory held his breath as the shadow of a figure appeared at the right hand side of the frame; it stopped, briefly, before rounding the edge of the doorway and entering the room.

"Who are you?" Gregory asked. "Why didn't you answer when I called out earlier?"

The figure – it was a man – was dressed in a dark overcoat with the collar pulled up around his face. He wore a large-brimmed hat – a fedora, Gregory thought – and it was pulled down over his eyes. He just stood there inside the doorway, saying nothing. Gregory took a few steps towards the stranger, but stopped when a voice suddenly rang out across the platform.

"Greg!" it called. "Can you hear me?"

"Maureen?" Gregory said in surprise. Then louder: "Maureen! Is that you? Where are you?"

He headed for the ticket office door and past the dark figure without a further thought. Outside on the platform, he saw a light in one of the other buildings and headed that way. There was no sign either on the door or above it, but it was open and Gregory could see that it was the café/gift shop – he went inside.

There was a mug filled with hot tea on one of the table tops and he went over to it. Picking it up, he took a sip – it was tea, and just the way he liked it. But who had made it and placed it there? Maureen? He called his wife's name once more – softly this time.

"Maureen? Are you here?"

There was no-one behind either of the counters, and no answer came in reply to his question. Gregory sighed in frustration – where *was* everybody? This was a railway station; it should have had some people around, even at this time of the day. He left the room and turned right towards what he thought must be the exit. His assumption was correct, and he could see, through the archway, a well-lit street. Try as he may, he could not force his feet to cross the border between the platform and the cobbled surface before him.

"What the…?" he said, shaking his head. He turned at the sound of footsteps.

It was the shadowy figure in the dark coat and fedora. The man – if that *is* what it was – had been following him silently along the station platform, and now stood about ten feet away holding out an arm. What did it mean?

"Who are you?" Gregory asked, but there was no reply.

He heard Maureen calling him again and returned to the café; she was not there, of course, and the mug of tea had disappeared. The lights were still on, and this time Gregory noticed that there was a poster on the wall – it was the first indication of where he might be. The wording, however, was incomplete and he could only make out the phrase *'Come to Pick…'*

"Pick what?" he said to himself, and then realised what it was that he was seeing. "Pickering!" he exclaimed. "Of course! This is Pickering station."

Rushing outside once again, he saw to his relief the familiar wrought iron pedestrian bridge which linked the two platforms. Thoughts came rushing to his head – they had been on holiday, Maureen and himself, in North Yorkshire, and had called at Pickering on the way back from Helmsley to their rented accommodation in… where? That he could not recall, but this was most definitely Pickering and Maureen was calling to him from somewhere close by.

Silence had returned – he could no longer hear his wife's voice, and the only other figure was the dark stranger following him from room to room. Gregory started to sit down at one of the tables in order to think things out. His legs began to give way, and he leaned on the back of a chair for support. The silent, dark figure moved slightly closer. Gregory began to feel dizzy and, more by luck than judgement, seated himself at the table. His head was beginning to throb and he held it in his hands, trying to will the ache away. A sharp pain had him gasping suddenly and the headache disappeared to be replaced by a spasm in his back and legs.

"What's happening to me?" he whispered.

Slowly, as if being pushed gently by some unseen force, Gregory began to slide out of the chair and onto the floor. He landed with a gentle bump, and shook his head to clear his vision which had suddenly become quite hazy. He gripped his arm as a numbing sensation started to make its way along the limb and down towards his left hand and across his chest,

"Blood pressure's dropping!" the nurse said, suddenly.

"Greg!" Maureen said, as the doctor stepped between her and the bed.

"Stay back, please, madam," the doctor said.

"He's flat lined!" the nurse said.

"Summon the crash team, nurse," the doctor replied. "I'll start CPR – tell them to hurry!"

'Heart attack,' Greg thought from his position on the floor. Now he understood. His doctor's warning six months earlier came back to him after the minor infarction that he had suffered following a particularly strenuous run.

Of course; he was beginning to remember now. They had been sitting in this café eating lunch after walking around the town and visiting the castle. Maureen had said that he didn't look very well, but he had dismissed her concerns and said that it was just that they had been walking for too long in the heat.

"That was it," he said to himself.

He had slumped as he had tried to raise his mug of tea to his lips. The mug had fallen to the floor, disappearing from his line of sight. He remembered that he lost feeling in his right arm and leg and had slipped gently to the floor.

"Maureen!" he had called out in fright, and then everything seemed to go dark.

He recovered consciousness some time later and there was bright light all around. He had blinked but no words would come when he tried to speak. Maureen was there and he tried to smile but that wouldn't work either. She reached out to him across the hospital bed… and everything went dark once again. All he could hear was her calling out to him.

"Greg! Greg! Can you hear me? Are you there?"

The memory faded and Greg started to ease himself up off the floor of the café. The shadowy figure was still there – watching, saying nothing. With an effort, Gregory eased himself back into the chair and took a series of deep breaths. A train had pulled into the station, and he could hear the hiss of steam as it ground to a halt. Surely this was the last train of the day – if he got aboard perhaps it would take him to where Maureen would be waiting.

"No," he said to himself. "Don't be stupid! The train isn't real; I'm hallucinating – none of this is real. I'm in a hospital bed somewhere. My God! Am I dying? Is that what this is all about? I feel all right now – maybe I'm getting better."

Gregory laughed at his own confused reasoning. If he had been with his wife when the heart attack happened she should be here right now, but she wasn't. All that there was was this shadowy figure, arm extended, inviting him to come along… somewhere. That was when he heard the announcement. It came in typical, old-fashioned British Railways style.

'Will passengers for the last train from Pickering please make their way to platform one where departure will take place in two minutes. There will be no further services from this station today.'

Gregory walked slowly at the side of the shadowy figure out of the café and towards the waiting train. His thoughts had all been in vain and this was indeed the last train that he would ever take. Sitting down in the first carriage that he boarded, Gregory also realised that these, his thoughts, his train of thoughts, would also be his final ones – the last train that would ever cross his mind.

The Long Mile

It's the final leg of the run and you know in your heart of hearts that it'll be the longest, most exhausting 1,760 yards of the route that you've set for yourself.

"I'll pace you," comes the offer from a range of friends, and you're extremely grateful for the company along the way and the escape from the drudgery of a scene from '*The Loneliness of the Long-Distance Runner*'.

"Great!" you reply, not thinking that, along their allotted part of the route, your section pacer will try to engage in conversation which you would dearly have liked to avoid.

Anything that interrupts the pattern of breathing will take away a small piece of the concentration that's vital to your completion of the run – especially as there is a substantial amount of sponsorship resting upon your arriving at the predetermined point at the end of the ten miles. Yes, you heard it correctly – ten miles.

If that wasn't bad enough, you finally, and with supreme effort for an amateur runner, turn the last corner onto the finishing straight only to find your five year old son hopping out of the family car that's been following in case of need. He speeds off to the finishing post to acclaim himself the winner of the race. Twenty-six years later you are still being reminded of that fact, and that a small boy can beat his dad into a cocked hat.

No, The Long Mile is not something to enter into without much thought and soul-searching, and when your nephew gives you that title for a short story you feel honour-bound to comply.

I felt thoroughly drained that afternoon back in 1995 and it wasn't until we went shopping to Sainsbury's later on that I suffered the full effect of what I'd done. I made the mistake of leaning up against one of the supermarket's fixtures for a brief moment while my wife was examining joints of beef... and nodded off. A sharp prod to the ribs brought me back to reality, and a chocolate bar, purchased especially for the purpose, had my blood sugar surging back to its normal level. The effect was electric, and all the lights came back on with a bang.

"Fancy a walk round IKEA?" my missus asked.

I was caught unawares in the middle of a Deric Longden novel, and replied with what I can only describe as a suicidally non-committal answer which was interpreted as assent. It was too late to back out.

"Okay," I sighed, putting the book aside.

Little did I know at that moment, that I had just signed away hours of my life in the quest for items of furniture for my son's new house. Don't get me wrong, I'm not against a little shopping, but IKEA? You need a fully equipped survival kit for one of those places, and it wasn't made clear to me at the time that the IKEA in question was in Leeds – not a little out of our back yard. When we got there, it was to discover that only part of the shopping list was available in store. The rest of the items were in... Sheffield. Only when leaving the Steel City did 'we' decide to call in at our LOCAL store because we would be passing that way on our trek back home.

You see, I reckon that by the time that you've gone from the entrance to the Market Place and then the checkouts at these places, you will have inevitably covered The Long Mile.

When I was at school, a mile was four times round the running track on the playing fields. I can deal with the corners on a running track – they're regular in shape and come at you in expected places. To cover the same distance in IKEA you have to follow the arrows on the floor or else run the risk of becoming lost and never being able to get out of the place – a thought that fills me with dread.

These arrows are cunning and have been manufactured especially by a team of highly-trained Swedish shopping gurus intent on depriving you of as much of your hard-earned cash as possible in the shortest time available on any given day of the week.

I can only look at so many lounge layouts and kitchen displays without feeling faint – fortunately they come complete with a ready supply of chairs where I can sit and recover while the rest of the team do whatever it is that they came to do. They can always collect me on their way to the next area – this has worked fine so far, but I do worry that one day I will be forgotten and end up a lonely figure as the lights go out at the end of the day's trading. With the café and fast food bars shut, what on Earth would I do all night?

No, The Long Mile is not an enterprise to be embarked upon with flippancy, and a certain amount of serious training should be undertaken prior to getting involved in it. You could begin carefully with a series of tentative walks up and down the stairs at home – that way, if fatigue sets in there is always the kettle in the kitchen and a welcoming armchair not too far away in the lounge. Sustenance in the form of the biscuit barrel would also be close to hand.

This could be followed by an extensive tour of the garden, stopping off for a rest at one of the two sets of tables and chairs positioned strategically around the lawn whilst remaining conveniently close to the back door with its connection to the kettle and biscuit barrel – do you start to see the ease of the training regime now?

One could then ramp up the pressure by walking down the side yard to the front garden and repeat the process there whilst revisiting the back garden with its resting points for the second time. This preparatory routine is essential to avoid the severe cramps and strains which would inevitably follow a rash excursion to IKEA unprepared.

The word 'mile' originated from the Roman *mille passus*, or 'thousand paces' which measured 5,000 Roman feet. About the year 1500 the 'old London' mile was defined as eight furlongs. At that time the furlong, measured by a larger northern (German) foot, was 625 feet, and thus the mile equalled 5,000 feet.

I'm not sure what the gurus in Sweden would have made of this, but to my mind 1,760 yards is still an awfully long way to travel unnecessarily. The Romans had an empire to run so they would probably not have given it a second thought. For me, it's worth a third or fourth thought and then a lie down in a dark corner, preferably with a bottle of Newcastle Brown close at hand and the TV remote within easy reach.

You can't rush these things, and with our local IKEA conveniently hidden behind a stand of trees on the A610, I intend to avoid rushing into the place as often as I can.

Thunder and Rain

Dennis Marks scowled at the figure across the other side of his desk. Roger Mainwaring was the CEO of Waterfords Bank in the City of London. The financial institution was one of the oldest in the square mile, and its chief was well connected to many within the Metropolitan Police and also the city council – this was the first time that they had crossed swords, and the DCI sat with gritted teeth at the intrusion into police matters by a member of the public.

"You do realise that this is highly irregular, don't you?" Marks asked. "All reports of crime should go through the proper channels. I'm not even sure how you managed to get yourself into my squad room."

"Chief Inspector," Mainwaring said, smiling slyly. "People in my position have ways and means of circumnavigating obstacles to their progress. I mentioned my problem to the Assistant Commissioner during our round of golf this morning." He paused as Marks phone began to ring. "Shouldn't be surprised if that's him right now."

The DCI picked up the receiver. "Marks!" he snapped. "Yes, sir," he said, suddenly much less abrasive. "I see. Of course; I understand. Well, with the current caseload I'm not sure that… very well, sir. I'll get onto it right away."

Replacing the handset with a certain amount of force, Marks glared across the desk at the now smug figure of the Waterfords CEO. The man had nerve - that was for certain; he also had the connections to ensure that he could grab the attention of one of Scotland Yard's finest detectives.

"Okay, Mr Mainwaring," the DCI said. "It would seem that I have my orders. What is it that I can do for you?"

"Thank you, Chief Inspector. Your help really is appreciated, despite what you may think of my methods."

"Peter," Marks called as his DI passed through the squad room. "Got a minute?"

Peter Spencer entered Marks' office and took the seat indicated by his boss. Marks made the introductions.

83

"This is Peter Spencer, Mr Mainwaring. We've worked together for quite a while and I'm sure that he and I should be able to give you the best that New Scotland Yard could offer. Now, you were about to say what it is that's on your mind."

"Indeed, Chief Inspector," Mainwaring replied. "And it's a matter of some considerable delicacy; The City would react quite dramatically if what I am about to divulge to you was to become common knowledge."

"Okay," Marks said, irritability beginning to come to the surface again. "Just tell us straight if you would, please."

"Waterfords has been… how can I put it without sounding over dramatic? Robbed is probably the best word in the circumstances."

"I've heard nothing on the news," Spencer said, frowning and looking across at Marks.

"No, you won't have," Mainwaring replied. "I only found out myself this morning when the bank opened. Our CFO rang me at home just as I was leaving for the office. In a nutshell, our systems have been hacked and a certain amount of money has been removed from our accounts."

"How much?" Marks asked.

"Five billion pounds," Mainwaring replied, his voice trailing away.

"Five…?" Spencer said, astonished.

"Billion," Mainwaring finished the sentence. "That's right, Inspector Spencer – *billion.*"

"But surely there should be some trace of where the cash has gone," Marks said.

"Ordinarily, I would have to agree with you, Chief Inspector. However, in this instance all records of the transaction have been deleted from our files – we simply do not know what has happened to the money."

"Computer records can't be completely erased," Spencer said. "They can be deleted so that you can't see them, but they stay on the system. The only way of completely removing them would be to reformat the computer drive that contains them. Has that happened?"

"No," Mainwaring replied. "None of our other files have been touched. Our CFO discovered the theft when he compiled the usual reports first thing this morning and found that his accounts did not balance. It was a simple matter for him to find out which account was short, and that's when he rang me."

"And the five billion…" Marks began.

"Represents a significant portion of our working capital; without it we cease to function as a bank. It's only seven years since the 2008 crash and a scandal of this magnitude could shake the British economy to its foundations. It's vital that we find out who has the money and get it returned to us."

"I see," Marks replied. "Now I can understand why the AC has pulled me off all other duties." He turned to Spencer. "Looks like you'll have to clear your desk as well, Peter."

"There was also this," Mainwaring said, handing over a piece of paper in a clear plastic wallet. "It was found inside one of our strong rooms this morning."

Marks took the wallet and read the contents of a note printed on a sheet of A4 paper:

Thunder and rain
It's pouring again
Pouring your funds to the needy.
What you made from the Crash
Has become quite a stash
Of cash to the poor from the greedy.

"I assume that this was found at about the same time as your CFO discovered that the money was missing," the DCI said.

"Yes. Paul Wilson unlocked the vaults as soon as he found the discrepancy, and that note was lying on one of the tables inside the room. It must have been put there sometime close to the end of business last Friday."

"Is there CCTV footage for the time period in question?" Spencer asked.

"Yes, and we can identify those entering and leaving the room in the course of their duties, but none of them appeared to be carrying anything resembling the note."

"In that case," Marks said, "Peter and I will need to speak to all those appearing on the footage without raising any concerns. I assume that only the three of us and your Mr Wilson are currently aware of the situation."

"Absolutely," Mainwaring replied. "Paul's extremely loyal to the bank and completely discreet."

"No time like the present, then," the DCI replied. "I suggest we make our way to Waterfords without delay."

"We have five people entering and leaving the vault between four-thirty and five when the bank closes," Paul Wilson said as the four of them sat watching the CCTV footage from the previous Friday. "As you can see, none of them seem to be behaving oddly, and all have valid reasons for accessing the vaults at that time; it's where we keep most of our daily printed records."

"You still do that?" Spencer asked.

"Of course, Inspector," Wilson replied. "The idea of a completely paperless office is a myth. We still need actual hard copies for some of our business."

"Who was the last to leave the vault?" Marks asked.

"That would be Donna Reagan," Wilson said. "There she is now," he pointed at the screen where a grainy image showed a woman leaving the room. "Four fifty-seven, and the vault was closed for the weekend three minutes later."

"Is there coverage of the table where the note was found?" Spencer asked.

"No. It's not in an area of the vault deemed necessary for that level of scrutiny."

"So it would be possible for any of the five to place it there without being seen," Marks said.

"Yes," Wilson replied. "We have absolutely no idea who could have put it there."

The interview with Paul Wilson and Roger Mainwaring lasted for a further half hour before Marks and Spencer left the bank. They departed knowing not much more than they did when they arrived save for the names of the last five individuals to leave the bank's vault on the final day of the previous week. They were, however, surprised at the information which came their way when they returned to New Scotland Yard.

"Sir," Jim Grainger said as they passed his desk. "There's a lady asking to see the officer in charge of the Waterfords investigation." Grainger was the Desk Sergeant on Marks' floor. "I showed her to the squad room and there's a WPC with her."

"Thanks, Jim," Marks said, looking at Spencer and raising his eyebrows. "Who the hell leaked that out?" he whispered.

The woman sitting at the end of the squad room and just outside Marks' office rose from her seat as the two detectives approached.

"Chief Inspector Marks," she said. "My name is Elizabeth French and I think that I may be able to help you in your enquiries regarding Waterfords."

"Come into the office please," Marks said. "It's a little more private for the matters that we have to discuss."

Elizabeth French followed Marks into the room and took a seat to one side of his desk. Spencer pulled up another chair on the other side of it. A woman in her fifties, she had auburn hair, brown eyes and behaved in a confident manner which Marks found slightly disturbing when she next spoke.

"I'm here to confess to the theft of the five billion pounds from Waterfords over the weekend," she remarked. "However, before we go any further might I suggest that you invite Mr Mainwaring to come along to our meeting – what I have to say will be, I'm sure, of great interest to him."

Marks, though initially stunned into silence, nevertheless made the call to the bank and within half an hour Roger Mainwaring was shown into his office. He stared at the DCI's visitor in amazement.

"Donna," he said. "What are you doing here?"

"Donna?" Marks asked. "No, Mr Mainwaring, this lady, who has admitted to the removal of funds from your bank, is Elizabeth French."

"If I might be permitted to explain, Chief Inspector, all will become clear very soon." She turned to Mainwaring. "It was quite easy to infiltrate your bank once I'd changed my identity, Roger."

"But your qualifications... they are outstanding..."

"Again, quite easy to come by if you know the right people," she said. "Listen and you might learn a little humility. You had, in your employment, a man by the name of Sidney Woodson, didn't you?"

"Yes," Mainwaring replied. "Although he is no longer with us."

"Yes, I'm aware of that," Elizabeth said. She turned to Marks. "Sid Woodson was a financial advisor employed by an asset management company wholly owned by Waterfords. Gerald, my husband, and I took advice from him on the best way to manage our pensions when Gerald reached retirement age…"

"The company of which you talk operates quite independently of the bank…" Mainwaring began, but was cut off midstream.

"But is owned one hundred percent by you and consequently answers to your board for all of its actions," Elizabeth said, scowling at him. "Despite our instruction regarding risk profile, Woodson chose to ignore our wishes and ploughed all of the pension money into more speculative ventures."

"How on earth did you…?"

"Manage to find that out, Mr Mainwaring?" she said. "Oh, when you're as driven as I am and learn the correct skills you'd be amazed at what information can be dug up." She turned to Marks again, who had been watching in fascination at the exchanges. "Woodson drained our pension pots and all of our savings - we lost the lot when his gambles turned sour. It wasn't just us, though. There are ten other couples whom I managed to track down, and they had all suffered similar fates at the man's hands."

"How much is involved, Mrs French?" Marks asked, as Mainwaring sat in silence.

"For Gerald and I? Four hundred and sixty thousand pounds. However, when you take the other ten couples into account as well, the total amount runs to over three million."

"Mr Mainwaring?" Marks said, turning to the banker.

"Chief Inspector," he replied, wiping a handkerchief across his brow. "It would have been made clear to all of the couples at the start of their investment portfolios that the values could go down as well as up…"

"Agreed," Elizabeth French said, "as long as Woodson had stuck to our risk profiles. He didn't and we lost all of our savings. We hold your bank responsible for the losses, Mr Mainwaring. We're looking for restitution of all of the money that he gambled away."

"I don't think I can help you there, Mrs French," the banker said, regaining some of his composure.

"In that case," she said, sitting back and folding her arms, "you can kiss goodbye to the five billion pounds."

"You'll go to prison for theft," he replied. "You've already admitted to taking the money."

"Money that you'll never be able to trace, Mr Mainwaring. Chief Inspector," she said to Marks, "how much time will I serve for the crime?"

"Seven years is the maximum, Mrs French," the DCI replied. "You won't get any time off, though, because you are refusing to give back the money." Marks smiled inwardly, now realising where the woman was going.

"I can stand that," she said, turning back to Mainwaring. "That's a lighter sentence than the one that *you'll* suffer at the hands of your board and The City once the news gets out. I tell you what I'll do," she said, smiling. "I'll return all of the money in exchange for written agreement from Waterfords to compensate all of us for the losses we've suffered at the hands of Sid Woodson. We will, of course, expect that to be topped up by the gains that we would have enjoyed had our original instructions been followed."

"Well," the banker said. "I'll have to consult..."

"According to calculations that I've made, the figure we're looking for should be in the region of three and a quarter million pounds. However, as you're trying to wriggle your way out of it I've just added a further two hundred and fifty thousand to that. Are we going to settle on three and a half, then?"

Mainwaring looked at Dennis Marks. The DCI sat back, smiling and shaking his head. He looked at Peter Spencer who was fighting hard to keep his composure. Marks cleared his throat and spoke to the banker.

"Mr Mainwaring," he said. "I think the lady has you by the throat. I agree that she has committed theft, but as she has offered to return all of the money to you I would say that there was no intention to permanently deprive the bank of the billions that she took. Now, if you want my advice, strictly off the record, swallow your pride, come out of hiding behind your company profile, and settle up. If you don't, Mrs French will certainly go to jail where, I would imagine, she will be accorded the status of a modern-day Robin Hood. You'll never see the money again as I assume that she has hidden it well beyond your reach, and you will end up out of a job. Did I miss anything?"

"No," Mainwaring replied.

"Good," Marks said, clapping his hands. "Now, all you have to do is confirm to Mrs French that her monetary demands have been met and then you can heave a sigh of relief and decide where you are going to 'hide' the compensation payment in your books. For DI Spencer and I, well, we can go back to being policemen instead of your lackeys. I think we're done."

The three of them watched as Mainwaring made his way slowly down the office and out of the squad room. As Elizabeth French rose to leave, Marks raised a finger.

"Yes, Chief Inspector?" she said. "Was there something further?"

"Oh, just humour my curiosity," he replied. "Was there just the briefest of moments when you considered keeping the lot?"

"You'll never know," she replied, smiling. "You'd never have found me if I hadn't come forward."

"Just one other thing," Marks said. "The poem you left in the vault…"

"Thunder and rain?"

"Yes," he said. "Why 'Thunder and rain'?"

"Where did you think I got my new name?"

"It's German!" Spencer exclaimed. "The literal translation would be '*Donner und Regen*'. That's how you came up with Donna Reagan, isn't it?"

"It is," she replied. "Just goes to show how easy it was to fool Roger Mainwaring."

Why Me?

"I'm not going, and there's nothing you can do to make me!" Toby said, slapping his spoon down into the middle of his Cheerios.

Milk erupted in a fountain and the breakfast cereal flew from the bowl and across the table. Waldorf and Statler, their two pet cats, scrambled away across the floor from the table where they had been patiently waiting for any stray morsels which might have come their way.

"That was stupid!" Maria exclaimed, coming across from the kitchen sink and wiping away the mess that Toby had created. "I don't spend all my time cleaning up after you; you're going into school and that's all there is to it. Now go and get ready; you'll be late if we have any more of these tantrums!"

"But why me?" Toby asked, his bottom lip jutting out like some diving board. "Why is it always me? Why can't somebody see what the bullies are doing!?"

Tobias Milligan had been at Walker Street School for just over six months since he had moved to Bradford following the repossession of their Leeds home. The mortgage on the house had fallen into arrears on several occasions but, under Maria's careful financial handling, the building society had relented in their threats until the latest round of failures to keep up the payments. They had been forced to leave the three-bedroom detached property in Armley, and Tobias had relocated to an inner city school which was undergoing Special Measures. He was not at all happy at the move.

The bullying had begun a couple of weeks after he first appeared at the school. At first it was not too serious; as a new face amid the thousand or so at Walker Street, he had become the focus of a few snide remarks made behind his back and he had chosen to ignore them, believing that time would wear away his tormentors' enthusiasm. He had been incorrect in that assumption.

The taunting soon escalated into some of his property disappearing while his attention was elsewhere, and when that failed to gain the desired response he came out of school at the end of one day to find that his bicycle had been vandalized. Both tyres had been punctured in several places, his pump was missing, and all of the lights had been smashed – he had been forced to push the cycle all the way home, running the gauntlet of laughter and jeers all the way down Walker Street until he was clear of the area.

"It's not fair!" he said, stomping away from the breakfast table and into the lounge where he threw himself down on the sofa to sulk. "They pick on me because they know that they can get away with it!"

"Who are 'they'?" Maria asked, wiping her hands on a towel as she followed him from the kitchen.

"Well, there's a group, and a boy called Stephen Pickersgill seems to be the leader. He's a big lad and the rest just follow him around like sheep. He's the one who started it all when I first went to the school."

"Can't you tell anyone at Walker Street?" she asked. "What about the Headmaster? Mr…"

"James?" Toby sneered. "He's about as useful as a chocolate fireguard. You never see him out of his office – he must think that Special Measures don't apply to his school. I tell you, the place is a joke. Can't we move somewhere else?"

"You know that's out of the question. We only got this rented house by a stroke of pure luck. I showed you the letters from the building society – they just lost patience and I can't really say that I blame them. We're stuck here until we get back on our feet financially."

"Well, I'm not going back into Walker Street – they can shove it!" Toby said, crossing his arms in defiance.

"Look," Maria said, her voice softening with the hardening of his resolve. She brought his bag and placed it by the side of the sofa. "There's a bus from the end of the street in about ten minutes. It'll get you to school just in time – we can always look at getting the bike mended at the weekend…"

"No!" he shouted, picking his bag up and throwing it across the room. "I've had it with the place. What can they possibly do to me that'll make things any worse than they already are?"

"Listen to me!" Maria wagged a finger in his face. "You need to grow up and face the problem head on. Tell someone at the school about it!"

"I'd like to punch Pickersgill's lights out," Toby said, ignoring her remark. "If I could just get him on his own…"

"Don't even think about that!" Maria exclaimed. "They'll kick you out of the place and we'll have to move again. Where do you think we'd end up then? This place is fine until we can sort out something better. You need to make more of an effort!"

"Why me?" he whined. "Why is it always me? Why do I have to go back into that school?"

"Because you're one of the teachers, Tobias; that's why! Do you think that teaching is easy? I've done it myself and you simply can't let the kids get the better of you! Now get your bloody coat on, pick up that bag you threw across the room and bugger off to work. I've got things to do and I don't want you under my feet all day!"

The Ghost in the Garage

Ron Harvey stood back and took a deep breath. He held it as long as he could and then let it out in a single gasp. His heart had skipped a beat when he took his first peek under the tarpaulin, but now it was turning somersaults at the revelation of what had lain beneath its protective covering. Locking the doors of the garage, he returned to the main buildings where his wife, Brenda, was coming out of the front door of the house.

"Well?" she said. "Is it there?"

"Oh, yes," he replied, scarcely able to hide his enthusiasm. "And in much better nick than I thought."

Now in their late fifties, the Harveys had run a Bentley dealership on the outskirts of Derby for the past twenty or so years. The business had been very profitable and, with its reputation for fair dealing, had built up a client base that extended throughout the length and breadth of the country. With an offer from a Texas-based global auto dealership that neither of them thought they could refuse, Ron and Brenda signed the papers and walked away with a substantial amount of cash in their bank account. This was the opportunity that they had both been working all of their lives for.

The property that they had just viewed had been on the market for almost a year, and with house prices now stabilising twelve months after the 2008 crash, its price had, Ron felt, reached a level at which he thought he and Brenda would be comfortable paying. It would, of course, need a fair amount spending on it in order to bring it back to life, but with the amount that Dwight Cranshaw had paid them for the dealership they felt that the necessary repairs and renovations were well within their spending power. Brenda had been particularly impressed with the inside of the house. Ron had headed straight for the pair of outbuildings where the estate agent had told him there may be something of a surprise. The previous owner had died leaving no relatives to inherit the property, and the entire lot was sold as a package. For Ron, it felt as if all of his birthdays had come along in one go.

"It's going to take a while," Brenda said as they got back into their Corsa for the fairly short trip to their current home in Breadsall. "We're due to move out in a couple of weeks. Any idea where we're going to stay?"

"Caravan, dear," he said, smiling. "One of those luxury ones. There's plenty of room to accommodate it and keep out of the builder's way. The grandchildren will love it spending their summer holidays with us while their mum and dad are at work."

"What about the film crew?" she asked.

"No, there'll not be any room for them as well."

"Silly bugger!" she said. "You know what I mean."

Ron had been in touch with one of the TV networks with their ideas for a grand designs project, and after a site visit to explore the possibilities the director and producer had agreed to feature the property as work progressed. It was another activity that he felt would hold the fascination of their eight-year-old twin grandchildren.

Brenda and Ron took the decision, very early on in their project, to leave the logistics of the renovations to the experts and decided to employ a skilled project manager to take care of all ongoing construction matters. With their hands, therefore, firmly on the purse strings, they were able to relax while the house took shape in accordance with their wishes. Brenda acted as liaison with their manager, Steve, while Ron busied himself with the contents of the outbuildings which were not a part of the present project. Brenda shoved open one of the double doors, her hands laden with a tray of tea and cakes.

"How's it coming along?" she said

Ron came out from under the car's bonnet, wiped his greasy hands on an old rag, and sat down on an upturned box, leaving the only chair for his wife.

"Well, the roof's intact, and that explains the fair condition of the interior. It's obviously been in here for quite a while and the tyres are all shot. From what I can see of the engine, it's going to need a complete overhaul but I reckon I can do that. The joists are strong enough to take a block and tackle so I can do all the work myself. I can get any parts I need from people I know in the trade. It's just going to take some time and, let's face it, we have plenty of that."

"Spooky in here, though, isn't it?" she said, shivering slightly.

"Not as dark as it was before I rigged up some lighting, but yes, there is a kind of atmosphere about the place. I keep mislaying tools and they turn up in places around the garage where I know I haven't been."

"Hmm," she said. "On that note I think I'll leave you to it. Don't let your tea go cold."

Ron took the last mouthful from his mug and put it back onto the tray. Picking up the final morsel of his cake, he finished it in one go, stood up and stretched in readiness for the next phase of the job. Brenda was right; there *was* something unusual about these outbuildings and it wasn't the weather. With summer on the horizon, temperatures were in the high teens until around tea time. No, there was definitely something odd; each time that he seemed to be stuck for an idea, the workshop manual that he'd found in an old cupboard seemed to be open at a page that offered him a solution to his dilemma. It was almost as if he had some invisible helper turning the pages for him. He shrugged and got back to work.

The shadow flitting across the wall at the end of the building sent a sudden shiver down his spine. Ghosts? He didn't believe in ghosts. So what was it that was moving around the place? Was someone messing around with the car? Ron unclipped the lamp from inside the bonnet and walked slowly down the side of the vehicle, picking up a large spanner from his toolbox on the way.

"Okay," he said. "You've had your fun. Come on out and let me see who you are."

There was no sound, and it occurred to Ron that he hadn't heard anything at the time the shadow passed across the far wall. With evening now closing in, all that he could hear was the wind blowing through the trees and moaning through the gaps in the outhouse doors. He shook his head, returned to the front of the building, switched off the lamp and locked up.

"So, what do you think that it was?" Brenda asked after they had washed up following their evening meal.

"No idea," he said. "At first I thought that it might be somebody messing around, but the back walls are solid and they'd had to have come right past me. I suppose I must have been feeling tired; it has been a long day working on the car and some of the parts have seized up. I'll take another look in the morning."

"No ghosts, then?"

"Come on, Bren; you know me better than that."

The following day saw a significant step in the progress of the house restoration. With new windows installed, the entire building was now watertight and work could commence on the interior. Brenda took more interest with the project manager and began the process of selecting fittings for all of the rooms. Consequently, Ron was left more to his own devices than before, and he tried to focus intensely on getting his own restoration project back on the road.

He had identified the parts in the engine that would need replacing and had managed, not without some difficulty, to track down spares for all of the components which would enable him to get it running. This, he believed, was the most important part of the job, and it took him the better part of the day to reassemble and lift the 7.7 litre engine back onto its mountings. With the block now bolted firmly back into position and all of the connections in place, Ron stepped back and wiped the sweat from his brow. He took a deep breath, slipped into the driver's seat, said a prayer and started the engine. It fired first time and settled into a pleasing humming sound.

"My, but that went well," he said.

"Yes, it did; didn't it?"

The voice – it was no more than a whisper – seemed to come from the rear seats, and Ron turned sharply to see who it was that had answered his question. There was no-one there, and the hairs at the back of his neck came smartly to attention; he shivered at the sudden cold feeling that went right through him. He killed the engine and got quickly out of the car. Walking round to the rear of the vehicle, he shouted abruptly.

"Okay, damn you! Who are you and what do you want with me!?"

Once again there was silence, and once more Ron thought that maybe he was letting the atmosphere in the outbuildings get to him. He decided, this time, to try and find out a little more about the property than the estate agent had told him and Brenda. On the following morning he paid a visit to the local library.

The librarian thought for a moment before raising a finger. "Follow me," she said. They made their way to the local history section where she pulled a small soft-back booklet from one of the shelves. "It was called Hanbury House at the time that I think you are referring to. It had been in the Hanbury family for several generations before the last of the family, Hubert, died a year or so ago. He was something of a vintage car enthusiast from what I can remember. Does that help?"

Ron thanked her and assured her that he was fairly certain that it would. Returning to the house where progress was now speeding along, he was met by Brenda who was trying to explain to him the layouts of the rooms now that she had made all of her choices. That he wasn't listening became quickly apparent.

"What's wrong?" she asked.

"You know what I said about not believing in the supernatural?"

"Yes," she said, slowly. "So what?"

"Well, I think we might have a ghost in the garage after all."

"What?" she said. "Are you serious?"

"Oh, I don't know, Bren," he replied, steering her towards the caravan. "Let's put the kettle on while I tell you all about it."

Brenda sat silently through her husband's monologue about the work on the car, the shadow on the wall, the pages in the workshop manual, and the voice in his ear. He then related his trip to the library and the discovery of the name of the previous owners and the hobby of Hubert Hanbury.

"So, is it this Hubert who's been around the place all of this time?"

"I don't know, but one of the things that the librarian said just before I left the library was that the old man died before being able to get the car back on the road."

"Maybe it's his ghost that's trying to help you. If you finish the job perhaps he'll be able to rest in peace."

"Now you're taking the mickey out of me, woman," he said in mock reproof.

"No, love," she said, ruffling his hair. "I can take the mick in much better ways than that. Come on, you've had a tiring day; you can have another go in the morning. If you get it back on the road, you could take the grandchildren for a spin in it."

Despite being on the alert for anything unusual, there were no other spooky encounters as Ron's work on the vintage car approached its end. The body work was in remarkably good condition and required only the minimum of restoration which he carried out himself. As he gave the bonnet its final polish on an evening two weeks later, he stood back and looked at his reflection in the paintwork. Taking a deep sigh of satisfaction, he took off his overalls, dropped them in a corner and turned to close the door and lock it.

"Thank you." The voice – it was not a whisper this time – came from the shadows at the rear of the building.

Ron stood frozen to the spot as a figure emerged from the gloom. It was that of a man, probably in his eighties, with silver hair and bright blue eyes. He was dressed in a tweed suit and was wearing a highly polished pair of brown boots.

"I owned it from new, you know," he said. *"It was my pride and joy until my wife died; I couldn't take it out after that and it's been here ever since. She loved riding in it, and now you've put it all back together. I'm very grateful."*

Ron had no time to reply, as the figure smiled again and slowly began to disappear. A summer breeze wafted gently past him as evening began to fall. The car, he decided, would have its first run out the next day.

The grandchildren were there bright and early. It was a Saturday and the whole family was set to travel on the car's inaugural trip since its restoration. Paul, the older of the twins, raced Ron down to the outbuilding and stood there, hopping from one foot to the other as the rest of the family approached.

"Is there really a ghost in the garage, Grandpa?" he asked as they approached.

Ron, always one for a good tale, had regaled his grandchildren since their early days with stories of mysteries and adventure, but on the previous evening had slipped seamlessly into the world of ghostly goings-on. His daughter had not been too pleased, but the evening had passed without incident and the two children had slept soundly enough.

"Yes, there is!" Ron replied on the morning of the following day. He paused dramatically with the padlock key in his hand. "Want to see it?"

"Yes please!" the twins cried in unison.

"But it's just a car..." Paul, the boy, said with a certain amount of disappointment as the doors opened.

"Not just *any* car, Paul," Ron replied. "It's a Roll Royce – a Rolls Royce Phantom!"

The Midnight Train

James Peterson awoke with a jolt. The train had shuddered and then ground to a halt, almost as if someone had pulled the communication cord. He rubbed the side of his head where it had bumped sharply into the window at the side of him.

"Bloody hell!" he cursed. "What was that?"

There was no answer to his question, and he stood up from his seat to be greeted with a completely empty carriage. His eyes widened in surprise; he was sure that the entire train was jam packed with commuters when it left Kings Cross, and yet there wasn't a soul to be seen. Stepping into the aisle, he made his way down the carriage towards the connecting doors to the rest of the train. It was cold – much colder than he remembered when he'd got on in London.

There was nobody in the connecting carriage or, for that matter, in any of the others at that end of the train. Retracing his steps, he proceeded to the opposite end. Returning to his original seat, he sat down in amazement – he appeared to be the only person on board. He looked out of the window; it was dark outside. No, not just dark – pitch black. There wasn't a light to be seen and although the train was rocking as it now raced along the tracks again, he could not estimate its speed without some point of reference outside. Surely by now it should have passed some settlement or other. A strange feeling began to settle in his stomach.

"This is crazy," he said to himself. "I must be going mad."

"No, not mad," said a voice from behind him. "Just a little confused."

James jumped and turned around to see a man sitting in the seat on the opposite side of the gangway and one place back. He looked old, maybe in his seventies, and wore what looked like a railway company uniform, though James did not recognise the badge above the peak of his hat. He was smiling, and there seemed to be a sadness in his demeanour.

"Who are you?" he asked.

"Oh, my name isn't important right now," the man said. "What matters is that you come to realise what's happened and where you're headed for."

"Okay, so explain."

"That will come later in the journey; we have more people to collect before I can begin to deal with things like that. I have to go now – it looks as though we're pulling in at our next stop."

James stared out of the window. He could feel the train slowing down, and when he turned back to where the man had been sitting he found himself alone once more.

"This is nuts," he said, taking his mobile phone out of his jacket pocket. "Better ring Sue and tell her that I'm going to be late."

His eyes widened in surprise. Not only was there no coverage, but his screen displayed only one message:

'All calls are ineffective from this location.'

"What?" he said. "That's bonkers. How can calls be ineffective? No network has that kind of message."

He switched the phone off and then turned it on again. The message remained the same. He took the battery out and reset the phone to its factory settings. Still the message persisted. He couldn't even access his list of contacts. The sudden realisation hit him that he was cut off from the outside world and alone in a train that he had boarded at Kings Cross in broad daylight.

The train came to a standstill but, try as he may, James could not see anything out of any of the windows in the carriage. Suddenly there was noise coming from the next carriage along the train, and he hurried to the connecting door. Through the glass he could see other people taking seats to either side of the gangway – there were four, and all of them wore puzzled expressions as they sat down. The old man, whom James assumed to be the guard, had ushered them along from the doorway at the far end, said something that he could not hear, and left again.

James pulled open the door and went inside.

"Where have you come from?" he asked the man nearest to his end of the carriage.

"Not sure," he replied. "I'm Steve. One minute I was walking down New Street in Birmingham, the next I was getting onto this train."

"What station? New Street? Were you catching the train?"

"No," he replied. "I was leaving a pub where I'd been having a pint with a friend. We were heading for Villa Park for the game, and then... I don't know; everything went black."

"What about you?" James asked a woman on the other side of the aisle.

"Shopping at the Bull Ring Centre," she said. "My name's Julia, and I'd just come out of H. Samuel on the Lower Mall. I remember slipping... then, like Steve, nothing. Where are we all?"

"No idea," James replied. "Same sort of thing happened to me. Can any of you remember anything else?"

There was a communal shaking of heads, and it did occur to James that he couldn't remember at all where he had been prior to waking up on the train. He had nothing in his possession – no bags of any kind, not even a newspaper. His phone didn't work and he now realised that he couldn't find his wallet. Had he been mugged and knocked unconscious?

"We need to find that guard who showed you into the carriage," he said. "I reckon he's the key to what's been happening. I spoke to him before you joined the train and I think he knows a lot more than he was letting on to me."

"Where's he gone, though?" Julia asked. "He vanished as soon as we'd all sat down."

"I'm going back to my carriage," James replied. "He turned up there just after I'd searched the whole train. Maybe he'll come back now that he's got you all settled in."

"I wouldn't hold your breath, mate," Steve said. "Looks like the train's slowing down. Wonder where we're pulling in."

"No use looking out of the windows," James said as the guy peered through the glass. "There's nothing but pitch darkness out there."

The train was indeed slowing down, just as it had before, and then came to a complete stop. Nothing happened in the carriage they were occupying, but up ahead towards what James believed to be the front of the train, he heard a door close very firmly. The train then slowly began to move, picking up speed quickly as it recommenced its journey.

"Any idea where we're headed?" Julia asked.

"Haven't a clue," James replied. "Wait here and I'll come back when I've taken a look towards the noise of that door."

"Before you go," Steve said. "Have you checked your watch?"

"No, why?" replied James.

"Might be worth a look; all of ours have stopped at twelve."

James pulled up the sleeve of his jacket and stared in surprise. His watch had also stopped at what he thought, bearing in mind the darkness outside, must be midnight. Where on earth was this train going at midnight if, indeed, all of their watches were correct?

James reached the other end of the train before he set eyes on the guard. The older man was seated right at the end of the carriage and watched him all the way along its length before the merest hint of a smile appeared on his face.

"I understand that you've been looking for me," he said.

"How…?"

"Oh, I get to find out lots of things without ever being specifically told," he said. "Come and sit down. I'm not going to get any peace until you find out what it is that you want to know, am I?"

"No," James replied, sitting down opposite the old man across the table. "Who are you, anyway?"

"I suppose you could call me Maurice," he said. "It's as close as I can think to a name that you'd understand."

"You're confusing me. Why would I not understand? What's happening to me… and the rest of the people on this train?"

"Yes, well; I was afraid that this would happen at some point," he began. "There really is no easy way to tell you this, James. You're dead."

"Dead? What..? But I'm here, talking to you. How can I be dead? I have a wife and two young children."

"Have you taken a close look at some of your travelling companions? Do any of them look… shall I say, 'vacant'?"

"Well, of the four who got on after I did, two of them weren't very communicative, and there are some new arrivals who just seemed to be sitting staring into the air."

"That's exactly how it's supposed to be. You see, the three of you shouldn't be holding conversations at all; it's very rare for anyone to retain cognitive capabilities after what's happened to them. Three of you... well, that's unprecedented."

"Right," James said. "Let's have it. What's going on? You said that I'm dead, so that must mean that we all are. Where are we going?"

"Let me explain some background first. You might all have noticed that your watches have stopped at midnight."

"Yes."

"This is the Midnight Train. We, the ones running it, collect the essences of the recently deceased and transport them for reprocessing."

"Reprocessing? You make us sound like waste," James said indignantly.

"In a way you are," Maurice replied. "When you all die, we take your consciousness and recycle it. It gets sort of distilled down into a new set of electrical impulses. Sometimes things go slightly awry, and that's when we get stories of reincarnation cropping up; it's uncommon but it does happen."

"So, are all of us heading for some kind of distillery, then?"

"More or less. Once we're done, none of you will exist either corporeally or spiritually. The new arrivals don't know what's happening, but it would seem that three of you do; it's most unfortunate."

"Well, can't you just let us go?"

"Oh no," Maurice said. "That would never be allowed. Once you're on this train your life is over. Letting you out would cause the most terrible problems. As you see from your watches, time means nothing aboard the train but it has continued as normal for those left behind."

"But we've only been here for less than a day. What difference could it make?"

"Listen to me, James," he said, slowly. "Time has no meaning here. How can you go back to a place outside of that?"

Despite trying very hard to make James understand what had happened, Maurice shook his head and said no more. There was no point – the man before him simply was not going to accept his fate. James returned to the carriage where Steve and Julia sat waiting and he explained, as well as he could, what Maurice had said to him.

"Can't we just make a run for it?" Steve asked.

"There are no handles on the carriage doors. They only seem to open from the outside when there is a fresh set of people getting on the train."

"Okay," Julia said. "We just wait until it slows down again and then jump off when the last of the entrants are on board. This Maurice will have enough on his hands without having to chase after the three of us."

James had to admit that it was the only idea likely to work, and jumping off the train into the unknown was, he thought, more preferable than sitting around waiting for a fate that he was loath to confront. Nevertheless, it was some time before the slowing down of the train had them looking at each other expectantly.

"Okay," James said. "We need to be in one of the empty carriages; let's move into the next one now that ours seems to be half full. That will give us the best chance of an open door."

His reasoning was correct. As the train drew to a halt there was a movement from the doors at either end of the carriage. They had positioned themselves in the seats nearest to the entrance and now waited for the last of the new passengers to finish getting on board. As expected, Maurice was the last in line as he tried to organise them to their seats. He had not spotted James, Steve and Julia in the small corridor forming the connecting passage.

"Now!" shouted Steve, and they leapt from the train into the darkness. They hardly heard Maurice's voice shouting at them as it faded into silence.

"What now?" Steve said as he brushed the grass from his clothing.

The fall from the train had been cushioned by the grass of an embankment, and they had rolled down it, coming to rest gently at the bottom of the slope close to a fence separating the railway from an adjoining field,

"I seem to be okay; what about you, Julia?" he said.

"Fine," she replied. "Why don't we head for the nearest road and see where that takes us?"

"Good idea," James replied. "Once we've found out where we are, we can all work out the best way of getting back home."

Sticking to the edge of the field, the three of them had walked for around half an hour when Steve spotted a house in the distance, and they climbed over the fence at the edge of the meadow. The building stood, like a toll house, at the bend of an unclassified lane, and they saw, about two hundred yards up the incline, a stream of traffic passing across its end. Fifteen minutes later, they stood at the crossroads where a church was located on the opposite corner.

"Well, that gives us a clue," said James, pointing at the church notice board. "St John's, Aldercar. Now all we need to know is where the hell Aldercar is."

"Look," Julia said. "Right under our noses." She pointed to a signpost on the opposite side of the road. "M1, it says. Think we should go that way?"

The walk, through the village of Langley Mill, took them to the A610 and they managed to flag down a car to take them the rest of the way to Junction 26. There, Steve and Julia departed – the two of them staying with the driver who was heading for Birmingham. James, heading north for Sheffield, remained on the slip road hoping for a lift in that direction. It was an hour before anyone took pity on him, and he fell asleep as soon as the car had joined the northbound carriageway.

"Sheffield coming up," the driver said, nudging James and bringing him out of his slumber. "Where d'you want dropping off?"

"Oh, the first turn-off will be fine. I can make my way home from there, thanks."

Junction 31 for Sheffield (East) took James along the A57 and a not inconsiderable walk to his home in Woodthorpe. Opening the gate at the end of a short path on Melville Road, he knocked on the white front door, wondering how he was going to explain to his wife, Sue, the fact that he had lost his keys. An odd thought occurred to him that the place looked somehow older than it should.

107

The door was opened by a girl. James estimated that her age would be around five years old, and before he had time to speak she had turned to yell over her shoulder.

"Granny! There's a man at the door!" She turned and ran back inside, leaving the door wide open.

A woman came out of a room at the end of the hall, wiping her hands on an apron and mildly berating the youngster for her carelessness. As she came out of the gloom of the interior, James began to get an uneasy feeling in the pit of his stomach. As soon as she stepped into the daylight, he gasped in surprise.

"Sue?" he said, eyes wide in amazement.

"No!" she exclaimed. "It can't be. You're... you're..."

"Dead?" he said, finishing off her statement. "No. I'm here. I got stuck, but I'm home now."

"No. You can't be. The train – you died on the train. The doctors said that it was a massive brain aneurysm. No-one could have saved you."

"But I've only been away for a day," he said.

"It was fifteen years ago, James. We were all at the funeral. You can't... how did you get here? You look just the same as you were on the last day I saw you alive. I'm forty-three, James. That little girl is our granddaughter, Chloe; she's five next week."

"Rachel has a daughter? I... I..."

"You can't stay here, James. Bill will be home soon; how am I going to explain you to him? We've been married for ten years and he brought me through some dreadful times after you..."

"Yes," James said. "I can see how that would be awkward. Is Rachel around? Can I see her? What about our son, John?"

"No, please don't do anything like that. Rachel's been in and out of psychiatric care since you died, and it was only getting married to Tony and having Chloe that finally brought her out of clinical depression. If she sees you again after all this time it might tip her right back over the edge."

"And John?"

"Living in Australia now. I get a letter from him when he can remember to write. You know what boys can be like." She smiled, sadly. "I don't know what's happened to you, James, but it's all in the past; you can't stay here. You do understand that, don't you? I'm sorry, but I have to go back inside now."

Behind the closed door, Sue broke down in tears at the love that she had lost so suddenly fifteen years ago and which was now standing just the other side of the front door. She looked through the spy hole as the man she once held so dear walked slowly down the path and out of her life once again.

Revenge Time

"Fired?" Sean Howard said, incredulously. "Why? I mean… what for?"

"Not fired," Lesley Reed replied. "The company is simply letting you go."

"Semantics!" Sean retorted. "You're firing me and you know it. After all that I've done for you and that sister of yours, you're treating me like a piece of merchandise!"

Sean had come to the company eighteen months earlier as its first accountant. Lesley Reed and Helen Wright, her sister, had set up *Reed & Wright Literary Agents* in the spare bedroom of Helen's home with a single PC and a telephone line. Selecting a niche in the market, they soon acquired a reputation for reliability and professionalism. Within a year they had taken on extra staff to operate a small office on a local business park and now, ten years down the line, the company turnover and staff numbers had exceeded all of their expectations. When their bookkeeper left to move to Scotland, the sisters felt that the time was right to put their finance department on a more formal basis. Sean Howard was chosen from a field of a dozen candidates to carry out that project.

"Helen and I need to move the company forward much faster now, and we feel that the time has come to hand over the finance function to someone with a professional qualification."

"Bullshit!" Sean spat out the word, safe in the knowledge that he was, in the light of his coming dismissal, safe in expressing his feelings in such a vitriolic manner. "I put my studies on hold so that I could devote more time to streamlining your accounting system. You're better placed now than you ever were to make inroads into the competition. Look at what I did with your cash flow. Your credit control was a joke, and I've reduced customer payment time by three quarters. Where do you and Helen think that all the money in the bank account has come from?"

"Yes, yes," she said, shaking her head at the incontrovertible truth of what Sean had said. "Nevertheless, it's the opinion of Miles and Shaw…"

"Oh!" he said, mockingly. "Those jokers you call your auditors? You should have stayed with Oldroyds; at least they know the ins and outs of the trade. I did advise you and Helen not to make such drastic changes. I could cope with new bankers and solicitors, but Terry Barlow is a prat."

Barlow, a family friend of the sisters' mother, had managed to persuade Lesley and Helen that having someone at the financial helm with an official accountancy qualification would enhance their profile considerably. Miles and Shaw provided a short list for the sisters to peruse, and recommended one candidate in particular.

"There's no need to take that tone," Lesley said, irritated at Sean's demeanour. "Mark Potter…"

"Potter?" Sean said. "He's the nephew of Colin Miles, their senior partner; talk about nepotism!"

"She sacked you? Just like that?" Sean Howard's wife, Debbie said as he slumped into a kitchen chair. "Can she do that?"

"I've only been there eighteen months," Sean replied. "No employment protection, see? I called at Stanfields employment agency on the way home. Gillian reckons that she can find me plenty of temporary and contract work until I get something permanent, so we're not going to be stuck for cash."

"But you won't get as much as you did with *Reed & Wright*."

"I know, but we'll be okay for the time being," he replied. "I just feel so angry."

"Wasn't it JFK who once said 'Don't get mad, get even'? Well, maybe that's what you should do. Wait your time and then… I don't know; do something that'll really rattle the two of them."

"Maybe I will, Debs," he said. "But I'm not going to let it rule my life; I need to move on. Gillian's set me up with an interview tomorrow."

"Wow! That was quick."

"I know; she's good at what she does. Fancy dinner out? I need some calm right now."

Sean had been working on a project for an engineering company in Huthwaite, just off the A38 in Nottinghamshire, for around six months. It was an interesting assignment involving fixed assets, but not the kind of work that he had in mind on a permanent basis. He had been home for around an hour and was washing up after dinner when Debbie came to the kitchen holding the phone.

"It's Nicola for you – she says it's 'interesting'."

Sean dried his hands, took the phone from his wife and went into the lounge where he slumped into an armchair and put up his feet. Nicola Wainright had been his deputy at *Reed & Wright.*

"Hey, Nic; what's up?" he said.

"You better be holding your sides, Sean. Are you sitting down?"

"Yeah, why?"

"Well, and this better not come back to bite me, our two sisters are up the creek without an accountant."

"Wow!" Sean said. "Mark Potter's gone, then?"

"Potter? No, not him. He never made the cut. Helen didn't like him from the off. They set on a guy called Brian Roberts and he's made a right mess of things."

"How?"

"Lied to them about his qualifications apparently, and when they confronted him he upped and walked out. He had no idea how to run the finances and wouldn't listen to me when I tried to help. We could do with you back here."

"Not going to happen after what they did to me," Sean replied. "Why don't you take it on? You're good enough."

"Don't want the hassle, and Tony'd kill me if I did. He says I spend too much time there as it is. Sure you wouldn't change your mind?"

"You'd be the first to know if I did."

Howard pondered silently for a while after he'd put the phone back on its cradle. He walked into the kitchen to make himself and Debbie a drink. She turned from the cupboard where she had been stacking their clean dinner pots.

"What was that all about?"

He gave her the gist of Nicola's news, and she laughed out loud at the predicament that the two sisters now faced. Her face turned suddenly serious.

"You're not going to consider going back, are you?"

112

"Not likely," he said. "But do you remember what JFK said?"

"Yes, why?"

"Well, I'm nipping out for an hour. There's something that I need and it may just fit with the advice that he gave."

He was back just after seven that evening with a parcel under his arm. He took off his coat and went into the lounge where his wife was sitting watching TV. She switched it off.

"Okay, what's the secret?"

"This, my love," he said, opening the parcel, "is a two terabyte external hard drive. Enough storage space to accommodate the entire IT system of an SME."

"What are you planning?" she said, sidling up closer to him.

"I'll tell you if and when what I have in mind is successful. Just going up to the study for a while."

Downloading the remote access software was a cinch for Sean. He had used the same programs when he was at *Reed & Wright* for working from home. He was certain that neither Lesley nor Helen had the faintest idea how tech stuff like that worked, and his only concern was whether Brian Roberts had stumbled across it and disabled it. He called up the main screen and logged in.

He smiled in satisfaction. Once *Reed and Wright's* IP Address had been entered into the remote portal, he was delighted to see that, despite his dismissal, nobody had thought to disable his user name and password. It took only seconds for him to gain full and uninhibited access to the entire company set up. Writing a simple script in SQL, he began the download of the whole file system on the company's server. Looking at his watch, he reckoned that it would take around an hour to complete the task – time for a celebratory glass of wine with Debbie.

"Okay, what have you got?" she said as they stared at the screen later that evening.

"A complete backup copy of their data files together with all programs, protocols, permissions... in fact, the whole shooting match."

113

"So, what now?" she said, puzzled. "What good is that going to do you?"

"It's not so much a case of what good it'll do *me*, but more a matter of what harm can be done to the sisters."

"I'm not with you."

"You will be in a minute. Just watch this."

Having unplugged the external hard drive, Sean switched the screen view to the *Reed & Wright* file server. Calling up the Windows administration tools, he selected the option 'Format Disk'. Navigating through the drop-down box, he homed in on the C drive on the company's system. Holding his finger over the 'OK' button, he turned and smiled at his wife.

"Correct me if I'm wrong," she said. "But won't that delete all of the stuff on their system?"

"No," Sean replied. "If I deleted it all, someone would be able to restore it. That might take a day, but it'd still be there. What I'm about to do is reformat the entire disc – scrub it clean and make it as it was when the system was first installed. They'll lose everything."

"But won't they know who's done it?"

"Ordinarily I'd agree with you, but in this case all that they *might* be able to discover, if they ever manage to get the system up and running again, is that Brian Roberts accessed it shortly before it went down – I logged myself out and then used his logon and password to get back in."

"But they'll know that you used our PC, then."

"Yes, if that's what I did," he said. "However, nobody thought to ask me to return the company laptop, and that's what I used. All I have to do now is reformat that and then chuck it in the river."

"Just remind me never to annoy you," she said. "More wine?"

Nicola Wainright's words proved to be rather prophetic when she and Sean had their conversation about the state of *Reed & Wright*. He was at home alone one evening on the week after the file purge at the company, Debbie having gone out with a couple of friends. The telephone rang in the middle of a live match in the UEFA Champions League; he muted the sound.

"Hello?"

"Sean, it's Lesley; I need your help."

He paused, taken momentarily aback at the call and the tone of voice at the other end. His silence did not go down too well.

"Are you there!?" she snapped. "Or are you just being difficult?"

"Excuse me?" Sean replied, now fully understanding what was going on. "How dare you take that tone with me? You fired me – remember?"

"Yes. Yes," she said, back tracking suddenly. "It's just that we have something of a crisis at the company and we don't know where else to turn."

"Oh dear," he said in mock concern. "I thought you two had everything firmly under control. Don't you have some high-powered accountants to advise you?"

"We fired them; they turned out to be as poor as you'd said. We're back with Oldroyds and they suggested that we get you back here."

"I wouldn't come back to you if you were the last job on the market," he said.

"Please, Sean…"

"Oh, it's 'please' now, is it? What happened? Your pet finance guy leave you in the lurch or something?"

"We didn't set him on," Lesley replied, her voice shaking. "We brought in a guy by the name of Brian Roberts and he's done something to the IT system… we can't access any of our data."

"So, tell Red Ridge; they should be able to help."

Red Ridge was a Birmingham-based software house that had supplied and installed all of *Reed & Wright's* computer hardware and software, and were responsible for maintaining it.

"They won't talk to us since Brian upset them just after he joined. We don't have a support contract any longer and I only found out about that last week."

"Well, you are in the mire, aren't you?" Sean was having a hard time keeping a straight face and hoped that it wasn't becoming apparent down the phone line.

"We're prepared to double the salary you were on when you left…"

"When I was fired, you mean."

"Yes, of course," she said, now capitulating completely. "Will you do it?"

"No," he said. "I won't." He ended the call.

"Word gets around quickly when companies hit trouble," Harold Palmerson said. "The way that I see it, Lesley, you're in a fix. Once your bank gets wind of the depths of the problems you and your sister are facing, they'll pull the plug. You'll be out of business and penniless."

"So, what are you suggesting, Harry?" she replied.

Palmerson was the Chief Executive of *'Books Are Us'* one of the larger literary agencies in Birmingham, and a rival of *Reed & Wright*. Helen and Lesley had known him professionally for a few years and had, on occasion, attended social events in the trade hosted by his company. He had long coveted the rising stars in *Reed & Wright's* stable of authors and once more returned to his favourite topic – a takeover.

"I'll take all of your shares at face value – it's more than they're worth right now if what I hear is true."

"That will still only give you forty-nine percent - our bank owns the remainder."

"I know, but once they get wind of your problem, I'll be able to pick those up as well. Think about it – I'll give you and your sister forty-eight hours."

"What now?" Helen asked as the call ended.

"We can't function with the system down, and Red Ridge won't help. I rang Sean and he all but laughed in my face."

"I told you not to get rid of him, but you wouldn't listen and I was daft enough to let you talk me into it."

"Water under the bridge, now," Lesley said. "We'll have to sell out to Harry and just try to start again. I'll ring him."

"That was quick," Palmerson said.

"No sense in prevaricating," Lesley replied. "Draw up the necessary paperwork and we'll both sign. We don't really have any alternative, do we?"

"Not that I can see," Harry replied. "I'll be in touch."

The takeover of *Reed & Wight* by *Books Are Us* was a hot topic in the literary world but none of the underlying causes came to the surface during the negotiations or the final settlement. Harry Palmerson smiled at the figure on the opposite side of his desk and raised a glass.

"Let's drink to a successful beginning, shall we?"

Sean Howard raised his own glass in agreement. "Cheers," he said.

"Well, let's get off to Nottinghamshire and finalise things with those two sisters. I'd imagine that you're going to enjoy this part of it, aren't you?"

"Like you wouldn't believe," Sean replied. "Your car, I presume?"

An hour later they were ushered into the board room at *Reed & Wright* by Nicola Wainright. She winked at Sean as she closed the door and returned to the finance office. There was an edge to the atmosphere as the sisters stared in surprise at their former accountant, now taking his seat at the side of the company's new owner.

"You know Sean, of course," Harry said, smiling.

"Yes," Lesley replied, frowning. "We er...."

"What's going to happen to us?" Helen interrupted, seeing her sister at a loss for words.

"Well, I rather thought that I'd leave that to Sean," he replied. "Sean?"

Sean Howard paused before answering. He had almost tasted this moment from the day that he'd been in touch with Harold Palmerson. Of course, he couldn't tell his new boss exactly what had happened at *Reed & Wright,* but he was certain that the man was astute enough to realise that something out of the ordinary had happened to the company.

"Well, *'Books Are Us'* don't intend to close down the premises of their new acquisition; that would sort of negate the goodwill that was a part of the purchase price. Consequently, all of the staff will be retained and all of their employment rights will transfer over to the parent company..."

"But us," Helen said. "What will happen to us?"

"Oh," Sean said. "I thought that it was clear enough. Neither of you will be required – you're both fired."

The Lemon Tree of Life

I had no idea about lemon trees until the day my daddy planted one in our back garden in 1965. He bought it from our local nursery and it wasn't much to look at back then, but I was only six years old at the time, so what did I know? My name's Lily and I guess my life's been tied up with that old tree, one way or another, for so long that I hated to leave it now I knew that we'd be moving.

I'd lived in Ridgecrest, California all my life up to then. It's a city in Kern County, along U.S. Route 395 in the Indian Wells Valley, adjacent to the Naval Air Weapons Station at China Lake. It was incorporated as a city in 1963. Well, that's enough of the geography lesson – doesn't mean a hill of beans to me now. I left all of those memories behind. Daddy's job ended when the plant on the north east side of town closed down, and I lost touch with all my friends. There was a new job waiting for him in North Dakota. It's up near the Canadian border too; it was sure cold after California.

"Can't we take the tree with us, Daddy?" I'd asked him the week before we were scheduled to leave.

"No, honey," he'd said. "It'd be too rough up there for it; wouldn't last more'n a year or so."

I cried that night. That tree had been like a friend since I was knee high to a grasshopper, and I couldn't imagine what life'd be like without waking up each morning to see it shaking in the breeze. Guess I was about to find out.

We stripped the tree of its fruit before we left – Mama used to use a lot of those lemons in her cooking and we didn't know what prices would be like up north. I had this crazy idea that I could maybe raise another tree from the pips, but Daddy just patted me on the head and said that I was bein' foolish. I did it anyway.

He built us a greenhouse when we'd settled in. Nothing big – just room enough for Mama to set some of the herbs that she'd need for the cooking and then plant them out in the garden. The factory where Daddy was working was in Bismark, and he and Mama found us a nice house six miles west of the city. It had a good sized garden where we could grow some of our own food as well as the flowers that Mama liked to put around the house. I read up some on how to grow fruit from lemon pips, and figured that it couldn't be that hard. Just to be sure, I planted a dozen or so of those pips in plant pots and babied them as if my life depended on their survival.

I watched them every day, checking for the first sign of a green shoot, but it was a slow process even in the warmth of the greenhouse, and I began to worry as fall approached. Daddy bought a small paraffin heater to make sure that they had the best chance of making it through the cold weather. I'd almost given up hope when the first three shoots appeared one Sunday morning.

"Mama! Mama!" I shouted, running into the kitchen. "Look! They've started!"

I handed her the three pots and she smiled at me and asked when the fruit would be ready for the first batch of drizzle cakes. We all laughed that day and I began to scope out the garden for likely places to plant them when they'd grown big enough. I was devastated one cold winter morning when I got up and realised that I'd left the greenhouse door open after I'd come in the previous evening. I rushed down to the garden to take a look. The seedlings were all dead – blackened by the hard frost that we'd had overnight. I ran into the house crying bitterly and flung myself into Mama's arms.

Daddy went down the garden to see if there was anything that he could do. The paraffin heater should have provided enough warmth, but I hadn't checked its tank and it had gone out. I felt so useless. I was brushing my tears away when I saw him come out of the garden and into the kitchen holding a single pot.

"Looks like this little one might have survived," he said.

I took the pot from him, wiped my eyes again and stared in disbelief. There, just poking its first leaf through the compost, was the tiniest shoot you ever saw.

"Thanks, Daddy," I said, and gave him a big hug. "I'll make sure that this one doesn't freeze."

That little seedling stayed in my bedroom for the rest of that winter. I placed it on my bedside cabinet, out of the way of the cold of the window but with enough light to keep it going until spring. Come March it was a full five inches tall and had more leaves than I ever thought it would back on that winter morning. Daddy said we should call it The Live Lemon Tree, but I told him that was silly; it should be The Lemon Tree of Life, because it had made it through the winter despite my carelessness. So, that's what it was, and as the year passed it just went from strength to strength.

It took six years for that tree to produce lemons for Mama's drizzle cake, but it was the best cake that I'd ever eaten. We'd planted it in the sunniest spot in the garden and made sure that it was protected each fall from the cold of the North Dakota winter. I know that lemon trees aren't supposed to do too well that far north, but this little sucker was as tough as old boots and just kept growing and growing. By the time I left high school for NDSU in the fall of 1977 it was over six feet tall.

Daddy died that November.

I came home from college and took over the running of the home. Mama seemed to have lost interest in pretty much everything, and it was left to me to look after Tommy and Luke, my two brothers who'd been born in North Dakota after we'd moved up there. They were eight and five. We scattered Daddy's ashes around the base of that lemon tree, said a few words and then got back on with our lives. Mama grieved long and hard but came out of it by the end of the summer and things started to look up again. I went back to college that fall and picked up my studies – Agriculture and Botany.

I spent my summer holidays under that tree, drinking lemonade and reading my college books. I'd made a few friends, and Tommy and Luke took over some of the work around the house. We had some high old times around the barbeque in the evenings, and Mama met up with Jake, a farmer from the neighbouring county. They seemed to get along pretty well and the boys liked him. I wasn't so close – too many memories of Daddy, and when they got wed I thought that it was time for me to move out.

I graduated from NDSU in 1981 and, at the age of 22, met and married a corn farmer from Iowa named Ted. I'd been staying with a college friend called Marie in Charles City and we'd been on a night out at a hoedown. Ted and I hit it off right from the start and it was a real whirlwind of a romance. We pitched in with his Mom and

Dad on their farm, and they'd said that he'd be taking over the place pretty soon. With my qualifications, everything seemed set fair.

At the back end of 1983, we got word that Mama and Jake had been killed in an automobile accident in Florida where they'd been on vacation. Mama would have been fifty-six three weeks later. Tommy and Luke were both kids, and there was no-one else to look after them until they grew up, so me and Ted upped sticks and went back home to North Dakota.

There were lots of folks at the funeral, and we gave Mama a real good send-off. It was kind of quiet around the house when they'd all gone home, though, and I set the boys some work to do to keep their minds off things until me and Ted could work out what we were going to do. There was a parcel of land at the back of the house and nobody had ever bothered with it. It was all scrubby and nothing but weeds ever seemed to grow there, but Ted came up with the idea of raising pigs. I was doubtful at the time, but his Mom and Dad gave us some money to get the thing started and it kind of took off. A couple of years later we had over sixty of the critters and folks were beating a path to our door for the meat.

Back then, in 1992, there wasn't much in the way of competition and we made ourselves a good living on that parcel of land. The lemon tree was still going strong, and I learned to make Mama's lemon drizzle cake from the recipe book that she'd left. That tree was twenty-three years old by that time and over twenty feet tall – we had to get a ladder to reach the highest fruit, and that was another money-maker by the time that we'd had our fill of the crop.

The boys were now both in their twenties and had left home to make their own ways. Tommy had graduated from Harvard and was now working in the DA's office in Chicago, while Luke ended up working in Seattle for Microsoft. Me and Ted would have liked a family of our own, but it just never seemed to happen, so we got on with our lives and ploughed all our energies into the farm.

I'm fifty-one now, and as I look out across the garden with a glass of wine in my hand I have to admit that life could be a whole lot harder than it turned out. That old lemon tree is still pushing towards the sky; it's getting a little gnarled around the trunk nowadays, and I know how that feels! Seems my whole life has been tied up with that plant and its fruit. I called it 'The Lemon Tree of Life' and Daddy had laughed at me, but as I watch Ted coming up the garden with the latest basket of fruit I wonder which of us will last longer – me or the tree.

Winter's Creeping Chill

Gillian Rodway stood in her garden and stared at the sky with a sense of foreboding. The weather had taken a turn for the worse and the heavens looked full of snow. It hadn't really been anything remotely like daylight for the past couple of days, and the conditions seemed to be worsening by the hour.

She had taken a lease on the cottage to the north of the Derbyshire town of Hathersage in an effort to rekindle her creative writing juices after a number of false starts on her fourth novel. Originally from Derby, where she owned an apartment in Brookbridge Court, she had let the two-bedroom property and retreated to the relative peace and quiet of the Peak District, and had spent the summer trying to summon up an idea for another successful book.

Her debut novel, 'The Riders of Hell', had hit the Best Sellers list and had been optioned by one of the TV networks in 2007 for a future series. With the financial crisis of 2008 had come disappointment as the studio, though retaining the option, had postponed production until finances would permit the investment. Nevertheless, the novel had made her a substantial amount in royalties as her agent provided access to UK and international markets. She had become known across the world, and that success had been followed in turn by her second and third releases.

Now, however, she had run into every author's worst nightmare – writer's block. The summer had passed without a single idea coming to mind, and as autumn turned to the beginnings of winter there seemed to be nothing on the horizon save for the onset of the current spate of bad weather. It had rained almost non-stop for a couple of weeks, and now that damp had turned to bone-chilling cold as a north-easterly airflow was bringing the threat of snow. She took one more look at the sky and closed the door as the first flakes began to fall.

"Not good eh, Ramsey?" she said to the tabby stretched out before the fire. "Mind you, I don't suppose either of you two will be venturing out in this."

The cat turned his head slowly and blinked at her. He was one of a pair and, hearing the voice of his mistress and protector, the second feline occupant of the cottage, Macdonald, a black short hair, strolled into the lounge from the kitchen where he had been polishing off the leftovers from his companion's bowl. Gillian had been the proud carer of the two since they had been presented to her as kittens by her father, George. A lifelong Labour supporter, Rodway had thought it amusing to name them for his Conservative daughter – it had been the source of some amusement for both of them ever since.

Macdonald strolled over to Ramsey, sniffed thoroughly at his left ear and then settled down before the fire. Seeing both cats singularly ignoring her, Gillian went to the fridge, took out the bottle of Hock which she had started the day before, and poured herself a generous measure. Returning to the lounge, she settled into her armchair and picked up the Stephen Booth novel which she had been reading. As one, Ramsey and Macdonald turned to face her and stared intently.

"Okay," she said with a sigh. "I'll put another log on the fire. Do either of you realise how much I spoil you? Do you even care?"

Stepping around the two recumbent forms, she reached into the box where a pile of cut logs had been placed at the weekend and removed the largest that she could find. Placing it carefully onto the embers, she turned to find that both of them had apparently fallen asleep.

"Thanks, Gill," she said to herself with a heavy dose of sarcasm. "You really are a peach."

Picking up the novel again, she wondered to herself if Booth also faced similar problems with writer's block – he seemed to churn out his *Cooper and Fry* stories with consummate ease; maybe she should write and ask him – perhaps not.

The snow had come with a vengeance during the night, and when Gillian opened the door the next morning she was faced with a three foot high drift. Ramsey and Macdonald took one look (each) and turned tail for the comfort of the fireside rug. She had planned to brave the cold but clear weather and walk along Baulk Lane, following the course of Hood Brook. Perhaps, she thought, this would provide her with some inspiration for the new novel. Now that was out of the question and, after a satisfying breakfast interrupted only by the culinary demands of her two felines, she sat down once again at the screen of her PC and its blank Word document. It was still in the same condition some hours later, and in a state of desperation she donned coat, hat and gloves, retrieved her snow shovel from inside the back door, and set about clearing a path from the front door down to the end of the garden. The work took her around half an hour, and as she straightened up and rubbed her aching back, she noticed the figure coming down the road towards her cottage.

The woman, Gillian could not estimate her age from the distance she was at, was not dressed for the conditions and appeared to be struggling with a large holdall. The snow beyond the front wall had drifted almost to its top, and walking through it was clearly hard going. Nevertheless, the woman made it, though in a state of some exhaustion, shortly after seeing Gillian standing at her gate.

"I'm lost," she said, between breaths. "My car's up on the top road and it's stuck in this bloody snow. I don't suppose I could use your phone, could I?"

"Of course," Gillian said, ushering her through the gate and towards the cottage. "You're lucky to have made it down here, and it looks as if we're in for another flurry."

As if on cue, the first large flakes were followed by a more substantial fall and in a matter of minutes visibility was down to a few yards.

"Looks like the wind's getting up as well," she said to the woman who was now stamping the snow from her feet in the porch. "You're going to be fortunate to get anyone to come out to you in this weather."

"Damn!" she said. "Would you be able to put me up until it clears? I'm Elizabeth McBride, by the way."

"Of course," Gillian replied. "You're welcome to ride out the storm here. I've got the freezer well stocked. The Peak can be a bit unfriendly at times. Feel free to try your luck on the phone, though - it's in the lounge. I'll put the kettle on."

Going through the motions of preparing a hot drink, Gillian could not shake off the strange feeling that she had seen Elizabeth McBride's face before. She was still pondering all of the possibilities when she turned with a tray and left the kitchen.

"No dice," Elizabeth said when Gillian returned to the lounge, "I found three garages around here on my tablet; two aren't answering and the third just laughed."

"You're here for the duration, then," Gillian replied. "I'll make up the bed in the spare room. There's plenty of hot water, so make yourself as comfortable as you like. You look like you could do with something hot – homemade soup okay?"

"Oh, that sounds fine," she replied. "I hope you don't mind, but I looked through your bookshelf while you were in the kitchen. You're Gill Rodway, the novelist, aren't you?"

"Ah, yes," Gillian replied. "All writers like to be recognised, but I try to keep out of the way up here in the Peak – it makes for a quiet atmosphere for thinking."

"Oh, I'm sorry to intrude."

"That's okay, I'm stuck for an idea so it's not as if you were interrupting anything earth-shaking," she replied. "Now I come to think of it, your face seemed familiar to me as well, and it's just come to me who you are. You're Callum McBride's wife, aren't you? Isn't he something at Holyrood?"

"Yes," Elizabeth said with a sigh. "Private Secretary to the Lord Advocate. He's one of the up and coming in the Scottish Parliament. He's been an MSP for the past eight years."

"Wow! That must be an amazing thing – married to somebody like that."

"It was," Elizabeth said. "The first few years were great. We'd met at Edinburgh University where we were both studying law. After graduation Callum joined the civil service, and that was the start of his rise. I just rode along on his coat tails and carried on my job in the Procurator Fiscal's department; nothing mind-boggling but the salary was good and our lifestyle was amazing."

"Okay, so what are you doing down here in deepest Derbyshire?" Gillian asked.

There was an embarrassed pause, and Elizabeth took the opportunity to take a drink from her mug. Gill Rodway was an internationally known author and there had been times in the past when the spouses of government staff had been caught unawares when injudicious statements had appeared in the national press. She did not intend to become one more statistic, but she had to share what she had discovered with someone and did not know who, at this precise moment, she could trust. She took a look across the coffee table at the woman facing her and made her decision.

"Hiding," she said. "Or rather, trying to hide."

"From whom? What have you done?" Gillian asked. "Are you in trouble with the police?"

"No," she replied. "Well, not yet as far as I know. It's Callum; I left our home in Edinburgh five days ago and he'll be looking for me."

"I'm not surprised," Gillian said. "He must be worried sick."

"Perhaps so, but it won't be for my well-being."

"I beg your pardon; why not?"

"He's far more likely to be concerned at what I found out," Elizabeth said.

"I'm sorry, I don't understand; has he got a mistress?"

Elizabeth laughed. "If only it was that simple." She took a deep breath. "He left his laptop open one evening a couple of weeks ago when he was summoned to an emergency meeting at Holyrood. I found some disturbing emails from a man by the name of Hughie Aikin. I did some digging in the files back at the Fiscal's office and Aikin is linked to organised crime in Glasgow."

"So, your husband..."

"Could be on the payroll of one of our country's biggest and most dangerous criminals. Aikin's been arrested on a number of occasions for a range of serious offences, but nothing had been made to stick. If Callum's working for the likes of him, and it looks as if he is, I am in serious trouble. That's why I packed a bag and left when he wasn't at home. I took my car, but then I thought that he'd be bound to be able to trace it. Once I crossed the border into England I traded it in at a garage just outside Penrith. The guy there was amazed at me swapping the Lexus for a Corsa."

"And, the Corsa..."

"Is stuck at the top of the road where I abandoned it before coming down here. I don't know what else to do."

"Well, with this weather closing in it looks like you might have bought yourself a little time, but you need to go to the police with what you've found."

"That's easy for you to say, Gillian, but I don't know anyone down here... apart from you right now."

"It just so happens that I might be able to help," Gillian said. "In all the research I've done for my novels, I managed to strike up a friendship with a DI at the Derbyshire Constabulary. His name's Mick Brown and he works at their HQ in Ripley. I can give him a call if you like."

"But what will he be able to do?" Elizabeth asked, new hope suddenly coming to the fore.

"Well, if the evidence that you've got is solid, I'd imagine that he'd be able to contact the Edinburgh police and let them take it from here. It would certainly get you out of a hole and they should be able to offer you some sort of protection. I'm assuming that's what you'd need."

"That's an understatement," Elizabeth said. "Can we get on with it right away?"

"That's arranged," Gillian said, when she put down the phone. "Once this weather eases I can get you down to Ripley in my 4x4. We might have to hole up here for a few days, but I can't imagine Callum being able to get here in that time even if he knew where you are. Looks like you've made a couple of additional friends as well."

She nodded at the recumbent felines, one on either side of her guest. Ramsey and MacDonald, having risen from their fireside beds, were now staring intently at Elizabeth, who was stroking them.

"How long have you had them?" she said.

"Since they were kittens, but don't let those looks fool you – they're a couple of mercenaries. Once they get the idea that you're not going to be feeding them they'll be back to the fire."

129

The remainder of the day passed as normally as it could in the circumstances, and it was not until they were turning in for the night that Gillian raised the subject of Elizabeth's family.

"I'm an only child," she said. "Mum and Dad died some years ago, so there's only Callum and I – we have no children, so leaving him was not a problem."

"Won't he be able to trace your mobile? I assume that you have one." Gillian said.

"I did, but it ended up in the Tyne as I passed through Newcastle. I bought a pay-as-you go phone from Tesco – he won't be able to trace me on that. I should be safe as long as he doesn't manage to find the Corsa, and in this snow that's not likely. I kept away from main roads on my way south; I got a little lost and that's how I ended up here."

"Well, I checked the forecast for the next few days, and there's a thaw set to begin the day after tomorrow. We should be able to make our way up to the main road by then."

Gillian's assessment of their plight proved to be accurate, and on the following Wednesday most of the snow which had been blocking the road had gone, enabling her Range Rover to make it to the main road. A quick call to Mick Brown ensured that he would be available to speak to Elizabeth when they arrived at the police headquarters in Ripley.

"This is a fairly damning set of documents, Mrs McBride," he said, closing the file which she had passed to him. "I'm afraid that the Derbyshire Police can't take any action, but I will fax them over to the Procurator Fiscal's office in Scotland. In the meantime you ought to stay somewhere in the area in case we need to talk to you again. There's a Premier Inn just across the way."

"I can't use any of my credit cards – Callum will know where I am," she said.

"I'll take care of that," Gillian said. "You can stay there until this is all over. There's no chance of him tracing you if the room's booked in my name."

With accommodation secured and her safety now assured, Elizabeth felt relieved that her ordeal was almost over. A week later, after a nationwide alert, Callum McBride was apprehended and returned under police guard to Edinburgh to face serious charges.

Subsequent raids on a number of Glasgow addresses resulted in the smashing of a serious crime network in the city.

"I can't believe that I'm now safe to go home," Elizabeth said to her new friend as she packed her meagre belongings into the Corsa that she had left close to Gillian's cottage. "How can I ever thank you?"

"Give me a few months and you'll know how much help you've been."

"I'm sorry, I don't understand."

"Well, I was struggling for a new story when we met – I'd been tossing ideas around for a while, but nothing had come to the surface."

"What? Do you mean...?"

"What you've been through will make a great novel, assuming that you're okay with the idea," she said.

"Wow! Of course – will I be famous?"

"I'll change names, of course, but who knows? I got a call from my agent while you were involved with DI Brown. I had a TV deal on the back burner but the studio has pulled the plug."

"Oh, I'm sorry to hear that."

"Don't be. My agent had anticipated it, and it looks like Universal Studios are interested in making a film out of my first book, 'The Riders of Hell'. They also want options on all other published and future work, so watch this space."

"What will you call the new novel?" Elizabeth asked.

"Titles are always the worst part of writing a book, and they cause me all kinds of problems. This one, however, was an easy one to come up with. After all the scary stuff that you've been through, the fact that Callum might be creeping up on you and the trek you had through that winter weather, what else could it be than 'Winter's Creeping Chill'?"

131

When I'm Gone

It's kind of lonely around here now. As I look out of the patio doors I feel so isolated from the rest of humanity living their lives outside, running around like ants – not a care in the world. We always wondered, Bonnie and me, what it would be like to lose the other one.

"What will you do when I'm gone?" we would ask each other, never thinking for one single moment that the situation would arise; well, not this soon anyways.

"You'll find someone else, won't you?" she'd asked. "I'd hate for you to be alone."

We'd talked about the kids and the effect on them if anything ever happened to one of us. I didn't imagine being cut off from her and our two boys so suddenly. The car smash took care of that all right.

We met up at NYU in our second year. Bonnie was an English major and I was heading for the bar after graduation on the back of some good results. We both landed well-paid jobs and within five years had moved up the property ladder to a penthouse apartment in Manhattan. When the kids came along we moved out of town to Rutherford. It meant a half hour commute, but it gave the kids a back garden to play in and some of the time I worked from home. I made partner a couple of years later and the money just seemed to roll in without too much effort on the part of either of us.

"It's like a fairy tale, Dave," Bonnie would say with that cute smile on her face that I found irresistible.

We were on our way back from her Mom and Dad's in Buffalo when it happened. It was just after Thanksgiving and the snow came down hard when we were about half way home. The semi came right across the highway and took our Impala with it; I never saw it coming and they were gone – taken from me in an instant of madness. The driver was way over the limit – not that it matters much anymore. It won't bring us all back together. Never even got to say goodbye.

Patrick called; he's been helping me come to terms with what's happened. I've had a number of sessions with him but progress has been on the slow side. He tells me that nothing's going to change, but that I will pass over the grief if I just let it go. It's easy for him to say – he's not just lost everything that he holds dear.

"You can't keep hanging on like this, David," he said the last time we met. "It really is time to move on. Bonnie and the boys are beyond your reach now. I'm sorry if that sounds crass, but it's the way that it is."

"I know, I know," I told him. "The place just seems so empty, and I swear that sometimes I can see them and hear their voices. It's just so…"

I was interrupted by the telephone ringing, and Patrick shrugged his shoulders as I went over to the bookcase where it sat. I stood there, staring at it as it rang out; when I finally decided to answer it, the messaging service kicked in and when I turned to Patrick he was shaking his head. I looked back at the phone as it relayed the call.

"Hi, it's Lonnie," Lonnie said. *"We… um… Janice and I sort of wondered how things are with you. That's stupid, isn't it? Look, we just wanted you to know that we're here if you need us. You can come over any time you like… or we can come to you if that's better. We'll bring along a couple of bottles of your favourite wine and have an evening sort of… talking about, you know. Oh, well, just give us a call, yeah?"*

He was gone. Lonnie and Janice had been friends since before the boys were born, and I worked for a while at the same place as him before moving up the career ladder. We'd spent many an evening with them, and it was like being at home. I'd missed their company but now wasn't the right time to take up his offer.

"I can't share what I'm feeling right now with any of our friends," I said to Patrick, but he was looking at his watch and making signs that it was time for him to be leaving.

"Think about what I said," he told me.

"I will. Thanks for calling," I replied. "If there was just some way that I could get a message to her, you know. I'd feel a whole lot better."

"I do understand," he replied.

"There's times that I'm sure I can see them all here," I said. "Bonnie sitting at the kitchen table looking at some photographs. The boys running around the house or playing soccer in the garden. Then they fade away and I'm alone again – it's heart breaking. You do stuff like that, don't you? I mean, you're not just a shrink, are you?"

"Yes, I have done things like that in the past, but it's not as easy as you might imagine. I'm here to help you through this and move on." Patrick paused; he took a deep breath. "Let me think about it and we'll talk again next time I call."

Then he was gone, leaving me alone in what had been our home. The silence was almost deafening after the noise that the boys used to make. I walked into the garden and stood in the middle of the lawn, just breathing in the air – air that Bonnie had breathed in not so long ago. I saw Mrs Kowalski over the fence and was tempted to call out – just for someone to talk to – but I didn't. She straightened up from the flower bed where she'd been working. She turned suddenly and glanced in my direction; it was almost as if she didn't see me standing there, and she shook her head and returned to her plants. I went back inside.

It was unusual for her not to say anything; we'd been good neighbours ever since Bonnie and I had bought the house – maybe she was just embarrassed to speak. She wouldn't be the first – or last for that matter. I went back indoors and picked up our wedding photo from the mantle above the fire place.

"Why, Bonnie?" I said, tears cascading down my cheeks. "Why did it have to be like this? The boys too; how am I going to get through this without you?"

I must have collapsed onto the sofa – I woke hours later. The house was in darkness, but then I could hear movement in the hallway. There were footsteps coming my way, and I rose from the sofa and turned to the door. I'd only seen her in shadow or a vague kind of mist before, but there she stood – large as life and in full Technicolor.

"Bonnie?" I said. "Have you come back to me?"

She stopped in her tracks – the bags that she was carrying fell from her grasp and she frowned, cocking her head to one side.

"Who's there?" she asked. Oh, how I'd longed to hear her voice.

She took a few steps forward and stared intently in my direction. I looked around; there was no way that she couldn't see me. I was in the middle of the room and in the full glare of the light that had just come on. Her search of the house was thorough and she kept asking who was there. I sat down and waited for her to reappear, but she didn't come back and the entire episode ended. The bags vanished from the spot where she had dropped them. Just one more vision to torment me. I went upstairs to bed.

I don't recall getting up the next day, or shaving for that matter. I must be walking around in a daze – I'm even wearing the same clothes as I did... before. In fact, I can't remember *ever* getting changed; were these the same clothes that I was wearing on the day of the accident? Patrick called again – I didn't even hear the door open and close; does he have a key?

"Hello, David," he said.

"Patrick," I replied. "I'm so glad to see you. I think I must have been dreaming. Bonnie was here – at least I think she was. Then she disappeared; I tried to talk to her but she just ignored me and went upstairs. I didn't see her again after that. What's happening?"

"Do you remember that you asked me if there was a way that you could contact her?" he asked.

"Yes, yes," I said with some excitement. "When can you do it?"

"I managed to get in touch with Bonnie, and she took a little persuading. She wants more time to think about it, but I believe that we can organise a meeting quite soon. What you need to remember, David, is that these things might not go the way that you think they will. There are all kinds of problems that might crop up; I'd advise you to prepare for a surprise or two."

"What do you mean, Patrick?" I said, puzzled. "Why would she not want to talk to me? What's wrong?"

"Nothing's wrong, David," he said. "Contact with the other side can be fraught with problems. I have to go now, but I will be in touch again soon."

Before I had chance to reply, he was gone just like before. I never heard the door close behind him. I sat down on the sofa again

– I seem to be doing a lot of that now. I was shaken from my thoughts by a knocking at the front door; it became heavier and more insistent the longer I delayed and I walked down the hall corridor and pressed my eye up against the spyhole. The figure on the other side was my mother.

"Anyone home?" she shouted – she never knows how to do anything discreetly.

I paused, my breath quickening by the second. She was the last person that I needed to talk to right now. My mother was a world expert on gushing, and it would take all of my will and determination to get rid of her once she crossed the threshold, I decided to ignore her.

"C'mon!" she yelled – the volume had gone up. "You can't hide yourself away forever. You have to face facts and the quicker you do the better you'll feel."

I seriously doubted that. She was the one who tried to persuade me that getting married so soon after graduating was the worst of all ideas. Bonnie had won her round in the end, but it had been a hard fought fight. I returned to the lounge – the blinds were closed. Maybe that would send the right kind of message. Silence returned to my life and I heard her car leaving the driveway. How I wished for a reply from Patrick.

It must have been almost a week when Patrick finally called again. How do I not hear that guy when he turns up?

"Good news, David," he said, waking me from what I assume must have been a nap. I seem to be doing a lot of that recently as well.

"What?" I said, rubbing my eyes.

"I believe that I might be able to organise a meeting between you and Bonnie."

"We can talk to each other?" I asked, not quite believing my own ears.

"I think so," he said. "We can do it today, but I'll need to set one or two things up first. Is that okay with you?"

"Of course!" I exclaimed. "Anything you want as long as I can see her and the boys once more."

"It'll be just Bonnie, I'm afraid," he said. "I think that it's unwise to involve the kids in this."

"All right," I said, a little disappointed. Anything would be better than nothing. "Just do whatever you need to do."

"Well, I'll need to move to the kitchen; we'll need a table at the correct height. I've brought along the equipment that I use; I assumed that you wouldn't mind."

"No, let's just do it," I said, leading the way out of the lounge.

I watched in anticipation as Patrick laid out a table cloth and lit a candle in the middle of the table. He closed the blind and reduced the light level to something approaching dusk. He then sat down and stretched out his hands. I hadn't seen Bonnie until that very instant. She sat down opposite Patrick and took each of his hands in hers. What was this?

"Is he here?" I heard her say. "You were in that trance for quite a while."

"He's standing right behind you, Bonnie," Patrick said. "Talk to him; I know he wants to talk to you."

I was stunned. There was my wife, clear as day, holding onto the hands of the man who was not only my shrink, but also a medium of some notoriety. I placed my hand on Bonnie's shoulder – it went right through and she shuddered slightly.

"Was that you, David? Can you speak to me?" she said.

Her words, her voice, brought tears to my eyes and I walked around to face her. I looked into those beautiful hazel eyes and now realised what it was that had happened. It wasn't me who had survived that crash but her and the boys. I was gone – dead. Now I understood things – Mrs Kowalski ignoring me, Bonnie not seeing me when she brought the shopping home, the lounge blinds being closed when I hadn't touched them. What was it that we used to ask each other? *'What will you do when I'm gone'*? Maybe now I knew – this was Bonnie's way of saying goodbye, and I needed to let her know that I loved her for the last time. It was my time to let go – to walk into the light.

"I'm here, honey," I said. "Give my love to the boys... and don't live another moment of your life alone. Goodbye, sweetheart."

The images began to fade as I left that room, turned, and headed towards the brightest light that I had ever seen.

One Caveat

One caveat was all that was needed. Just a single warning or word of caution and I would have been fine. But can you rely on it? No! You can't rely on anything these days; not even a hint from a friend to stop me almost ending up in serious trouble. I tell you, the world's going to hell and there's nothing that I can do to stop it.

Okay, that might be a little exaggerated, but damn if it's not how I feel right now. If I get out of this there's going to be payback for one poor sod! Want to know how it all started? Well pin back your ears – here it comes…

"Come on," Barry said. "Where's your sense of adventure? This could make us both rich!"

"I don't need to be rich, Baz," I told him. "What's wrong with being happy with what you've got?" I knew the answer, of course – he was skint.

He was always skint; ever since our schooldays Barry Phillips had empty pockets. Oh, he would start with money; it's just that he had an enormous problem in holding on to it. Now he comes to me with some scheme that he thinks will ease all of his – his, mind you – problems. He just needs me to put up the ante. Well, I won't.

"That's always your answer, Mark!" he snapped. "It's okay for you; you've got money coming out of your ears."

"Yes, I have," I said. "And it's staying in my bank account where it belongs until I find my rainy day. You seem to have one every week, Baz!"

"This is a dead cert," he continued. "You have to live a little."

"Oh, yeah, a dead cert," I said with a heavy serving of sarcasm. "Like the one that you put your shirt on at the last Grand National?"

"That was bad luck," he whinged.

"Bad luck?" I replied in amazement. "It was the first bloody fence, mate!"

We continued in this vein for a while, him whining and me winding him up. I knew that I'd end up caving in eventually, but it served my purpose to keep him dangling at the end of a piece of string. He had nobody else to turn to and the only collateral that he had for any kind of loan was his old MG. He'd inherited the car when his dad died some years ago, and it had stood rusting away in his garage ever since. It was an MGC GT 1968 in mineral blue, and in good condition would fetch around fifteen thousand pounds. The trouble was that it wasn't in good nick and he'd be lucky to get five thousand as it stood. He wouldn't have sold it to a stranger, anyway. I suspected that this was why he was trying to rope me in.

"It'll be different this time," Barry said. "I promise."

Oh, those words. Words that he'd used time and time again over the years. It was always going to be 'different' and this time he'd hit the jackpot. Well, I'd seen him fall down so many times and then get back up for more. The odd thing is that he always seemed to come up with funds for the next failure. This time, I thought, he'd overstepped the mark.

"What exactly is it?" I asked.

"I got a tip off," he said. "There's this company, not doing too well, and I've heard that a takeover's in the offing. The share price is rock bottom at the moment, but it'll rocket when news hits the Footsie…"

"Stop right there," I said, raising both hands to cut him off. "Are you crazy? Don't you know about insider trading? You could get jail time for that, not to mention your licence going down the drain."

Barry had been a trader on the London Stock Exchange for a few years, but all of his legal gains had gone down the plug hole with the hair-brained schemes that he'd got involved in. Now he was stepping right outside the rules and expecting me to follow like some demented sheep.

"I'm not coming in with you, Baz," I said.

"Well, lend it to me, then," he said, almost begging. "I'll pay you back – scout's honour."

"The car," I said. "Sell me the car."

"The MG?" he asked, stunned. "That was my Dad's. I'm going to fix it up."

"With what?"

"Well, what are you suggesting?"

"What's it worth as it stands?" I asked.

"If I do it up I could get over fifteen thousand for it," he said, his eyes glazing over at the thought. He snapped out of it. "Why are you asking?"

"Tell you what," I said. "I'll take it off your hands for ten thousand – all official; I want the log book. If and when your ship comes in you can buy it back from me. If you lose, I keep the car. Deal?"

"Do I have a choice?"

"Of course," I said. "You can walk away and our conversation never happened. Actually, I'd prefer it that way."

"All right," he said, glumly. "But I get first refusal on the car when the money comes in."

He was right about my financial situation, though. I was well off – hell I was rolling in it. But it was all mine, and earned legally. My dad started a car dealership and repair shop back in the 60s, and I sort of gravitated towards the trade after college. When he handed over control of the business in the 1990s, all I had to do was play a straight bat, treat customers fairly, and watch the money roll in. Barry's MG wouldn't pose a problem for me, and I had it moved to my house using the recovery vehicle from the repair shop. Once in my garage, I had it up on ramps and began the work.

There was nothing fundamentally wrong with the MG – the engine needed some work, it was true, but after a few minor repairs I had it running as sweet as a nut. The bodywork was the real issue, but with mates in the trade I soon had it fixed and resprayed, and within a month I could have used it as a mirror. I was just itching to show it to Baz.

I rang him at home and at work, but there was no answer. He'd not been seen by anyone for at least three weeks. It was strange for him to go AWOL like that, especially where I was concerned. I didn't start to worry seriously until a fortnight later – he'd been anxious to get his hands back on the MG and it was completely out of character for him. The phone call told me all that I needed to know. It was late on a Wednesday evening about seven weeks after I'd bought the car from him.

"Mark!" he snapped, before I'd even had the chance to say 'hello'. "Can we talk?"

"We are doing," I said. "Where the hell have you been?"

"Never mind that," he said, testily. "Do you still have the car?"

"You mean *my* car?" I asked, wondering where he was going with this.

"I want it back."

"So buy it from me," I said, getting annoyed at his attitude. "You won't recognise it now, and it's going to cost you more than the ten thousand that I paid for it."

"What!" he exclaimed.

"It's been completely overhauled," I said. "I've spent a fair bit on it."

"How much?" he said – I could sense a change in his demeanour.

"Another three grand – you need to come up with at least thirteen, always assuming that I want to sell it back to you."

"You promised…"

"I said you'd get first refusal, that's all. It runs like silk, and I've become sort of attached to it. Do you have the money?"

"I can get it."

"That means that you haven't," I said. "What about that little scam, sorry scheme, of yours? I thought it was going to make you rich."

"The takeover fell apart in the end," he said. "I lost all the money I'd used to buy the shares – the company went into administration when the buyers pulled out."

"You're screwed, then, aren't you?"

"I need the car," he said. I could almost see him on his knees. "There's something…"

"I know," I said. It stopped him in his tracks.

"What?"

"I found the little parcel when I was under the chassis, Very clever hiding it inside the false second exhaust pipe."

There was a stunned silence, and I thought at first that he'd hung up. I wasn't going to prompt him, and just bided my time. I could hear his breathing at the other end, and it was clear that he was becoming more and more desperate.

"What did you do with it?" he asked, his voice almost down to a whisper.

"I had a look. Nice little velvet bag, it is," I said, casually. "They really sparkle when you empty them out. Where on earth did you get them?"

"I was looking after them for... a friend," he said.

"And this friend," I said. "I'm guessing that he wants them back?"

"Just hand them over and you can keep the damn car!" Barry snapped.

"Temper, temper," I said. "They're worth quite a lot, aren't they?"

"What have you done?" he asked. "You've not been stupid, have you?"

"Me? Why would I be stupid? No, I just wanted to see if they were real. I popped down to Hatton Garden a couple of weeks back and had an acquaintance assess one of them for me. No questions asked, you understand, and it turns out that the one I showed him is a real beauty. Uncut, aren't they? My acquaintance reckons that he can cut it into at least three separate stones – says it's worth around forty thousand. I reckon you're minding close on a million quid's worth for this friend of yours."

Barry was close to hyperventilating by the time I'd finished, and it was becoming clear to me that he'd got himself into something way over his head. I decided to let him off the hook.

"Look, Baz," I said. "I'm not interested in the diamonds. You can have them back – I'm not getting into the kind of trouble that I suspect you're storing up for yourself."

He heaved a huge sigh of relief. "Thank Christ for that," he said. "I'll come over tonight – don't go anywhere." The line went dead.

I waited in all evening, and it was close to midnight when I finally gave up on him and went to bed. The diamonds were quite safe – stashed away in the concealed security vault that I'd had installed years ago for deeds, my will and so on. There was no way that anybody would be able to find it concealed within the panelling of my study. I realised that something had happened to him when I came home two days later to find that the house had been ransacked.

143

I had tried to warn Barry in the past about the waters that he was sailing into, but I may as well have talked to the wall. Obviously the owner of the diamonds had lost patience with my friend and wormed my address out of him. God only knows what he did with him afterwards.

So, there you have it. No caveat, not even one. Barry never told me exactly what the dangers were, but now that I know it's clearly time to hit the road. I went upstairs to the study – it too was wrecked – packed whatever clothing I could round up, emptied the safe, and headed for Dover. Thank God my passport was up to date; not sure what I'll do if anyone comes looking, but then again I do have a few shiny stones to help me on my way. Amsterdam looks good.

Time to Travel

"Call off the wedding?" I asked, incredulous. "You want to call off the wedding?"

"I know it sounds a bit abrupt," Tom said to me. "I just need a little time to think things over, Sandra."

"Think *what* over, exactly?" I asked, my voice and temper becoming more strident by the minute. "We've been planning this wedding for over a year now. What's to think over?"

Tom Halliwell and I had met at a friend's party a couple of years ago. We'd clicked almost immediately and my Mum and Dad thought the world of him. I'm Sandra Benson, and I'm as pissed as hell.

"I just…" He shrugged and looked down at his shoes. I remained silent, waiting for the joke to spring itself upon me. It didn't – he was serious.

"Do you understand what it is that you're saying, Tom?" I said, eventually. I'd calmed a little, seeing his obvious discomfiture. "My Mum and Dad have paid out thousands for our wedding and now you want to call it off."

"Not call it off exactly…" he began. My temper was rising again and I cut him short.

"Well, what the bloody hell *do* you call it? It sounds like you're calling it off to me! What is this, cold feet? If it is, yours must be a couple of blocks straight from the Polar ice cap!"

He stood there like some naughty schoolboy outside the headmaster's office, waiting to learn what punishment was to be meted out for the misdemeanours that he'd been caught committing. Something had clearly gone badly wrong with our relationship and the future which we had so carefully planned together. From the evening he went down on one knee before all of our friends to this surreal dialogue that was now playing out, I was at a loss to understand the line of logic that had brought him to his decision. He looked up at me – there were tears in his eyes.

"What? What is it?" I asked. It was like I'd stepped into a dream world where all of the normal rules no longer applied. Was I Alice, and was this the rabbit hole that I had fallen down?

"I can't..." he began again. This time I let him hang there. "I just need some time; I think I need to go away for a while; maybe some time to travel and get my head sorted."

"Time to travel?" I asked, a sudden chill eating its way into me. "How much time are we talking about? A month? Two? Three?"

"I've got my bags packed," he said. "I'm going abroad for a while."

"What about your Mum and Dad? What do they think?"

"No idea," he said. "I left them a note."

"A note?!" I said, my voice rising again. "And what about the invitations? Am I supposed to deal with them? Over two hundred people have been invited to the wedding and now you're skipping town and leaving all that to be dealt with. What are they going to think? Have you even considered the effect that this will have on me?"

"I'm sorry," he said – it was almost a whisper. "It's just something that I have to do."

He turned and walked out of the room – out of our flat. I heard the door click closed and he was gone. I collapsed onto the sofa and the tears flooded out. How could he have done this to us?

I took a deep breath as I walked down the street to the tube station. I suppose that it went as well as I could have hoped... or even deserved.

"Well done, Tom," I said to myself. "You're a real heel, y'know? As bastards go, you must be up there at the top of the pile."

That did nothing to ease the pain that I was feeling. I did love her; Sandra was the only one for me – I knew that in my heart of hearts, and despite what had happened to bring me to this point there was still a nagging thought that maybe, just maybe, I could have worked it through. The pictures were the things that swayed me.

They came in the post – anonymous poison without any way of identifying who had sent them. There were four in all; pornographic images of a woman and a man – a man who I'd never seen before, but a woman whose face I knew only too well. Sandra had deceived me. They looked like stills from a film and they made me sick to my stomach. She was smiling – clearly enjoying what was happening – and I'd rushed to the toilet and vomited into the bowl. I spent an entire day trying to work out what it was that could have persuaded her to get involved in something like that.

It wasn't money – we had enough of that between us to live on, and savings to cover the deposit on a property that we'd seen. I was relieved now that we hadn't committed ourselves to buying it.

It's selfish of me to run for it and leave others to face the music, but I don't know what else to do. I just couldn't bear the thought of people seeing her doing… that. What if any of my mates saw it? Some of them subscribe to porn sites, and surely the film would come to their attention sooner or later.

"Where to mate?" the man at the ticket booth at St Pancras snapped me back to reality. I had no idea how I'd got there from the moment I entered the tube station.

"Oh, Dover," I replied.

"That'll be twenty-eight ninety," he said. "You should have booked earlier – would have been half that."

"Yes," I said, not really listening. "Thank you."

The journey was almost two hours, and it gave me plenty of time to reconsider what I'd done and where I was going, but by the time I got off the train at Dover Priory I was none the wiser for the interval. I made my way to the ferry terminal and booked a one-way ticket for Calais.

Time flew while I was away from home, and I became more than competent in a number of foreign languages. That helped in finding casual work in the EU, and it was just as well since the money I had on me when I left London had long gone. I'll be honest, there were a few females whose company helped me through that phase of my life – nothing serious and certainly not likely to become permanent and, as the months turned into years, the memory of the day of my separation from Sandra was beginning to fade.

There were, however, relapses. They were usually brought on by the maudlin effects of alcohol, and on one balmy evening in Turin I slipped into a conversation with a young man in a bar which, under sober conditions, I would never have considered. How we came round to the subject of the aborted wedding I'll never know, but we did.

"And you left this lady because of something like that?" Gianni said. "If you loved her, I do not understand why you could behave in such a way."

"It's a British thing," I said. "We're not like you Italians; we're more reserved – stuffy, if you can understand that word."

"Si, I understand," he said. "But love... in my country love is everything and you can forgive even the most outrageous mistakes."

"So, you think I was wrong?"

"From what you have told me, Signor, this lady was crazy about you. Are you certain about the pictures?"

"Absolutely!" I said. "A face like hers – once you see it you never forget. She is beautiful."

"Then go back," he said, raising his glass and taking a generous swallow of the Chianti.

"I can't," I said. "I've ruined any chance of my family forgiving me." ·

The conversation continued in a less confessional manner for a while longer, but when we parted company I was still convinced that I had done the right thing.

"I don't suppose that you've heard anything from Tom, have you, Sandra?"

The question came from Harry Benson, my Dad. He had liked Tom from the first time that I'd brought him home. Their relationship grew even though Tom was an Arsenal fan, and Dad supported Spurs – that had been the topic of much light-hearted banter between them.

"No, Dad," I said, putting down the newspaper that I'd been reading. "It's been over two years since he took himself off across the world, and I'm not holding my breath."

"And you've no idea why he broke off your engagement?"

"No," I replied. "Look, we've been through this before. He wouldn't tell me why he suddenly got cold feet – he just left, okay?" I tried to get on with the paper but he wasn't letting go.

"Are you sure that you hadn't argued, love?" he went on. "Maybe you said or did something without thinking, and it upset him."

"Dad!" I shouted, throwing down the now forgotten paper. "Will you stop this going on and on?! Tom left and wouldn't tell me why – okay? As far as I can see he just got cold feet! Now, if you wouldn't mind, I really would like to forget all about him!" I stood up, left the room and slammed the door behind me, almost colliding with my mother on the way as she came in from the kitchen, clearly to find out the cause of our argument. "I'm going out!" I said as she stood there. "Perhaps you can talk some sense into him!"

"Well," Anne Benson said to her husband as she entered the lounge. "That sounds as if it went well; anything that I need to know?"

"I just don't understand why they split up," Harry said. "Everything seemed to be going along fine and then he just left. Cost us a packet when he did, mind. I'm still cross about that, but there has to have been a good reason – the lad didn't seem to be the type to just up and go."

"Well, I don't think harping on at Sandra will help. Remember how she was when it happened? She shut herself away for weeks. Come on, I've got tea ready; let's sit in here and watch the news while we eat."

Anne turned on the TV for the BBC Six O'clock News, but they had only just begun to eat when both were stunned at one of the headline stories.

'British tourist Tom Halliwell was arrested earlier today at Riyadh airport by Saudi police, who found ten kilos of heroin in his luggage. Mr Halliwell, from London, had been stopped by immigration officials in a routine check and denies all knowledge of the class A drug. We'll have more on the story as it develops.'

149

Harry and Anne looked at each other in stunned silence – surely this could not be the same Tom who had left Britain so abruptly two years earlier. Their attention was dragged away from the TV screen by the loud closing of the front door, followed by the sudden reappearance of their daughter.

"You've seen the news, then," I said, sitting down at the side of my Mum. "What the hell has he got himself into now?"

"He's said he didn't know anything about the drugs," Mum said. "I can't believe that he'd be so daft."

"Stupid, more like," I replied. "He runs out on me, leaves the country immediately and we hear nothing of him for years – and now, this. The Saudis have the death penalty for drug traffickers, don't they?"

"I read somewhere that they'd executed nearly fifty people since the beginning of 2018 for that," Dad said. "Surely the British government will step in. Innocent until proven guilty, isn't it?"

"Not over there," Mum replied. "It's the other way round. He's in a real mess unless the Foreign Office gets involved. The Saudis are an ally of ours, after all."

"I wouldn't hold out that much hope," I said. "Even if the government did get involved, he could be locked up for ages waiting to be tried, and then it's usually behind closed doors."

I was shocked. After all this time I thought that I was over him, but now this news had brought all the memories back to the surface. It was the following day that more facts emerged, and Tom's one phone call that the Saudis allowed him had started the ball rolling when his father contacted Downing Street with a plea for help. It seems that the Foreign Office is making overtures to the Saudi Royal Family to intercede.

It's a nightmare. I have no idea how it happened. I'd got off the plane at Riyadh and went to collect my luggage at the carousel. The brown bag was slow to appear, and many of the other passengers had collected theirs and were now heading for the departure gate. When mine eventually appeared there were only three of us left waiting for baggage. I picked the brown bag up and made quickly for the exit. The official standing in my way was pointing to a side room.

"If you would be so kind, sir," he said in almost flawless English. "We would like to take a look at your luggage."

"Okay," I said. "Can we make this quick? I have to be somewhere."

"I'm sure that it will not take too long, sir."

I should have known that there was something wrong from the tone of his voice - he was being way too polite, and his grip on my arm was too firm for my liking. I went along with him; I was, after all, in his country and knew that the Saudis did not like difficult foreigners. When they opened up the bag, the bottom dropped out of my world. I hardly remember the rest of the events of that day, and I was taken to jail to await my fate. It was a couple of days later that a man in a suit came to see me.

"Mr Halliwell," he said. "My name is Geoffrey Forbes from the British embassy. It looks as though you've got yourself into a spot of bother."

"The bag wasn't mine," I said, ignoring all of the formalities. "I have no idea where the drugs came from."

"But you told Saudi immigration that it was," he said.

"I was in a hurry, and it looked similar to mine – I just picked it up off the carousel. Can they do this kind of thing to me?"

"Mr Halliwell, it's no more than our own officials do at any of our ports, and taking one look at you I'm not surprised that they singled you out."

He had a point. I hadn't shaved for almost a week, and my clothes were the same ones that I'd been wearing for a few days. I must have looked terrible.

"However," he continued, "you may count yourself very lucky. The Saudis intercepted a known drug mule in Jeddah. He was carrying a bag similar to the one that you picked up in Riyadh. Looks like he made the same mistake."

"So, am I off the hook?"

"You may have to wait a few days while the authorities sort themselves out. The bag that he was carrying had all of your belongings in them. They've had to let the man go as he was not committing any offence, but he's lost the drugs he was carrying and I suppose his bosses will be none too pleased with him."

Forbes was right, although it was a further week before I was released - I took the first flight out and headed back to Europe. It was time to set one or two things straight and Sandra was the first person on my list.

"All right, all right. I'm coming; keep your hair on!"

I don't understand some people. Ring the door bell and then just wait. Don't go hammering on the bloody door just because nobody answers it straight away. I'd been upstairs washing my hair and was dripping water all over the floor and stairs. Unlocking the thing, I stood in amazement at the figure standing there on the step.

"You?" I said, the towel sliding off my shoulders and onto the floor. "What the hell are *you* doing here?"

It was Tom – the last person that I expected to see. He stepped forward and I stood aside as he went past me and into the hallway. It was an automatic reaction, catching me completely unawares.

"Hello Sandra," he said.

"Is that all that you have to say?" I retorted, recovering some of my composure. "Over two years since you walked out on me on the eve of our wedding, and all you can say is 'Hello Sandra'?"

"This is going to be difficult…" he began. I cut him off.

"Difficult? I'll tell you what's difficult. Difficult is explaining to family, friends and the rest of the two hundred people that we invited to our wedding why you suddenly buggered off and left me to face the music – *that's* difficult!"

"I know, but…"

"Why did you leave, Tom?" I continued, ignoring his remark. "You never told me at the time."

"Well, I suppose I owe you an explanation…"

"No kidding, Sherlock," I said. "Come on then, let's take a seat – I'm all ears." I walked into the lounge, leaving him to follow if he chose to. He chose to. "Sit down, why don't you."

"It was the photographs," he said.

"What photographs?" I asked.

"These," he said, pulling a brown manila envelope from his bag.

I took it from him and slid four pictures out onto the coffee table. My blood ran cold at the sight of them, but I quickly realised what it was that had happened.

"You think that this is me?" I asked, pointing to the woman.

"Well, yes, it is," he said. "I recognised your face."

I peered closer at one of the photos. "It's my face all right, but didn't you look at the rest of what was there from the neck down?"

"What do you mean?" he said.

"Tom," I replied, flinging the picture at him. "We'd been seeing each other for two years – don't you know what I look like from the neck down, particularly naked?"

"Well, um," he faltered.

"Have you never heard of Photoshop? Don't you understand how easy it is to fake a photograph? Did you really think that I would do something like that?"

"Well, now that you put it that way..."

"Yes," I said. "I *do* put it that way. Now you come back here as if nothing happened and you think that you can just breeze back into my life. It's not going to happen, Tom."

"Oh, you mean...?"

"We're finished. We were finished the moment you left. I've moved on; I'm over you and, incidentally, I'm getting married in three weeks' time."

"Married?" he said. He looked shell-shocked. "Who to?"

"Peter Thorpe."

"Peter? But he was going to be my best man," he said.

"Yes, he was, and he's been very supportive over the past year or so. He's not the idiot that you are, and when he popped the question I said 'yes'. You're not invited."

How ironic. I suppose it's no more than I deserve, really. It wasn't Sandra in the photographs and I should have known that at the time. How could I ever have thought that of her? And now she's getting married to the bloke that I considered my best friend back then. A man who, by his own admission when we were younger, was a dab hand with Photoshop.

Talk about being stabbed in the back. I wonder how long he'd been hankering after Sandra, seething with jealousy while we were making our wedding plans. He really suckered me in with those fakes. Shall I tell her? Probably not – that would really set the cat amongst the pigeons. I told her at the time that I needed time to travel; maybe that's what I should do now – there's nothing left for me here any longer.

Deafening Silence

"You do realise that what you're saying amounts to mutiny, don't you?" Robin said. "You could land yourself in a whole heap of trouble."

"I know," I replied. "But what else is there to do? We've been moaning like hell about the situation for God knows how long – it's time to put up or shut up."

I'm Paul Handford, and Robin Phelps is probably the only person that I could trust at this point to keep what I've been grumbling about close to his chest. We arrived at the place at the same time along with about half a dozen others. What none of us realised at the start was how it was run. In charge was Adrian Hiller, and we pretty quickly nicknamed him 'Hitler' because of his attitude and the way that he kept order using a cabal of lieutenants whose loyalty to him was absolute. We were not alone – in all, there must have been almost a thousand others 'trapped' beneath his jackboot.

"All right," Robin said, folding his arms and, for once, ignoring the pint in front of him. "What do you propose that we do? I'm assuming that you want me in on your nefarious scheme."

"Yes," I replied. "That's why I had us meet up here instead of one of the pubs closer to home."

We were seated at The Windmill on the way to Derby. No-one there would recognise us, and the table in the corner gave us clear sight of the door, just in case. He was right, though; if what I was about to suggest ever got back we'd both be for the high jump.

"Go on, then," he said.

"Hiller's got to go, and the rest of his team with him. The only way that we're going to be able to achieve it is to raise the entire place against him. He's so unpopular that he'd have no alternative if we play our cards right."

"And just how do you, or we, go about organising this rebellion of yours?"

"First we have to involve the other half dozen new starters – we can't trust any of the more established members right now; then, when we're both confident of their support, we bring in the rest. That would give us an initial force of about thirty if you discount Hiller's inner circle."

"Right," he said. "But that wouldn't be enough."

"I know," I said. "Let me finish. Next, we mobilise everyone else. That would mean assembling them all secretly and laying out the plan. I'm sure that it'll work as long as we all hold our nerve. Hiller's bound to try and face us down, but if we mount a campaign of non-cooperation there's precious little that he can do to force us to comply with his rules."

"With you so far, but what if he does? Those members close to him are a devious bunch and not beyond singling people out for special treatment."

"Then we fight fire with fire. Bullies don't like a challenge and if we stick together we can beat them. Then Hiller will have to go – he'll be powerless."

"So, you and I put your plan to the other new guys and see what they think?"

"I already know what they think. None of them have been here more than a few months and they're already looking for ways out. If we lay this out before them our first target will have been achieved. I'll put the word out tomorrow."

And so I did. To my great relief, all six of the new members fell in with the suggestion without a murmur. Robin and I then began the process of allocating tasks to each of them in order to recruit as many of the others to the cause. I had few doubts that we'd succeed in amassing a large number to our side, and anyone suffering from cold feet could be left behind. Within a week our number had swollen to nine hundred and ninety and, at a mass meeting, details of the plan to oust Hiller and his cronies were laid out for all to see.

There was much nodding of heads and murmuring of support, and I was overjoyed at the prospect of seeing him and his allies out of the gates for good. The only remaining matter was who would take over, temporarily at least, his position as leader. Robin suggested that I do it, but as organiser of the 'coup' I was reluctant to be seen as the megalomaniac who had ousted an established regime for his own ends. I said that we'd face that issue when the time came.

The plan of action was set for a week on the following Monday.

First thing in the morning Hiller was to get the shock of his life.

I would make the announcement to all assembled before he had the time to appear.

I did not sleep well during the weekend prior to our takeover bid. I couldn't eat; I went for walks but felt no better when I returned home, and even the cat avoided me. Saturday rolled agonizingly slowly into Sunday and that went on forever. When I woke up on Monday morning, my first port of call was to the bathroom where I was as sick as a dog. Breakfast was, of course, a non-starter.

The drive to what was, potentially, my Temple of Doom seemed to take an age, and when I rolled the Corsa into the car park at eight thirty there was a small crowd gathered at the gate. Robin was there and was quick to disperse them as he came up to the car.

"Ready?" he asked.

"Not really," I replied. "I've burned my boats though; we've crossed the Rubicon. Now it's time to stand together. We mustn't falter at this late stage or there might never be another chance."

He nodded, smiled, and patted me on the back. We had to work fast, though. Hiller would be arriving soon and it was important to address those assembled before he had the time to work out what was in the wind. I marched into the hall and up to the platform at the front. All conversation stopped as I took up position at the podium where Hiller would normally be standing at this point in the day. There was a deafening silence as I looked out at a sea of faces. I cleared my throat and saw, at the back, that Hiller and his group had appeared at the end of the short corridor leading into the room.

"There are going to be some changes," I began, amazed at the steadiness in my voice. "Some of you are aware of the situation that has been proposed regarding the removal of the Headmaster, Mr Hiller, and some of the senior staff. I have to tell you now that we, the remainder of the teaching staff, are assuming control over the running of the school and its curriculum."

There was a gentle murmur amongst the assemblage of the pupils and the other staff members. I looked at Hiller, who had now come into the hall; his face was blank – there was no trace of emotion where I had expected outrage. I could feel his eyes boring into me as he stood there, his gown wrapped across his chest and his diary in his arms. Then, and only then, he smiled. It was a knowing smile, an evil one; it was the kind that makes you think that you've

157

overplayed your hand. I looked at Robin; he had turned and was also looking at Hiller as he stood at one of the entrance doorways to the hall. He turned back to me and I expected him to give the 'thumbs up' – he didn't.

Hiller moved. He made his way, very slowly and with measured tread, down the side of the hall and up the stairs to the stage at the front. He paused, looked at me again and smiled. It was the smile on the face of the tiger, and I had the sickest feeling in my stomach that I had ever experienced. He walked to the podium where I stood, and waved me to one side – I moved automatically. I looked out at the assembled crowd, longing for the uprising that Robin and I had been planning. It was then that I noticed that the six other new starters were missing.

"Looking for confederates, Mr Handford?" Hiller said, calmly. "I think you'll find that those you believed would support your little escapade are no longer employed by the school." He paused to let that sink in. "I think you and I will have a little chat after assembly in my office. Now, would you kindly leave the stage and take up your usual place with the rest of the staff?"

For a moment I was frozen to the spot, lost in an instant of time and trying to rationalise what had just happened, or not happened as was the case. Hiller smiled once again and raised his eyebrows to dismiss me from my elevated position. You could have heard a pin drop as I walked across the stage – the short journey to the back of the hall seemed to take forever. Once there and with the rest of the staff, I looked to my side where Robin was seated.

"What the hell just happened?" I whispered.

Robin didn't answer. He just stared straight ahead, ostensibly listening intently to what Hiller was saying. I may be wrong, but I thought there was just the hint of a smile at the edge of his mouth. Had he betrayed me? How could I have been so wrong? I nudged him and he looked at me at last. His eyes were empty; I couldn't read him. He just shook his head and tapped his watch – it was our signal to leave discussion until later.

"Mr Handford," Hiller said as I entered his office directly after assembly. "Take a seat."

I sat down. My stomach was churning; I was now almost certainly out of a job, and there wouldn't be a school in the country that would employ me after the events of this morning. The silence

158

was deafening and I was struggling to see what I should do. Should I tell him to stick the job and simply walk out with my head held high? Should I sit through what would almost certainly be a disciplinary hearing witnessed by his secretary? Should I try to rope Robin in and attempt to shift some of the blame after he had clearly betrayed me? My questions were academic as Hiller broke the spell.

"You have to understand what being a headmaster is all about, Mr Handford," he said. His voice had that piercing quality and sent a shiver down my spine.

I felt like the leader of an escape committee now in the office of the camp Commandant and soon to face a firing squad. I made no reply.

"Did you seriously think that your scheme had any chance of success?" he asked. "When you're in a position like mine, you have to have your spies constantly alert, and Warren is one of the best that I've ever had in my time here; he's a really clever lad who knows which side his bread's buttered."

Warren! Colin Warren, the head boy, and one of the more vociferous supporters amongst the sixth form who had attended our early meetings. The one senior pupil who I had recruited personally. Robin and I had singled him out amongst the seniors, along with a number of the prefects, to carry the plot amongst the upper school. Robin had not betrayed me after all. A similar number were picked from the fifth form to muster the remainder, and yet it had gone spectacularly wrong. In the midst of my despair, I became aware of an increasing volume of noise outside the window. Hiller frowned and rose from his desk to find out what the commotion was all about. He opened the window to be greeted by a cacophony of noise. I followed him and saw, to my amazement, that the car park was full of staff and pupils shouting and waving banners, most of which bore the phrase *'Hiller Must Go!'*

There was, to one side, a much smaller group comprising Hiller's inner cabal of staff, Warren, and a few of the other prefects clearly loyal to the establishment. At the front of the massed gathering stood Robin, pointing directly at the headmaster and shouting the same command. Then, as if summoned by some unseen signal, the chant changed.

'We want Handford! We want Handford!'

I stepped forward, easing past the Headmaster, and raised my hand. The noise ceased immediately – the silence was deafening.

Do It Again

"You're a bloody disgrace!"

The not-so-subtle comment came from a green-shirted figure in shorts and football boots, standing in the centre circle with arms akimbo, and was aimed at one of the established professionals further up the pitch at the Osmaston End of the ground.

"I pay you to score goals, not take corners!"

Karl Chambers had come up through the club's youth and reserve teams much in the way of a number of other players in the first team squad, but this was his first experience of a training session under the watchful eye of the football club's imperious and autocratic manager.

"Karl," the man said, waving an arm in the youngster's direction, "Get over there and take that bloody ball off him before he hurts himself. You can take the corner and we'll see if he can actually find the net!"

Chambers trotted self-consciously over to the corner of the Osmaston End and the Co-op Stand, retrieved the ball from the now admonished England international, and placed it carefully in the quadrant. He looked up into the penalty area and made a quick assessment of where he was actually going to place the kick. There was a lot of pushing and shoving going on in front of the goalkeeper, and Karl decided that his best plan would be to just fizz the ball in there and let them sort it out for themselves.

He took a step back towards the crowd barrier, took a deep breath, and sent in a wickedly curving corner kick. Everything slowed down as the ball made its unerring trajectory first out from the goal and then, as if caught by some evil gust of wind, back toward the crossbar. The keeper had come out, clearly expecting the ball to continue on its original path, and was caught completely flat-footed by its change of direction. It nestled neatly in the far top corner, much to the surprise of all those in the penalty area. There was an unexpected silence, broken seconds later by the rasping voice from the half way line.

161

"D'you see?" it said. "That's the bloody way to take a corner! None of you lot saw that coming, did you? Well done, Karl! Now then, lad; let's see if you can do it again! It's the sort of thing that we might need against Everton on Saturday."

Karl was stunned. He hadn't moved from the corner of the pitch from where he had just taken the aforementioned kick. The ball found its way back to him, and he placed it once more in the quadrant. His mouth had gone as dry as the Sahara and he suddenly had an urgent need to go to the toilet. He didn't think, on balance, that putting his hand in the air and saying *'Please Sir'* would go down terribly well. He stepped back to the crowd barrier as before and wondered what the hell he was going to do for an encore.

From a short run-up, he curled an inswinger with his left foot high above everyone in the penalty area and arrowing for the far post. The previous kick had been an outswinger – initially – and taken with his right foot. The change of angle completely baffled the keeper who chose, this time, to stay rooted to his line. The tall left back, coming in late at the far post, met the ball with the centre of his forehead and it arrowed into the back of the net, bulging the roof. Once again there was silence in the area save for a hissed 'Yes!' from the full back who, quickly realising that his was the only voice, muted any celebration. The figure from the halfway line bellowed out again.

"Brilliant! David Harvey would never have sniffed that one!" he said. "Right, that's it for today! Well done young Karl!"

"Seriously?" Karl's father said when the lad told him the news. "In the first team against Everton? But you've only just joined the training session."

"I'm only on the bench, Dad," he said. "Probably won't get on the pitch."

"But it's experience, lad," he replied. "You've broken into the first team; think on – this is how young Steve Powell made it."

"There's a team full of top class players with the Rams, Dad," Karl said, trying to cool his father's enthusiasm. "I really would be lucky to get any time against Everton."

They left the discussion at that but, as match day approached, Karl could feel the atmosphere in the house starting to build. It got a little more intense when he came home with match tickets for his parents.

"Co-op Stand?" his Dad said, eyebrows shooting up to the ceiling. "Smack in the middle an' all! You have done us proud, son. Just score the winning goal now, eh?"

Karl's shoulders slumped. As if his parents being there wasn't bad enough, the old man was now expecting the impossible. He avoided any further conversation on the subject for the remainder of the week, and when Saturday morning came he was out of the house before his father had woken up. He was at the stadium well before the rest of the players, but ran straight into the manager as he was making his way to the Home dressing room.

"Karl!" he exclaimed. "Just the man I was looking for. Come into the office, son; I need a word with you."

Chambers followed in the man's wake, fearing slightly for what he thought was about to happen. Perhaps the boss had been having second thoughts after the training session and was now going to break the news that he would be dropping Karl from the match day squad. He took the seat offered and tried to keep his breathing even. The manager stood by the window, leaning back onto the frame.

"Got a bit of a problem, I have," he said, more quietly than Karl had expected. "Steve Powell's failed a fitness test and it's set me a slight conundrum. D'you think that you can last ninety minutes this afternoon?"

Chambers was stunned into temporary silence. This was one of the finest managers in the English game, and he was asking *him* how he felt about playing for the Rams. He swallowed in a dry throat, acutely aware that any hint of indecision would probably cost him his chance.

"Yes, Boss," he said. "I do. I'm ready."

"Excellent!" was the reply. "Well you've certainly got here early enough. Go out there onto the pitch and try to settle yourself into the role. You'll be playing right side of midfield and I'm having you take any corner that we get – okay?"

The Baseball Ground pitch usually resembled a mud heap at any time after the end of October, and tended to be heavy on the legs. He was fortunate to be playing on the right flank where there was

163

still some grass; anywhere in the middle would need far more stamina. Fortunately that was where Archie Gemmill ran the length of the pitch, so Karl would not have those conditions to contend with.

In no time at all the intervening time slipped away and he was in the dressing room with the rest of the team, listening to the final instructions given out by the management team. With kick-off time fast approaching, there was a knock on the door from the match referee to summon the team, and he was lining up behind his heroes ready for the fray.

Karl stuck to his brief and for the first quarter of the game he saw very little of the ball, keeping instead to his task of shadowing Mike Bernard – one of Everton's midfield dynamos. Then came a space on the right flank and Gemmill waved him up the field, planting a perfect pass directly into his path. Taking the ball in his stride, Chambers headed for the opposition goal, and side-stepped a tackle en route to the byline. His cross was blocked by Steve Sergeant and the ball went out for a corner. He looked over to the dugout – the manager was pointing at him; Karl knew exactly what was expected.

Placing the ball in the quadrant, he backed away towards the Pop Side and looked up into the penalty area. Derby players, anticipating a re-run of the training ground routine, were clustered around the penalty spot leaving a clear sight into the goal mouth. Everton players looked around in puzzlement – it was customary to put at least one forward on the goal line directly in front of the keeper, but nobody was there.

The cross shot across the area like a rocket, swirling in the wind and leaving David Harvey, the Everton goalkeeper, in no man's land. This time, however, instead of ending up directly in the net, the ball was met with a thunderbolt of a left foot shot at the far post by Alan Hinton. Derby were one up and it was largely down to him.

Congratulations went on for a while as it was Karl's first taste of glory, and the half faded to its end with no further action. Chambers' head was still spinning when the second period began and he was soon in the action. Far from marking Everton's Mike Bernard, Karl now found himself being watched closely by the very same player who had clearly been given revised instruction during the break.

"Pull wider," Gemmill whispered to him. "Watch Hinton on the other flank and let's see if we can pull them out of shape. With a bit of luck I'll have a wee bit more room down the middle."

Karl trod the right touchline as if he was a tightrope walker, and Bernard followed him across the pitch. The gap was momentary, but enough for a pass to be slid right into the path of Kevin Hector who made for the penalty area. With only the goalkeeper to beat, the tackle from behind brought the inevitable penalty which Gemmill duly despatched to make it 2-0.

The two-goal cushion lasted only five minutes before John Connolly reduced the arrears, and Karl was forced to track back as Mike Bernard seized upon the upswing in Everton's confidence to make inroads down the Derby left. However, in taking his eye off the ball he was robbed by the youngster who, with his opponent now out of position and struggling to recover ground, raced into the Toffees' territory and sent a defence-splitting pass into the path of David Nish on the left – the full back made no mistake and it was 3-1. At eighty minutes, Karl, clearly showing signs of fatigue, was substituted and left the pitch to a standing ovation. The match ended with the score unchanged and his parents were invited to the boardroom after the game to congratulate him and the rest of the team.

"It was only a game, Dad," he said at home that evening, but with *Match of the Day* cameras at the ground they were able to relive the game.

"Aye, lad," his father said. "But you made two of the goals today, and I'll bet you get some rave reviews in tomorrow's sports pages."

Karl never got to see those newspaper headlines the next day. He was awoken with a thump as the floor came up to meet him when he turned over and fell out of bed. His mother was up the stairs in an instant to see what had happened.

"I'm okay, Mum," Karl said, rubbing his head. "Just had a strange dream, that's all. I'll be down in a minute."

Yes, he sighed to himself in disappointment, it had all been nothing more than a dream. No training with the Derby first team, no injury to Steve Powell, and no heroics on the Baseball Ground pitch. He laughed to himself for his foolishness; what was it that

Clough had said to him? 'Do it again'? That was really funny now, back in the real world.

Things turned another corner on the Monday morning as he was preparing to go to college. His mother came back from the front door with the day's post in her hand, and she was waving a letter in his direction.

"This one's got your name on it, Karl, and just look at the heading on the envelope. Isn't that the Derby County emblem?"

It was indeed a letter from the Baseball Ground. Karl had been turning out for a local team in the Sunday leagues for a year or so, and was known to be one of the best young players in the area. He opened the envelope and gaped in surprise at its contents.

"Well," his father said. "Come on; out with it – what does the thing say?"

"It's a trial, Dad," Karl replied. "They've invited me for a trial. This could be my big chance. I've made it in the local league – I wonder if I can do it again."

Mind My Toes

"Ouch! Watch where you're putting those feet of yours, Joe!" Wendy hissed as they made their way around the dance floor. "That's the third time you've kicked me – mind my toes you great oaf!"

Wendy Bartram and her husband, Joe, had been taking dancing lessons for almost a year, but he was still having trouble coming to terms with the intricacies of some of the dances that they had been learning at the group sessions in their local area. She had few problems in following the teacher's instructions, but her poor, long-suffering husband just couldn't seem to get to grips with the more complex footwork, and it normally resulted in a series of bruises to either of her feet; there had even been instances of bloodshed when his shoes came into contact with toenails exposed by her open-toed dance shoes.

"Sorry, Babe," he said with downcast eyes. "Just can't seem to get into the rhythm of this rumba."

"No kidding, Sherlock," she said, sitting down as the music ended, removing the targeted shoe and rubbing her throbbing foot. "We really need to do something about those great clod hoppers of yours."

Lovely as he was in normal daily life, dancing classes seemed to bring out the clumsiness in him and, try as he may, he didn't appear to be able to go through an evening without inflicting some sort of damage on her toes,

"A pity that we can't get a pair of shoes that'll do the dancing for you," she said. "Get me another drink while I try to coax some life back into this foot."

With Joe at the bar, Wendy stopped her massage and thought again about what she had just said. Since leaving school, she had joined a software company to work in IT at a junior level. She had learned the basics of computer programming and progressed up the company's departmental hierarchy, and at the age of twenty-seven, with almost ten years under her belt, she had become the departmental manager and chief programmer.

Finding the firm's in-house suite of programs restrictive, she had, in her spare time, developed a much slicker and more efficient data processing platform, working under a language that she had written herself. Without a means of testing the new set of routines, they remained untried though, she believed, with enormous potential. What if, she thought, there was a way to develop the code into a way of helping Joe with his foot work?

In principal it would be quite straightforward – convert a basic waltz to a series of algorithms and program them into a microchip lodged into the structure of each shoe. Once that was accomplished, all she would have to do would be to persuade her husband to trust the shoes and just follow where they led.

"You look deep in thought," he said, returning from the bar with their drinks. "Am I in more trouble?"

"Hmm?" she said, looking up at him. "Oh, no; I just might have the solution to all of your dancing problems – we could turn you into the next Fred Astaire."

"Why am I suddenly worried?"

"Relax," she replied. "I'm serious. Can't tell you anything about it right now. I have to do some serious thinking, but the idea I've just had could save me a whole lot of pain and suffering. For the moment, just watch where you're putting your feet and mind my poor toes."

Joe didn't see too much of Wendy after work during the following week. As soon as dinner was over she was up in their study with the door closed as she worked away at the program that she had thought up. The initial layout was relatively simple to devise, and within a fairly short period of time she had a working model, albeit a CGI version, to develop further. At the end of another couple of days, the routine had been enhanced to encapsulate one of the more complicated sequence waltzes.

Now came the tricky part – installing the software into a pair of dance shoes that would react to the particular rhythm of the dance in question. The microchip that she had chosen for the task was at the top of the range, and was one which the manufacturer claimed was capable of learning as it worked. Wendy fixed the chip into a slot which she had made on the front portion of Joe's older dance shoes and set them on the floor.

She had programmed the steps to the waltz from the script that she had purchased from Riverbank Publications, and now set the shoes in the middle of the laminated floor. Holding her breath, she played the music and, after the count in, pressed the 'Play' button on the hand control that she had made. After a few stuttering steps, the shoes, like something out of Disney's '*Sorcerer's Apprentice*', seemed to take on a life of their own and produced a very fair approximation of the dance. She let it run through a couple of sets and then stopped it.

Now came the more advanced task of tuning the chip in to whatever tune and pace the waltz was to be danced to. She looked at the clock and decided that such a task was for another day. Feeling suitably smug, she deactivated the chip, logged off the computer, and put away the shoes in case Joe stumbled across them – he was quite accustomed to stumbling too much as it was.

"How did it go?" he asked, fishing for information when she came down the stairs.

"Oh, it's coming along," she said, not wanting him to know too much at this early stage.

"You've been up there for ages – want a drink?"

"Now, that would be really kind of you, my love," she said. "Good ideas take time to perfect, but I think you're going to be more than a little surprised at this one."

"Surprised, or shocked?" he asked.

"Just have to wait and see, won't you? Tell you what: if I can get it to work a little better you can try it out tomorrow. Okay?"

"What have I let myself in for?"

"Well, I did keep telling you to mind my toes."

"They look weird," Joe said on the following evening as he looked at what Wendy had done to his old dance shoes.

"Just put them on," she replied. "You've got nothing to worry about, and I'll keep the tempo down. Just remember not to fight them – just go with the flow."

"What are we doing?"

"A basic ballroom waltz," she said. "You know – the one where you *don't* tread on my toes, so we should be fine. Come on; ballroom hold."

Wendy turned on the music and they waited for the intro to finish. At the start of the first bar, Joe's shoes came to life and after the first faltering steps where he tried to take the lead he let the shoes take over. He and Wendy glided faultlessly around a cleared kitchen floor and, despite this first attempt, her toes remained untouched.

"What now?" Joe said, staring in amazement at the shoes.

"This is where it gets interesting. A fairly straightforward tango – we know this one as well, so there shouldn't be any difficulty."

There wasn't, and by the time that the dance came to an end Joe was enthusiastically demanding more.

"I can dance!" he said.

"No, the shoes can dance," Wendy replied. "You're just following their lead. However, if you stick with them, you'll learn a lot faster – it's called muscle memory and you'll do the steps without thinking about them. There's one more and that's all that I've done so far."

"Which one?"

"You're going to love this: the Verbena Foxtrot."

"The Verbena?" he said. "You've got to be kidding. I know *you've* picked it up, but I'm all at sea with it. We've had a fair few frank exchanges about it."

"Trust me; you'll love this one, Come on, there's plenty of room in here."

Joe was flabbergasted. He disliked foxtrots as a matter of principal – the principal being that he couldn't follow either the beat or the intricate steps.

"This is one too far, Wend," he said.

"Nonsense; you've seen what the programme can do; just relax and listen to the music."

Joe closed his eyes, hoping that his wife would take the lead and save him the trouble. He opened them in surprise when it became

170

clear that she wasn't, and that it seemed to be he who was taking the principal role. As the dance ended, she was all smiles.

"See?" she said. "It just shows what can be done if you trust the software."

"This is amazing!" he said. "You're a genius. How the hell did you manage to work it out?"

"Well, I could tell you, but then I'd have to kill you. Look on the bright side; it's saved me throttling you for treading on my toes."

"What now?" he asked.

"We take the shoes with us to the next session and get up for all of the dances at the social."

"But you've only programmed three into the microchip, and the next lesson's only a few days away."

"Oh, ye of little faith!" she exclaimed in mock scorn. "Now that the software is running okay it'll be a simple matter to insert the scripts for all of the dances that we do on a regular basis."

"How many are there?"

"About thirty I think, and I can have them done in time, so stop worrying," she said.

Tuesday evening came around all too quickly for Joe, but Wendy didn't seem the least fazed by time passing. She had worked every evening in the interim, writing out the code and completing the necessary test runs. By the time they were ready to go out she had twenty-seven more dances loaded into the microchips. She smiled at Joe and ruffled his hair as they locked the door and got into the car.

"That was impressive," Stella said as she came to the table where Wendy and Joe were changing their shoes at the end of the evening. "How on earth have the two of you managed to improve since last week? You, Joe; your feet were all over the place then, and I saw the agony on Wendy's face when you stepped on her toes."

"It's her," Joe began, nodding at his wife. "She's gone and…"

"Put him through some intensive practices," Wendy interrupted, frowning across the table. "I've also issued stern warnings about his footwork."

Stella looked from one to the other and raised her eyebrows. She'd known them for too long to miss the obvious gag that Wendy had metaphorically placed across Joe's mouth. She sat down and leaned across the table.

"Come on, you two," she whispered. "Something's afoot. Look, nearly everybody's gone; you can tell me – what is it that you're hiding? You haven't found a way of cheating, have you?"

Joe leaned back, smiling. "You might as well tell her, Wend," he said. "You never know, you might make a few quid."

"What's he talking about, Wendy?" Stella asked.

"Oh, what the hell," she replied. "I've written a computer program to help Joe get his feet right and stop him causing me all kinds of pain."

Stella laughed. "Yeah, right. Ooh! There's goes another one flying past the window!" She stopped laughing when she saw the serious looks on their faces. "You're not kidding, are you?"

"No," Wendy said. "The steps are written into a microchip in each of his shoes. They react to the music and a single verbal command from whoever's wearing them. From then on you just let the feet do the walking, so to speak. Want to try them? Your feet are about the same size as Joe's."

"Are you sure? You wouldn't be pulling my leg, would you?"

"As if," Wendy replied. "Play one of the dances from this evening and see what you think, but don't forget to tell the shoes what dance it is."

"I must be mad," Stella said, rising from her chair. "You've got me believing you and talking to a pair of shoes. I'll be at the funny farm next."

Stella spent half an hour mixing up the dances and talking to Joe's shoes, and by the time she sat down again and removed them, she was astounded.

"You know what you've got here, don't you?" she said.

"Yeah," Joe replied. "A reprieve from a death sentence."

"No, well yes, there is that," Stella said. "Seriously, though, this is one hell of a teaching aid. Just think of how many at tonight's lesson are struggling with steps – this is an amazing breakthrough. How much are they?"

172

"No idea," Wendy replied. "These shoes of Joe's are just prototypes; we weren't entirely sure that they'd work until this evening. He brought his other pair along just in case they didn't."

"How soon could you knock out a few more sets?"

"By next week I should think," Wendy said. "Why?"

"If they work as well as they did for the past half hour you could be onto a real money spinner. Get a price worked out and we'll talk again next week."

The four mile journey home took Joe and Wendy a little over twenty minutes, and when they sat down with a drink Joe broke the silence that had enveloped them since leaving the dance class. Stella's request had come out of the blue, and Joe knew better than to interrupt his wife, buried in her thoughts, on the journey back.

"What now?" he asked.

"Well, I can get the chips ready by next week without a problem, but what if she wants more? I'm not geared up to mass production."

"In that case, just take next week as it comes. The worst case scenario is that no-one will want them – that's down to Stella. But think on: if this takes off it might not just be dancing where you could make a packet."

"What do you mean?"

"Just try to see what it is that you've got, Wend," he said. "If this works for dancing, what other teaching could it be applied to? Languages? Music? The possibilities could be endless."

"But I couldn't do it all myself, and you don't know how."

"No, but you could set up your own company and licence the software out."

"You're right. I could set up a website and an on-line trading portal… but what would I call it?"

"Why not *'Mind My Toes'*? Just think of it, the website could be www.mindmytoes.com. Hey! You could pay me a commission for the idea."

"Not a chance, mate," she said, laughing. "You just concentrate on keeping your feet away from mine!"

173

Blood and Sweat

"Why have you stopped running?" John said, his breath coming in short, sharp bursts. "We have to be back in fifteen minutes if we're going to be in time for the meeting."

"There's something over there," Peter said, pointing into the bushes at the side of the track along which they had been taking one of their regular jogs.

"Where?" he asked, coming back to Peter's position. "I don't see anything, and we're going to be late."

"It won't take a minute. What if someone's lying injured?"

"What if it isn't 'someone' at all?" John replied, his voice now showing an irritated tone.

"It would be very neglectful not to even take a look."

"Oh, very well," John said. "We'll have to run faster for the remainder of the distance, though."

The light had not been good when they started their run – heavy cloud had masked the weak winter sun, and the temperature, cold as it had been at the outset, was now plummeting to the forecast freezing point by nightfall. As they left the track and made a cautious way into the undergrowth, a recumbent figure became visible in the shadows. It was a man – he was dressed in white and was lying on the ground.

"He's breathing," Peter said. "It's very shallow but he *is* breathing – we need to get him out of there; come on."

"Are you sure this is wise?" John asked, nervously. "I've heard of traps like this where people suddenly appear from nowhere, beat you up and then steal from you."

"Not likely at this time of day and in this weather. Who'd be daft enough to lie in wait in the freezing cold?"

"Okay," John replied, following his friend as he closed in on the figure.

"Look!" Peter said. "Do you see that?"

"It's blood," John said. "The guy's been beaten up – we need an ambulance."

The figure groaned; it was a low sound and seemed to be full of pain. The two young men stopped in their tracks and looked at each other. The man on the ground had turned onto his back and his face was now in full view.

John O'Reilly and Peter Fitzpatrick had been students at St Cuthbert's since leaving school and were now both in their second year. Divinity scholars, both were aware of the strict rules governing classes and course meetings, and were now running out of time.

"Get the car," Peter said. "We have to get him out of the cold or he's going to freeze. He doesn't look as if he can go anywhere on foot."

"But the meeting," John began.

"Will just have to wait – this guy's more important; now hurry! I'll put my top over him so don't be too long."

John was back a little while later and they poured the still semi-conscious figure into the rear of the vehicle; he lay on the back seats hardly moving, and was in no better shape when the three of them arrived at the flat that the two students shared.

"Who dresses like this?" Peter said as they brought the man into the full light of their lounge. "White three-piece suit, white socks, white shoes. What is he, some kind of ghost?"

"He's bleeding," said John. "Look at his head."

"No cuts or abrasions," Peter remarked, having taken a close look.

"Where's it coming from, then?"

"John," Peter said. "He's sweating blood."

"What?"

"Look at my hand. I just wiped his forehead and there's blood on my palm, but there's more coming from his pores where I wiped."

"Jesus, Mary and Joseph!" John said, crossing himself and falling to his knees. "D'you know what this means?"

"You're not serious," he replied, falling involuntarily to the same position. "It cannot be stigmata – they're only for the hands and feet. Surely he's not…"

"Christ," John whispered. "The Second Coming."

175

"But this blood; I don't remember anything in the texts about it."

"Yes there is," said John. "Wait there." He backed away from the figure on the sofa and went to his room, returning with his copy of the New Testament. "I remember something in one of the gospels. Ah, here it is; Luke 22:44."

"What does it say?"

"I'm not reading it all out, but apparently knowing why Jesus was overwhelmed to the point of sweating blood and what he did after, is a critical point of understanding who he claimed to be and why. He experienced what may be somewhat similar to a panic attack. But his experience was much more traumatic as evident of his sweat becoming like drops of blood falling to the ground. The reference was written by Luke, who was a doctor. His account of Jesus alone states that Jesus' sweat was like drops of blood, falling to the ground when he prayed about what was about to happen to him."

Having been engrossed for the last few minutes in the theological discussion, neither of them had noticed that their guest had sat up and was now staring directly at them. They both shuddered at the piercing gaze which seemed to penetrate right to the bone.

"איפה אני?" he said.

"What was that?" Peter asked. "Hebrew? Was that Hebrew?"

"I think so," said John. "I think he just said 'Where am I?'"

"So tell him."

"מי אתה?"

"Now he wants to know who we are," John told his friend.

John was about to frame his answers when the man passed out again and fell to the floor. They lifted him back onto the sofa and covered him up.

"Must be in shock," Peter said. "I think we should leave him for tonight, but one of us should keep watch… just in case."

"Shouldn't we call the police or phone for an ambulance?"

"And tell them what? That we think we just found Jesus and would they mind coming out and praying with us? No, best to leave stuff like that until the morning. Maybe this chap will be a bit more forthcoming by then."

176

Peter took the first watch over their guest, and occupied his time by reading up on sections of the bible that foretold a second coming of Christ and what it would mean for mankind. He got as far as the Book of Revelation, and could find no other references to the condition that the man had displayed, which he now knew to be that of hematidrosis - an excretion of blood or blood pigments in sweat which can be associated with a severe anxiety reaction triggered by fear.

He closed his Bible and looked at the recumbent figure on the sofa. The man seemed to be breathing a little more evenly, and Peter tried to reconcile what he now knew from his reading to what Christ must have been going through on the cross. Aside from the obvious agony, he had pleaded with God but had been forsaken – his despair must have been complete. By the time morning came and John had risen from sleep, there had been no further action from their stranger.

"My turn, now," John said, bringing two mugs from the kitchen. "Drink this and then go to bed. When you get up again we'll talk and decide what we're going to do."

Peter yawned, stretched, and took the drink. He told John about his reading during the night, and asked him to write down anything that their guest said during the day so that they could present a full picture to whatever authorities they were going to report to. John checked the man many times during his watch, but aside from tossing and turning in his sleep there was nothing further to report when Peter came down the stairs.

"So, what's the plan?" he asked John when they'd eaten. "Do we wake him up and offer him a cup of tea?"

"If he is Jesus, he's not likely to be needing anything to drink, is he? Being the Son of God does come with some benefits, I suppose."

"Don't be flippant – we need some help here. What about the Abbot?"

Abbot Seamus O'Connor was the Principal of the college, and a world renowned Hebrew scholar. He was also their head of year and a fierce disciplinarian – they would already be in some trouble for

177

missing yesterday's meeting. Involving him in the matter of their guest may not go down too well. On the other hand, keeping him out of the loop concerning a possible Second Coming could also have serious consequences. They decided on the latter option, reasoning that it was likely to be the lesser of two evils. He was at their flat less than an hour after receiving Peter's call.

"And you think that he's the one, d'you?" he asked with some scepticism. "What would make the two of you come to that profound conclusion?"

"Well, sir," John said. "Look at the way he's dressed – all in white. And would you take a look at him - long dark hair, beard, swarthy complexion. Do you not think that it could be him?"

"Did neither of you think to check the news bulletins last night before you came to your stunning conclusion?"

"No, sir," Peter said. "Why?"

"Why? I'll tell you why," O'Connor replied, sitting down in a chair and pulling it closer to the sofa. "This poor man was reported missing from the Meadowdale Care Home yesterday afternoon, and they've been scouring the area for him ever since. It you'd have called 999 as soon as you found him, not only would he now be back there but you'd also not be in bother for missing the evening meeting."

The unexpected guest chose that very moment to wake up and stared in confusion at three people in the room with him where there had previously been only two. He began with the same two questions that he posed the night before, but was this time rewarded with answers in fluent Hebrew with which he appeared to be satisfied. He then smiled and spoke, to Peter's and John's astonishment, in fluent English. The knock at the door was answered by O'Connor who returned with three members of the Meadowdale Care Home staff.

"His name's Gabriel," O'Connor said. "See, I listen to the news, boys – you should try it sometime. Maybe I'll see you at some of today's classes, d'you think?"

With that, the Abbot rose to take his leave and Gabriel, having risen from his 'bed' shook his hand in thanks. The two young men stood, feeling thoroughly embarrassed, in complete silence as everyone began to depart. As he stepped over the threshold, Gabriel turned back to face Peter and John and, with a smile said:

"אשרי טהורי לב, כי יראו את אלוהים."

He was gone.

"What was that?" Peter asked.

"Um, I'm not entirely sure," replied John. "I think he might just have *said 'Blessed are the pure in heart, for they shall see God.'*"

"Wasn't that one of the…?"

"Don't even go there. We're in enough bother as it is."

L'Appel du Vide

"What are you reading?" Claude Larousse asked of his friend, Bernard Bisset.

"This?" Bisset pointed at the paperback in his right hand. "Oh, it's an odd thing, really, and I was just looking through it as I had nothing better to do. Why do you ask?"

"Ah, now I see," Claude said. "I've heard of the author, Pascal Caron, and I think I may have read the book myself some years ago. Yes; 'L'Appel du Vide' – written when he was just a young man studying at the Sorbonne, and you are quite correct; it is an odd story. How far have you got with it?"

"Not very far," Bernard said. "I am having difficulty in following the plot, I must confess. I think that I may give up on it if it doesn't improve."

"Oh, I think that would be a mistake, my friend; the call of the void is quite an unsettling concept and Caron told it from a certain amount of personal experience."

"Really?" Bernard asked, suddenly distracted and forgetting the book for the moment. "Tell me more – I would hate to waste hours of reading if what you say is of no interest."

"Caron lived in a large old house just outside the Bois de Boulogne which had been left to him when his parents died. Their deaths, incidentally, happened in very unusual circumstances but the police recorded them as accidental. Pascal never believed that and tried to discover what had happened to them in the house on the evening that they died."

"What was the house like?" Bisset said.

"It was a three-floor mansion, built at the turn of the century and set in four acres of gardens." Claude replied. "The house had a grand entrance, with columns on either side of the main door. Inside was a hall decorated with paintings, tapestries and a Japanese screen. On the second floor, up a sweeping marble staircase, were private rooms. Separate bedrooms on either side of a private sitting room were more comfortable than elegant. Beyond that was the third floor, used as the servants' quarters and for storing clothes."

"So, how did it come into Caron's parents' possession?"

"From what I can recall," he replied, "the owner, a Monsieur DuBrett, got into severe financial difficulties and Caron senior, as one of his major creditors, agreed to take the house in full settlement of the debt."

"That was very generous," Bernard remarked.

"Not really," his friend replied. "There was little altruism in Caron's actions according to what I discovered. The house was valued at a far higher figure than the one that DuBrett was forced to accept, and he had very little alternative than to take the offer and clear much of the rest of his debts. He swore revenge upon Caron but died before he could carry out the threat."

"So, what happened then?"

"Well, according to local stories, the Caron family was beset with all kinds of problems when they moved into the property. Walls in the gardens fell down, plaster in some of the rooms crumbled and window frames collapsed. It cost Caron senior a lot of money to put right the destruction. Things went fairly quiet for a time, and then there was the incident of the parents' deaths."

"That's a really strange story… if it's true," Bernard said.

"I can't tell you whether it is or is not; as I said, it's all gossip and conjecture. The fact remains that Pascal moved back into the house upon the death of his parents determined to discover what had actually taken place."

"So he wrote the book to bring their fate to the attention of the public?"

"I don't know, but whatever the reason was it did him no good."

"Why?"

"He disappeared while at the house a few months after the book was published. No publisher wanted to take it on, and Pascal had paid all of the costs of getting it into print himself. When he was asked why he had done it, he said the there was a voice from the void that had told him what to do – that's why he called it *'L'Appel du Vide'*. The cost of the novel almost bankrupted him."

"He must have been mad to do it, then," Bernard scoffed.

"Funny you should say that," Claude said. "He did spend some time in an institution whilst in the midst of writing it. His behaviour had become rather erratic, and he caused some trouble at a local bar.

One man suffered a broken nose when Caron went wild and hit him with a chair."

"But Pascal recovered?"

"Yes, and paid an amount of damages to the man in question. He became a recluse after that, shutting himself away in the house and trying to find out what had killed his parents. It did him no good, though, as I said, and the place has been up for sale ever since. Nobody seems to want to take possession of it."

It had been over a week since the two friends had met, and during that time the story of Pascal Caron had occupied most of Bernard Bisset's waking hours. He had finished reading 'L'Appel du Vide' and had begun to experience the oddest feelings that he was, in some way, being drawn to the house where the writer had spent his last days. He rang Claude Larousse and they arranged to meet at a coffee house on the Champs Elysees the same afternoon.

"So, what was the hurry?" Larousse said as they took seats close to the window with their drinks.

"I finished the book," Bernard replied. "It is a strange piece of work, as you implied it would be. He talks about a voice from the void, and says that it seemed to be that of someone almost sitting upon his shoulder and whispering into his ear."

"Well, I did tell you that he was considered to be odd – he was institutionalised for a while," Claude remarked. "I believe he was diagnosed with schizophrenia."

"You did say that the house is up for sale, did you not?"

"Yes, and it still is. There has been little or no interest for quite some time now. Why do you ask?"

"I wondered whether it would be possible to take a look around the place," Bisset said, watching his friend's reaction.

"I should have known," Claude replied. "You just can't leave well alone, can you? Ever since we were students, you always had to go around sticking your nose into things that…"

"Just answer the question, Claude." Bisset said. "Is it, or is it not, possible to take a look?"

"Oh, I suppose so," Larousse replied. "As agents for the sale we do have the keys to the property, and I could say that you were interested in, at the very least, looking at the possibility of renting…"

"Excellent! When can we do it?"

"Patience!" Claude said. "These things cannot be made to happen overnight. There are forms to be completed and procedures to be followed. It will be the start of next week before I can find a slot in our schedule for you. We do have other clients, you know."

"Oh, very well," Bernard sighed in disappointment. "That will have to do. But if you get a cancellation could we not fit it in earlier?"

"Yes, we could," his friend replied. "However, that is unlikely, so don't hold your breath."

Bernard tried to suppress his anticipation by carrying out a little research into the writing of Pascal Caron. There was very little written about him, 'L'Appel du Vide' being his only novel. He had submitted some short stories to a few Paris publications, and on the whole they had been well received. That had been some time earlier and he had, seemingly, faded from the literary world.

Time seemed to drag for Bernard and, despite a number of trips out of Paris, he appeared to have a lot of time on his hands after work and was becoming anxious for the day of the viewing. Finally it came around and he met Claude Larousse at the same café as the week previous, and they made their way to the Bois de Boulogne for the long-anticipated visit.

"A bit spooky, isn't it?" Bernard said as they drove through the gates and up the drive towards the house.

"Neglected, I think you mean," Larousse replied as they pulled up. "It's been empty for some time; you've been reading too many horror stories for your own good. Come on, I'll let you in."

Bernard's words turned out to be rather prophetic; as they stepped up onto the veranda the moss-covered planking caused Claude to stumble. He fell awkwardly and let out a scream of pain. It was clear to Bisset that his friend had been seriously injured, and the ambulance staff confirmed a broken leg when they arrived some ten minutes later.

"Look, Bernard," Larousse said, between breaths of oxygen. "Take the keys and have a look around. Just make sure that you get

183

them back to the office by the end of the day. Take my car home with you and keep it there until I see you again."

As the ambulance sped away, Bisset turned to look at the Caron house and slotted the front door key into its lock. It was very stiff, almost as if there was someone on the inside trying to prevent him from turning it. It gave with a sudden jolt, and the force of release sent a sharp pain all the way up to Bernard's shoulder. He rubbed his aching arm, cursed loudly, and turned the large metal doorknob.

The door opened in protest with an eerie horror film creak, swinging back slowly on its hinges. The inside was dark and it took a few moments of being over the threshold for Bernard's eyes to grow accustomed to the gloom. He was standing in a large entrance hall that looked for all the world as if it had been lifted straight from the pages of a horror novel by Guy de Maupassant. He blinked; there was nothing but a few sinuous cobwebs blowing from side to side in the draft from the now open front door. He wrinkled his nose.

"My God, what a smell!" he said.

He walked further into the hall, noting the large portraits hung from the walls on either side of him; he hoped that it was his imagination, but the eyes seemed to be following his every move. Bernard Bisset had never been the type of individual to let his feelings run away with him, but the accident to his friend just seemed to have come at the most inopportune moment; with nobody to corroborate what he may or may not find in the house, he might just be judged to be the same kind of person as Pascal Caron. The noise, a dull thud, brought all of his senses back to the matter before him.

"Hello!" he shouted. "Is there anyone there?"

Of course, there was not, and Bernard mentally kicked himself for being so foolish. He did not feel foolish when the voice whispered in his ear. The words were not very clear, but the goose bumps on his arms and the hairs prickling at the back of his neck certainly were. He felt the need to walk to the left of the staircase and into a gloomy alcove; there was a door at the end which, when opened, appeared to lead into a large kitchen – this was clearly where the servants would have worked. The voice whispered again and once more Bernard was drawn further into the property.

184

"What now?" he said to himself, coming towards a solid wall. "There's no way out of this room unless I go back."

Once more the whisper, that still, small voice, the call from the void, '*l'appel du vide*', urged him forward. The writings of Pascal Caron had defined the call as being akin to the 'fight or flight' concept that comes with the sudden surge of adrenalin in times of crisis. Bernard was feeling that now, and took more steps in the direction given.

He was now up against the far wall, and stood in puzzlement. There was nothing to see, and yet the call had been quite insistent.

'*Poussez!*'

The word was clear – much clearer than the earlier instructions. He pushed against the wooden panelling before him.

Nothing.

'*Plus haute!*'

Bernard slid his hands higher up the panel, pushing against it continually.

'*Au sommet!*'

There was a rail near the top of the wall; it was similar to those from which paintings would be hung in a grand salon. He pushed hard.

There was a 'click', and part of the rail slid backwards. A panel, expertly concealed in the wall, slid slowly open. It was pitch black beyond the gap which had been revealed. Bernard reached into his bag and removed a torch. He shone it into the void. Was this the 'vide' of which Caron's book had spoken? There was a stairway leading downwards into the blackness, and Bernard placed one foot onto the top step. He hesitated; going back into the kitchen, he fetched a chair and wedged it firmly against the panel to keep it open. There were no handles on either side of this 'door' and to be trapped behind it would mean almost certain death from starvation or thirst.

Carefully, he made his way downwards, not knowing how far the stairs led. The torch was powerful enough only to light the immediate area before him and there was no way of knowing just how large the 'void' was likely to be. Suddenly his right foot hit level ground and he breathed a sigh of relief. He looked back up the stairs and was reassured to see a faint light to lead him back up to the ground floor.

"Okay," he said to himself, more as a means of reassurance than anything else. "Let's see what we have down here."

He had gone but a few steps when his foot stubbed against something. He had been looking forward and not at his feet. He shone the torch beam down at the ground and gasped in horror at what he saw.

"My God!" he exclaimed.

There, before him, lay the skeletal remains of some poor unfortunate who had clearly become trapped down in this cellar. After the initial shock had worn off, Bernard stooped and took a closer look. The head was twisted at an unnatural angle – the neck was obviously broken. Were these the last remains of Pascal Caron? Had he come down to this dark place looking for clues as to the deaths of his parents?

"But why?" Bernard said to himself. "The bodies of the parents were found in the house upstairs. There would be no reason for him to come down here... unless..."

It was at that moment that there came from above the sound of a chair being dragged across the kitchen floor. Bernard froze – he looked up; the pale light shining down the stairs was becoming fainter and fainter. With a suddenness that shook Bernard to his very soul, the door panel closed with a soft 'click'. He was trapped.

He was trapped and there was no-one upstairs to rescue him.

Claude!

Claude would know where he was.

No, Claude was in hospital and would be there for at least a couple of days.

Then he would be at home while his broken leg mended.

No – he would miss his car; he had told Bernard to take it home with him to be collected later.

Later – that was the word. How much later would Claude be before he thought to reclaim the vehicle? It may be weeks!

"This is my fate," Bernard said to himself. "Whatever is here in this Godforsaken house has trapped me in the same way that it trapped poor Pascal."

He shone the torch around the room. There was nothing down here – not even anything to sit upon. He slid downwards, his back against the wall, until he was seated on the cold earth of the cellar floor.

It would, indeed, be three weeks before Claude Larousse felt mobile enough to arrange for the collection of his car. Only then would he think to revisit the former Caron residence, merely to find that his friend had vanished without trace.

.

.

.

The Dancing Clouds

Sayeena looked up at the sky and shielded her eyes from the glaring sun. There was not a cloud to be seen and it had been like it for too many weeks now. The legends all told of periods like this, but in the sacred books there had come the rains to end the drought. The dry season arrived every year without fail, but it was usually short and the tribe had, by this time, normally gathered in sufficient supplies to last during the period when the streams had all but dried up.

There had, even then, been a trickle of water in the beds but now there was nothing but dust. Their animals scratched the surface in search of moisture but there was none to be found. The spiny cactus plants were the only things that could survive, but even they had little stored up inside their tough skins.

"We have to harvest the cactus," her father, Poultos, said. "Without its sustenance we will surely all die."

"What if others come and take them, Father?" she asked.

"Then the men will have to stand guard and protect what we have on our lands, my daughter. Life is so precious that we dare not allow strangers to come onto our territory and steal the only form of food that is available to us."

Though the cactus harvest was not great, the tribe did manage to fend off incursions from neighbouring groups, but all too soon they were running out of supplies. The council of elders met one evening and took the momentous decision to abandon their homes on the prairies and head instead for higher ground where the temperatures would be cooler and food, hopefully, more abundant.

The trek was long and arduous, and a number of the older ones succumbed during the journey. These the tribe buried with all due ceremony but without the sanctity of their sacred burial grounds which they had left behind them. At last they came to the foothills of the Dagra Range – a ridge of high mountains whose lower slopes would provide shelter and food until the time was right to return to the plains.

Reaching a level plateau, they pitched their lodges and began the hunt for food. All across the plains, the Carabus, the large quadrupeds that supplied all of the tribe's needs, had headed west towards the Mushka River – a journey that they alone could endure, taking with them Sayeena's people's staple source of food. They wasted nothing of what the large beasts could provide – meat, skins for clothing and even bone for the making of tools and weapons. Other alternatives would have to be found,

"How long must we stay here, Father?" she asked one day a few weeks later.

"I am unsure, Daughter," he said. "If the drought does not break, we will be forced to stay through the winter season and see what the following spring and summer bring."

Sayeena was a clever and resourceful girl. Though a child of only ten summers, she had learned from her mother and all of the other women in the tribe the skills that she would need in womanhood. Indeed, there were other abilities, unusual for a female, which she picked up from her older brothers Manja and Taruq. Neither, in their childhood, had managed to better her in the arts of fighting and weaponry. She was a skilled archer and had demonstrated, on several occasions, the ability to hunt and kill small animals for food.

However, as the summer and autumn turned to the first hints of the cold that was to come in the winter months, Sayeena experienced her first taste of the chill that was going to be the tribe's future for the coming period. She also came to realise what it was to be the prey rather than the predator.

Two scouts returning from the northern edges of the new wintering grounds reported sightings of a pack of Wolver – a four-legged carnivore normally specialising in deer or smaller grazers. With the migration of their usual food source, these medium sized predators had been known to attack small groups of people and make off with their young. The group, the scouts said, was heading directly for the winter camp.

Tharana, the chief of the council, ordered a squad of twenty archers to head out of the camp and intercept the pack.

"Take to the trees," he said, waving an arm to illustrate the instruction. "The sap from the bark will prevent detection until they are past your positions. Take down as many as you can."

The sap from the underside of the tree bark was normally used for flexing the wood that the tribe used for its bows, but also had the property of concealing the smell that the wolvers would detect. Silence in the trees would render the bowmen almost invisible. The squad set off.

Sayeena, knowing that she would be forbidden from taking part, slipped away whilst preparations were being made and took with her a small flask of the sap. She waited, concealed, until the group had passed her position and then followed without being detected. She heard the command to halt and watched as the squad leader, her father, dispatched his troops amongst the trees. When everyone else was positioned, she selected her own platform and shinned skilfully and silently into her own nook. Now they waited.

The wolver appeared half an hour later; they walked slowly, pausing from time to time, sniffing the air for danger. Sayeena could see the first three animals as they entered a clearing beyond the far line of trees. Poultos had positioned his squad wisely to set up a killing field in which the wolver would be caught in a cross fire descending upon them from above. He raised his hand to ready the archers.

The pack leader looked back as the last of his group entered the clearing. Some had caught small mammals on the way and all now paused to make the best that they could of the meagre meal. With the wolvers' attention now distracted, Poultos dropped his arm in silent command. The deadly rain of arrows fell with unerring accuracy upon the pack that had been heading for the tribe's camp and a more satisfying meal.

Animals screamed in agony in their death throes, all thoughts of food now forgotten. In minutes not a single wolver remained standing, and the archers began their descent from the trees to bind up the animals for the trip back to the lodges. The meat would be tough and gamey but better than nothing, and the pelts would provide extra clothing for the coming colder weather.

Sayeena, disappointed at not having been able to take part in the kill, came down from her own hiding place to face the displeasure of her father when he found out that she had disobeyed an unwritten rule that females took no part in any hunt. She had approached without being seen, and was now ten yards from Poultos. He did not see her, his back being turned, and had not noticed a sole wolver which lay wounded to his left. The animal, struggling to its feet, now crouched for a killing pounce which would take a man off his feet. The wolver's leap was silent and accurate as the animal sailed through the air aiming for Poultos' head.

The screech of agony had Sayeena's father turning in surprise to see the animal twist in mid-air as the arrow pierced its throat and took it to one side of its intended target. Sayeena stood, motionless, as the recoil from the bowstring continued to reverberate, her eyes fixed in concentration.

"Sayeena!" Poultos called. "What do you think you are doing?"

"Saving your life, Father," she said, finally approaching from the base of the tree that had concealed her.

"You… you should not have…"

"Been here, Father?" she said, as others in the squad now approached, their faces split with grins.

"Yes, well," he replied, unable to remain annoyed in the circumstances. He turned instead to the squad. "Why did none of you check that all of the wolver were dead? Why leave that task to a child?"

All semblance of humour was checked in an instant, but he turned to his daughter and winked. Sayeena knew that she was, on this occasion, off the hook, and marched with the rest of the group back to the lodges with their booty.

The winter was a long one – longer than many of the tribe could remember, and when the rains failed to appear for the second successive year, they remained in their new home for a further season.

Sayeena had, like all of the other children in the tribe, listened to the tales told around the lodge fires by the elders during the colder weather. One of the ones which transfixed her the most was that which foretold the advent of the rainy season.

"The clouds will dance," Mithraya said, waving her aged hands in the air expressively. "It is prophesied that the rains will not return until the skies are full of their magic. When the air darkens to herald the swirling mists the gods will unleash the life-giving waters and we shall return to our true homes."

She had not been allowed to read the texts until her twelfth summer but, now of that age, she was fascinated by the legends that they contained. It was in that year that she also attracted the attention of a young man by the name of Wheda. Wheda was the oldest son of her father's friend, Galla, and they had grown up in neighbouring lodges.

Wheda made his intentions clear in the time-honoured way, and asked Poultos for permission to 'address' Sayeena. Their courtship followed the traditional route and, at a ceremony at the end of spring, they became betrothed. It was the following day that the clouds danced.

"See the rainfall, Sayeena," Wheda said as they looked out of their new lodge. "The gods bless our joining and the tribe shall now return to its traditional home. The Carabus will soon return and all will again be well."

She smiled at her handsome man and squeezed his hand. This was truly the turn in her people's fortunes, and their children would be able to grow up on the lush plains instead of the harsh surroundings of the winter lodges. The rainy season had truly begun, and the tribe packed up all of its belongings and headed for home.

The Carabus numbered in their tens of thousands, and the dust clouds heralding their coming could be seen from miles away. When they finally arrived, it was a time of great rejoicing and feasting, but not a beast was taken that could not be fully used. Years passed in seeming abundance of food, clothing and happiness and Sayeena had all but forgotten the close call that her father had had with the wounded wolver. It was inevitable, the sacred texts had said, that misfortune could not be held at bay forever, but the loss of Poultos in the Carabus hunt was a bitter blow.

Isolated momentarily in a small group of the beasts, Poultos' mount had shied in fright at the sight of a saken, rearing from its slithering path in the dust. It bucked unexpectedly and threw him into the path of two stampeding beasts. By the time that other riders had arrived at the scene he was taking his final breaths. He died the same evening.

The death ceremony was long and ceremonial as befitting Poultos' status as one of the elders of the tribe. Sayeena's family were distraught at the loss of their head, but with Manja, now of twenty-three summers, as its new leader they placed his body on its stilted platform in the sacred burial grounds and consigned it to the gods.

The dancing clouds appeared each year after Poultos' death, and the tribe flourished as never before. Sayeena and Wheda brought forth three children of their own who, in turn, made the two of them grandparents to a family of six others. Each night, and now an old woman of fifty-eight, Sayeena regaled the grandchildren with tales from the sacred texts, and also told of the adventures from her childhood in the first winters spent in the foothills of the Dragas.

When her time finally came, ten years later, she held the hand of her husband and smiled one last time.

"I shall go to dance with the clouds now, Wheda," she said. "Do not grieve, for I shall see you all again when the rains return each year. The dancing clouds will bring me back to everyone, and all that you will have to do is look up and there I shall be."

The Optical Road

Han Pearson flipped the switch on the control panel, stood up, stretched, and made his way to the back of the flight deck where the galley area was located. The auto pilot would take care of the trajectory upon which he had set the *Phoenix,* and he could now look forward to a hot meal and a decent period of sleep before he reached the next set of co-ordinates.

"Beef and ale pie, lots of mash, gravy, and please yourself about the vegetables," he barked into the food dispenser – retro meals were a firm favourite of his. "Oh, and gimme a cold beer to wash it down."

Pearson had been on board the freighter for three weeks and was currently on assignment to the Orion sector to pick up the latest delivery of berrillium crystals needed for the power plant on Gallek IV. The trip was a regular one and paid well, but it was as boring as hell – he was nothing more than a glorified delivery boy and longed for some excitement to while away the interminable time that he spent on board the one-man ship.

He took his meal from the hatch in the machine and sat down at the only table in the galley area. He took a generous swig of his beer, wiped his mouth with the back of his sleeve and got stuck into the food. He had to admit that the grub was good – far better than he'd tasted on other ships where he'd served, but then this menu was tailored to suit his requirements so he shouldn't really have been surprised.

The warning beeper from the flight console had him frowning as he placed his empty plate into the dispenser that would take care of its cleaning. Ambling back to the pilot seat, he stared at the flashing red light in puzzlement. He looked across the array of controls for any sign of malfunction but everything appeared to be working correctly.

"What's wrong with you, asshole?" he said to the light, knowing full well that there would be no response – the *Phoenix* was not that sophisticated. AI it certainly was not, which is why he almost fell out of his chair when a voice responded.

Well, he assumed that it was a voice, but the background static made it hard to be absolutely certain.

"Who... call... hole?" The words came through in a very crackly form, and he had to listen again as his silence elicited more.

"What... mean... language... like... hear me?"

Han adjusted the communications console in an effort to clean up whatever signal was coming through to him.

"Can you hear me?" he said.

"Yes," said the voice, much cleaner now. "Who are you calling an asshole?"

"What are you doing on this frequency?" Han asked. "It's supposed to be reserved for military use."

"Which military?" the voice asked. "There's no military involved."

"Hold on, hold on," Han said. "Just who the hell are you, and why are you hailing me?"

There was silence at the other end, and for a moment Pearson thought that he had lost the connection. There was then what sounded like a rustling of paper and someone turning the pages of a book.

"You still there?" he asked.

"Yeah; just gimme a minute."

"Who... are... you?" Han asked, deliberately.

"Hey," the voice said. "No need to be like that. I'm Sam and I'm in control. Who are you?"

"Sam? I don't know any Sam," Han said. "I'm Han Pearson - just what do you think that you're in control of?"

"It says here 'The Optical Road'. Don't you know that?"

"What's to know?" he replied.

"Where exactly are you, Han?" Sam said.

"En route to the Orion sector with a delivery to collect."

"Orion? That's not right. What are you picking up?"

"Berrillium, if it's any of your business," Pearson said.

"Of course it's my business," Sam replied, tetchily. "I own the *Phoenix*."

"You what?" Han exclaimed. "Nossir! You do not; this ship is mine – bought and paid for. I run this route regularly. I've got sole freight rights all through the area."

"Nope," Sam said. "You're wrong. It's says here, and I quote: *'You are the owner of the freighter 'Phoenix' and the mission is to evacuate all survivors from Gallek IV following the attack by the Renagi.'*"

Pearson was dumbfounded. This Sam person was right off the grid; he dug out his manifest and read it from top to bottom. It clearly named him as sole owner of the freighter, so this dumbass didn't know what was going on.

"Better check your paperwork real good, buddy," he said. "I got certified ownership documentation right here in my hand. Time for you to get off my wavelength."

"The Optical Road is mine," Sam said. "I bought it last week and this is the first time that it's been set up. Just how did you manage to muscle in on me?"

"Okay," Pearson said. "Audio's not getting us anywhere. Can you switch to visual? I'm transferring this transmission to the forward view screen."

"Hold on," Sam said. "I'll have to check my hardware for compatibility."

Pearson leaned back in his chair and shook his head in puzzlement. Either Sam could switch to visual or not – there was, he thought, no issue about compatibility. This situation was becoming more and more bizarre. He checked the route clock; he still had a further twenty-three hours until the next trajectory change and this one would require a hyperspace jump.

"Hey," he said. "You there? I got a route change coming up tomorrow and I can't have any delays or I'll lose the franchise."

"Yeah," Sam said. "I think I can do it. I just need to make a few adjustments to the control file, but it will need a reboot so I'll go offline for a few moments. Now that I know where you are I'll be able to reconnect."

"Knock yourself out," Han said, swinging his chair around and going back to the galley; he felt the urgent need for a strong, black coffee.

196

Sitting there at the table with his feet up, he pondered the conversation that had just taken place. This... Sam person was clearly deranged in thinking that the *Phoenix* belonged to anyone other than him. And what was it with this so-called rescue mission? He didn't take passengers – they were far too much trouble. He had swallowed the last mouthful of his coffee when he heard a hail from the cockpit area. Sighing in exasperation, he hauled himself to his feet and made the short journey back to the console. It was Sam.

"Hey," he said. "All rebooted?"

"Yes," Sam replied, "and I've managed to reconfigure the control file to initiate a visual format. Ready?"

"As I'll ever be," he said.

The forward view screen flickered briefly, down, Han thought, to the slight incompatibility that their two systems were trying to rectify. Suddenly all of the static disappeared and he was staring at the face of the person that he had been arguing with just half an hour ago.

"Oh," Sam said, leaning back from the screen.

"Ah," said Han, scratching his head and smiling in amusement.

"You don't look like you sound," Sam remarked.

"And boy, have I made an error of judgement," Pearson responded.

"Well, um, that's quite a ship you have from what I can see," Sam said.

"What's all that at the back of you?" he asked, trying to take the conversation in a different direction.

"Oh, just my room," Sam replied, looking over one shoulder. "I spend most of my time in here when I'm not at work."

"So, what's the story?" he asked. "You live alone?"

"Pretty much. It's just me and Bob since I left home. Dad died when I was eight and Mum remarried a few years later. The new guy made it clear from the outset that he didn't want me around, so as soon as I reached sixteen I packed my bags and left."

"That's tough," Han replied. "Who's Bob?"

"Oh, he's my cat, want to see him? He's right here on my knee – won't leave me alone most of the time."

Up before the screen appeared a not-too-impressed tabby who had clearly been napping before being so rudely interrupted. Sam put him down on the floor and turned back to the screen.

197

"What's going on with you, Han?"

"Similar story. Left school at seventeen. Mom and Dad both died when I was a kid and I was raised in an orphanage. Didn't like it and left as soon as I could. Got a job with a freight company booking stuff in and out and they put me through Flight School. Got a pilot's licence by the time I was nineteen and started working with them ferrying stuff all around the quadrant."

"Hmm," Sam said, picking a box up. "That's not what it says you should be doing in the Optical Road manual."

"What manual?" Han asked. "What is it with you and this idea that you own the *Phoenix*? The Optical Road isn't some kind of game – it's the route through the quadrant where I make my living."

"Well, it says so right here on the box," Sam replied. "You are the pilot and I own the ship… and you."

"Me?!" he barked. "Nobody owns Han Pearson! I need to see that manual."

"How are we going to do that? Where did you say that you are?"

"En route to the Orion sector. Why? Where are you?"

"Droitwich."

"Where in hell's Droitwich?" Pearson said.

"England."

"England?" he asked. This was becoming annoying and he needed to bring the whole thing to a close. "What planet are you on?"

"Earth, of course," Sam said, nettled and starting to feel the frustration.

"Earth? But you can't be. Earth doesn't exist any longer and hasn't for thousands of years. What year is it where you are?"

"2016," Sam replied. "Why?"

"Oh boy, have we got a situation," he said. "Listen, Sam, it's 4593 where I am – that's a couple of millennia in your future."

"I don't have a future," Sam said, sighing and sitting forward with head cupped in hands.

Pearson thought about those words for a moment or two. Sam's situation was a very close match to his own and, but for the *Phoenix*, he would be in no better a position himself. He brightened.

"Say, why don't you come and join me here?"

"What?" Sam replied, suddenly sitting bolt upright. "In the future? How can that be?"

"Well," Pearson said, thinking quickly. "The ship is equipped with a transportation device that I use for loading and offloading freight. It's in the cargo bay, but it's quite safe. All I'd need are your co-ordinates."

"Co-ordinates?" Sam said. "Like on *'Star Trek'*?"

"Star what?" Pearson asked.

"Never mind. I'll explain another time. I don't know my co-ordinates."

"Well, how do you know where you are right now? Is there no system for working out a geographical position?"

"Longitude and latitude!" Sam exclaimed. "That should do. I can get it down to degrees, minutes and seconds. That should be accurate enough to pinpoint my flat."

"In that case, tell me what they are and I'll insert them into the ship's navigation system and see what it comes up with. I just hope that it can place you over two thousand years ago; I don't know if the star charts will go back that far in time."

In complete silence, the two of them waited while Pearson inserted the data that Sam had supplied into the ship's computer. It seemed to take an age before the message appeared on the screen:

<Calculations complete. Press 'Go' to complete the data conversion.>

"You seeing this?" Pearson asked, quietly.

"Yes, I am," Sam replied.

"You ready?"

"Yes. Will it…?"

The words were lost as Pearson activated the transporter from his pilot seat and left the cockpit in a hurry, making for the cargo bay. He did not allow himself to think of the consequences of getting it wrong. In the early days of transporters, there had been a number of fatalities… but he swept those thoughts from his mind.

"Hi," Sam said as Pearson appeared through the door at the side of the cargo bay. "I got here." She placed a box onto the floor and opened the lid. "Say hello to Bob; I couldn't leave him behind."

"So you did," he said, smiling. "Hi, Bob. Life's going to be a whole lot more interesting now that there are three of us aboard. Welcome to the *Phoenix.*"

Dear Mum

Please don't bother coming to look for me – it would be a pointless exercise. I've gone somewhere that you couldn't possibly imagine.

You've never taken much interest since Derek arrived on the scene and he's made it clear that he doesn't want me around.

They won't miss me at work, either, so don't waste time telling them that I've gone – they'll soon find some other drudge to do their work.

Remember those dating sites that you made so much fun of? Well, I found one that you'd never have dreamt of. I met a really nice bloke called Han, and I've flown off to be with him.

Samantha

Life's An Illusion

"Come on," Judith said. "It'd be a hoot. You've said yourself that we'd breeze most of those types of questions."

Judith, my wife, was referring to the latest episode of *'Life's An Illusion'*, one of the TV network's prime time family entertainment quiz shows. Aired on Saturday evenings, it was one of the flagship programmes that was raking in viewer figures that hadn't been heard of for many a year. Not since the days of the Morecambe & Wise Christmas Specials had they seen figures like it – over twenty million were tuning in each weekend to see the latest poor sods fail to win the star prize.

"I dunno, Jude," I said, wrinkling my nose. "I'd hate to be made a fool of by that slime ball of a host."

The quiz's front man, Mike Barton, was everything that I disliked in a person. He oozed what the Americans call schmaltz, and he seemed to have an ego bigger than the Shard. He made my flesh creep by the way that he appeared to manhandle the female contestants, seemingly with impunity, and the way that he whipped up the audience placed him firmly, in my mind, on the same pedestal as a mob leader. I smiled to myself – it would be nice to take him down.

"It would be like a walk in the park for us, Ted," she said.

I'm Edward Hawksworth – Ted to family and friends – and Jude and I have been married for close on thirty years. She was right, of course. In our spare time we, and our friends Ellie and Dave, like to take part in many of the quiz nights at a selection of local pubs in the area. We're good – there's no disguising that fact – and when we're not winning, we invariably come second. It's a laugh – no more – and the prizes are usually fairly modest. Nevertheless, there was something in what she said, and she'd been making the point for a few weeks now. Her opinion of Barton was the same as mine, and I could feel all resistance slipping away.

"Yes, you could be right," I replied. "There'd be the selection process to go through, though; they don't just let anyone onto these programmes."

"Better get our application in soon, then," she said, smiling. "Look, I made a note of the website address. No time like the present; come on, let's do it now. What could possibly go wrong?"

What indeed. I capitulated good-naturedly, not expecting anything to come of her suggestion, but was mildly surprised a few weeks later when we received an invitation to the television studios for a preliminary selection meeting. We sailed through the session and were given our slots on the show for a month ahead.

'Life's An Illusion' is a rarity nowadays. Most quiz shows are recorded in a studio before a live audience and are aired at some future date. This is not the case with the network's prime-time offering. The programme is aired live on a Saturday evening at eight o'clock. It must be a risky strategy, as there is no margin for editing out any, shall we say, 'unfortunate' occurrences during the broadcast, and this is presumably where the host, Mike Barton, came into his own.

Barton is one of the old school entertainers. Quick-witted, slick in his presentation and with a talent for ad-libbing when things go 'off piste'. He was poached by the network from their main rival to front the show at its inception, and had made it his main source of exposure to the nation. That said, he was one of the people I would be least likely to willingly meet for any reason that you could imagine. Therein lay the temptation of my wife's suggestion.

"How are you going to play it?" Ellie asked at one of our regular evening quiz meets.

It was interval time at our current event – a pub outside our usual catchment area. The interim scores revealed us to be way ahead of all of the competition and we hadn't even played our joker yet. I looked at Jude and shrugged, she took up the baton.

"We're going to play them at their own game," she said.

"What do you mean?" Dave asked.

"We've been watching very carefully when the final round comes up. Once the other three couples have been eliminated from the show, Barton presents the final pair with a single category. One of them has to provide ten answers in sixty seconds to win the top prize."

"So?" Dave said.

"So, have you ever taken a close look at the faces of those poor two unfortunates when the very subject that they *don't* want to see magically appears on the question board? We think that the round is loaded." Jude replied.

"I did some checking," I said. "Since the show began its run some years back, nobody has succeeded in walking away with the star prize – doesn't that sound odd?"

"I suppose you could look at it that way," Ellie said. "It could also be just a case of pure bad luck."

"Well, we're going to test that theory," Jude continued. "The four of us know how good we are as a team; I mean, it's not as if we spend hours and hours looking up reams of facts. It's just that we're exceptional at retaining information – simple as that. Ted and I are about to put all of that in front of Mike Barton and take him to the cleaners, aren't we, love?"

"Apparently," I said. "Another round of drinks?"

The day of the show was soon upon us and the journey from Birmingham to the theatre in Manchester gave us the time that we needed for last minute tactics. During the month between our screening and tonight's event, we had spent every spare moment researching the show, its format and particularly its host, Mike Barton.

On Barton we did a particularly thorough job. Every possible source had been used in order to identify traits in his character, mannerisms, preferences, and even the way in which he spoke in a variety of circumstances. By the time that we'd got into the car that day, we believed that we knew him as if he were a member of our family. That avenue had, in our opinion, been well covered. There was nothing that the man could do to shake our confidence.

"When you look back over the shows that we've been watching, you can see what he's up to," Judith said. "See the way that he's closer to the women than he should be – that's all designed to make them nervous. He gets right in the faces of the blokes as well – staring directly into their eyes. It's no wonder that they stumble over some of the easier questions. How many times have we yelled at the screen when people have got things wrong?"

"It's true," I said, listening whilst trying to concentrate on my driving. "I'll tell you something else: we're timed to be there at least an hour before the show begins. That means that they'll probably put all the contestants together in some kind of hospitality room where there's food and drink. That's also going to be a way of loading the gun."

"What do you mean?" Jude asked me.

"Think about it, love," I said. "What's going to be the likely consequence of drinking alcohol?"

"Oh, I see," she said. "It's going to have a blurring effect on the brain, you get confused, time-pressured, and hey presto! You make mistakes."

"Exactly," I replied. "So, let's keep off the wine or whatever else they offer. If we have to take a glass, find some way of getting rid of it. We need to keep a clear head – do that and we stand a great chance of winning and walking away with the top prize."

We rolled into the theatre at Salford Quays at around six that evening, and were shown immediately into what they referred to as the Green Room. It was about the size of our lounge at home and was furnished with a set of comfortable chairs. There was a table at one end laden with a selection of buffet food, and also what appeared to be a free bar – bottles of wine and beer in abundance. We gave each other a knowing glance and picked two chairs close to a large potted plant.

"Mr and Mrs Hawksworth?" the young woman with the clipboard said, smiling broadly at us. "I'm Melanie, one of the PR assistants. Welcome to the show and congratulations on being selected."

Jude and I murmured something instantly forgettable and smiled in return.

"The waiting on staff," she ushered in a young man with a tray laden with drink, "will give you everything that you need as regards refreshment. Please feel free to help yourselves to as much as you'd like. The show airs in around an hour, and Mr Barton will be down here about fifteen minutes before we go live in order to introduce himself and make sure that you're nice and relaxed."

With that, she vanished and we each took a glass of the wine offered.

"More like ramp up the pressure," I said as the waiter turned away. I dumped the contents of my glass into the potted plant and Jude did likewise. No-one seemed to have noticed and we settled back to put some small finishing touches to our tactics.

With around twenty minutes to air time we were done, and took a few moments to size up the opposition for the evening. There were three other couples, all partaking freely of the 'hospitality' and now well on the way to total confusion. Jude and I, on the other hand, despite taking refills and consigning them to the aforementioned pot, remained stone cold sober and sharp as a tack. You could almost hear six sharp intakes of breath as Mike Barton made his entrance. In true professional style he worked the room like clockwork, pausing at each couple and spending a predetermined number of minutes with each before moving on; we were last in the queue and gave him very little to work on before the five-minute warning had him retreating out of the room and towards the theatre stage.

"Well, here goes," I said. "Let's take the man down."

"Hurrumph!" Jude whispered as we left the room.

I was, I'll admit it, not completely prepared for the start of the show. Despite having seen all of the fanfare and lights many times on the TV at home, actually being there under all of those glaring theatre spots had me temporarily on edge. Jude must have noticed, as a sharp nudge in the ribs had my feet back down on solid ground pretty sharpish.

Burton descended, in true star fashion, a lavish stairway to one side of the stage to his signature tune *'The Eye of the Tiger'*. It's one of the pieces of music that boxers sometimes use when entering the fray and its roots seem to have come from Stallone's starring role in *'Rocky'*. He walked each step like a dancer, waving to the audience and seemingly oblivious to us poor souls who were about to be granted the pleasure of his performance. Coming to a stop in perfect time to the dramatic ending of the music, he stamped one foot and bowed to the audience like some gladiator. Having issued forth with the time-honoured greeting, he turned to us and smiled.

The next few moments, as each couple was introduced to those watching, were like some form of psychological torment – at least for those not completely sober. When it came to our turn, however, it must have become apparent to him fairly quickly that we, unlike the other six, were not going to be cannon fodder. Our chat was brief, he recovered himself, and the show began.

The format was simple. After a set of reasonably straightforward questions, one couple would be eliminated, much as they are on *'Pointless'*. There would then follow a set of tests of logic which, I have to say, were far beyond the capabilities of one of the remaining three couples who had partaken far too freely of the alcohol on offer in the Green Room. That left four of us to fight it out for the right to compete for the star prize. This time the questions were tailored to target each of us individually with no conferring between our respective spouses. Jude and I came away from this section as clear winners and we entered the final phase of the evening's entertainment.

"Well, congratulations to Ted and Judith Hawksworth for finishing as our winners for tonight!" Barton gushed. There was widespread applause from the audience, accompanied by whistles and hoots, all carefully scripted by two of the production staff holding large cards and standing at the front, out of camera shot.

He wandered over to us and led us from our positions at our podium to the centre of the stage. Having failed miserably to shake us during the preliminary rounds of the quiz, this would now be his last chance to derail our efforts. Barton's early career as a comedian of rather blueish tinge now came to the fore in a selection of not-too-polite attempts at humour at my expense. I shrugged my way through them and he turned his attention to Jude. I could have been put off by this, but we were well prepared.

We'd seen the antics that he'd got up to in the Green Room before the show, and the touchy feely way that he handled the women was, to put it mildly, distasteful. He'd run out of time to attempt anything like that with Jude, but now took the opportunity to try to make up for it. Placing an arm suggestively around my wife's waist, and with a card in his other hand from which he was, on the face of it, reading out further details that we'd been obliged to supply, he began, out of camera shot, stroking the side of her leg. I'd seen the smile on my wife's face and, although I had no idea what it was that she had in mind, was sure that Barton would regret the action that he'd just taken.

I was right. Sliding her hand around his back, she let it fall below his jacket and gave a firm squeeze to his buttocks. I would truly pay a substantial amount to have a picture of his face at that precise moment; he broke free instantly and, with a rather flushed expression, moved reasonably seamlessly into the final phase of the show.

"And so, ladies and gentlemen," he addressed the audience, "we come to the finale of our evening. Ted and Judith now have to decide which of them is going to step forward and challenge for the star prize." (There was a crescendo of a drum roll.) "Your dream home!" (There was a rousing and lengthy applause). "Yes, *Life's An Illusion* will provide funding, up to," (there was another drum roll) "… one million pounds! Yes, one million pounds, for the dream house of their choice!"

Barton paused at this point, licking his lips. Was he nervous? Did he sense that things were running out of his control? He turned back to us.

"So, Ted and Judith," he said, dramatically. "It's time for you to decide which of you is going to face the test."

"Go for it," Jude whispered. "Just remember what we discussed."

I stepped forward. "I'm going to take the test. Mike," I said.

"Step forward and face the board," he announced, dramatically waving an arm to the back of the stage where a large electronic answer board had appeared. "You'll now be faced with a single question requiring ten answers within a time limit of sixty seconds. For each answer I can only accept the first thing that you say; understood?"

"Yes," I said.

"Is there anything that you'd particularly like to see come up for the question, or is there something that you most definitely would not like to see?" he asked.

This was the clincher, and we had prepared particularly well for this psychological stage of the proceedings.

"Well, Jude and I have been taking part in quizzes for a while back at home, and there's always been one section that I'm not too good at – I really don't fancy football."

"Okay," Barton said. Was that the hint of a smile?

He blathered on for a moment or two, and my wife and I suspected that this was in order to enable the question setter back stage to take the opportunity of inserting the correct question to scupper our chances. Then came the reveal.

"Here, Ted, is the chance to walk away with our star prize. The category you are being set is… The FIFA World Cup!"

There was a gasp from the audience, and I saw Jude put her hands to her face in mock horror. I tried my best to look downcast and I think that Barton fell for it. I had him hook, line and sinker. Not only had I been a season ticket holder at Villa Park since my teens, but I'd also seen every world cup since Mexico 1970. However, I wasn't entirely prepared for the actual question itself.

"With the clock set at one minute, Ted," Barton said, "you are required to name all of the outfield players in England's World Cup winning team of 1966. To make it clear, we need the names of all ten of those players, excluding goalkeeper Gordon Banks, who played in the final at Wembley Stadium on 30th July 1966. Is that clear?"

"Yes," I said, as nervously as I could.

"Very well," Barton said, smiling once again. "The clock will start… now."

I worked from the back and mentally ticked each one off, pausing from time to time as if deep in thought.

"George Cohen, Ray Wilson, Nobby Stiles, Jack Charlton… Bobby Moore, Alan Ball, Bobby Charlton… Geoff Hurst… Martin Peters…"

I looked at the clock; it had been ticking down relentlessly even allowing for my artificial pauses, and I now stared at the ceiling in apparent appeal for help from on high. I knew that I was missing just one name, and as the time ticked down to five seconds I smiled and looked Barton dead in the eye. With two seconds left, I wiped that smug expression right off his face.

"Roger Hunt."

For an instant there was complete silence until the hooter went signalling that time was up. All of the names had appeared on the answer board as I had recited them and Barton was staring at it in complete disbelief. He shook himself and turned to the audience, who were now on their feet and cheering wildly. Judith ran across the stage to me and we embraced in delight. We'd beaten him; we'd beaten his show; we'd beaten the system loaded against us. We were backstage sooner than we thought and in a private room with members of the production staff and Mike Barton.

"How did you know the answers?" he asked. His earlier bonhomie was now a thing of the past. The TV network was faced with a one million pound payout that they had never anticipated, and much of the advertising revenue derived from their flagship show had now been swallowed up by our success. "You must have been cheating!"

"I trust that you're brave enough to make those allegations public, Mr Barton," I said, not a little forcefully. "You clearly thought that we didn't see you delay while your staff behind the scenes changed the sequence of the final question."

"I have no idea what you mean," he said, suddenly quieter.

"Well," I replied. "Let's put it this way. Millions of viewers saw Jude and I win the star prize tonight. What do you think the effect will be on you and the TV network if we go to the papers with the fact that you're now baulking on paying out? You call the show *'Life's An Illusion'* – it looks like your little illusion has just come unstuck."

209

Meet the Author

www.nealjames.webs.com

contact: georgius4444@hotmail.co.uk